BAD TIPS AND ROWI ACCUSED OF MURDERING MAKES IT A REALLY BAD NIGHT FOR A BARTENDER

Praise for Matthew Nunes' New Novel LAST CALL

"With intriguing characters set amidst the backdrop of an old-money summer in Newport, *Last Call* is like the drinks (and customers) Paul serves: classic, with a twist."—***Connie D, BFA, MBA, MLS (Master of Liberal Studies,) Asst Prof Humanities, Retired***

In Matt Nunes' first novel, *"Last Call,* Paul Costa is flawed and vulnerable — but he's also dangerous. Costa is a graduate of the US Naval Academy, but he also has street smarts that do not come from books. Following the death of his wife, Costa has become a bartender to find anonymity and solitude. But now he's been hurled into the headlines when he's accused of the murder a U.S. Congressman in the men's room of the very bar where he works. Dana Kilroy is an FBI agent and she's been tasked with pinning the murder on him. Primal heat develops between when they collide and Costa steps outside of the law to negotiate a world of strip bars and Washington, DC, elites. The novel is peopled with unlikely heroes who help Costa along his way, and malevolent villains who have raped, murdered, and plundered their ways to power.

Nunes' story is a refreshing throwback to the old detective stories with flawed protagonists and vulnerable women. It ran itself like a film noir, in my head, as I read it. accompanied by interior monologues from the main character. If they had made his novel into a movie in the 1940s, Humphrey Bogart would have been Paul Costa.—***John Silviera, past senior editor of Backwoods Home Magazine and the author of Danielle Kidnapped and TheDevil You Know***

LAST CALL is the first of a series of mystery novels featuring former Naval Officer Paul Costa, a man who thought he was seeking a quieter life for himself and his daughter in civilian life, only to find the biggest threats still lie ahead.

Trouble has a way of stalking Paul Costa. But when the latest trouble comes in the form of a very dead Congressman with a knife in his ear, the same knife Paul was just using, the same Congressman Paul just neatly ejected from his bar, he knows trouble's notjust passing through, it's come home to roost.

Paul had tried to retreat from life, and from pain, raising his young daughter, Marisol, alone after the death of his beloved wife. The former JAG attorney and Naval Officer needed roots, and time to heal, and his daughter needed a father who would be there for her, always, just as he promised he would be.

But being the prime suspect in a high-profile murder threatens to tear him from her. And that was something Paul Costa was not going to allow to happen, even if it means hunting down a killer who's already got Costa in his sights, and who knows the way to reach him is through Marisol.

LAST CALL

Matthew Nunes

Moonshine Cove Publishing, LLC
Abbeville, South Carolina U.S.A.
First Moonshine Cove edition March 2020

This book is a work of fiction. Names, characters, places and incidents are products of the author's imagination or are used fictitiously. Any resemblance to actual events, locales or persons, living or dead, is entirely coincidental.

ISBN: 978-1-945181-795
Library of Congress PCN: 2020903209

Cover and author image by Grove Schaffner; cover and interior design by Moonshine Cove staff

Former Merchant Marine Officer and bartender, with a short story appearing in *Suspense Magazine,* Matt Nunes spent years mixing drinks and keeping confidences, like his protagonist, Paul Costa. *Last Call* is the first in a series of mysteries, relying on Costa's unique blend of skills and experiences. Look for his next book, *On the Rocks,* coming soon.

www.matthew-nunes.com

To the real-life Marisol, thanks, Muffin, for putting up with me.

Acknowledgment

I owe a huge debt to my agent, Gina Panetierri of Talcott Notch Literary, for her commitment and persistence in keeping the story alive. She knows that there's nothing as pathetic as a storyteller who can't get an audience to read his story. Thanks to her, that pathos will be looking for new accomodations.

Thanks to Grove for exactly the cover I hoped for. You did your best for the author's photo, the face is what it is, old friend.

I'd like to thank the Downings of Taunton, for employment in their bar and some wonderful anecdotes. As well, I'd like to thank their customers for the same. It wasn't always fun, but it was never boring.

To those who think they see themselves in some of the characters, maybe you do, because knowing you enriched my life, and added something I thought would be special to the story.

Writers of fiction are essentially thieves, forgoing permission and borrowing this bit of a person, this snatch of conversation, this piece of reality, a first name here, a last name there, things that we wished had happened, or building on what really did occur. If I can claim to have a skill involved, it's bringing them into one big "what if," and taking the leap of faith. If I get the chance to have readers jumping with me, so much the better. Lots of people are involved, usually without knowing about it, and to them, I want to say thanks.

A special thanks to Annie, for always believing.

Last Call

Prologue

He stumbled into the men's room in the bar. If he could just make it to the toilet in time, he knew that he'd feel better. He was sweating, trying to fight the pressure he felt and the pain in his arm. It seemed as if there wasn't enough air on earth for him to breathe. The man used a partition to hold himself up as he stepped into a stall, and tried to balance himself to lower his trousers.

Whatever he'd eaten, he'd never felt it come on like this before. He was still fumbling for his belt when his legs gave way. One moment on his feet, the next lying on the floor of a public restroom. Rising to his feet crossed his mind, until he realized that it wasn't possible. Too tired, too much pressure and a burgeoning pain radiating from his midsection to his shoulders and back made it unthinkable. He sensed darkness closing in from the sides, until he could only see what was directly before his eyes. Just before he flickered out, he looked through the louvers at the bottom of the outside door, seeing the shadow of two legs. The door swung open. Maybe help was on the way.

He died thinking that it was a ridiculous place for a man with his position to be found.

Tuesday Night

"Whiskey sour, two Gimlets and a Tom Collins, please and bill it to my room" he said into the button just below my bow tie.

"Yes, sir," reaching up for glasses, down for mixing cups and the ice scoop, waiting for his eyes to meet mine. As they did, I shifted to one side, and his eyes followed without head movement, making it okay to serve him. A little older than I, he had an expensive haircut and a carved wedding ring. His college ring had gold Greek letters embossed into the stone. "Phi Kappa Delta." I saw three women and two other men at his table, talking quietly. They wore expensive, casual clothes, slightly rumpled and sagging from a full day of leisure. The men wore no socks, and their wives wore sandals with low heels or wedge soles.

They seemed to be three affluent couples, enjoying a vacation. Affluence was a common condition for a Newport summer. I imagined them golfing, or shopping at the waterfront, looking through the tiny upstairs art galleries on Bowen Street. One of the couples, their backs to me, was holding hands under the table. I swallowed against a suddenly tight throat. . Nothing to indicate that he needed watching. The man had perfectly groomed graying blond hair, and gestured with his free hand as he spoke. The hand he was holding belonged to a slim woman seated facing away from me, as well. None of the couples showed any signs of overindulging.

It was my first upscale bar in one of the hotels on the waterfront. The bar was decorated to look like an old passenger liner, including porthole frames surrounding mirrors and prints. The tables were glass set on old-fashioned ships' wheels. Ships' brass sidelights were converted to give soft, indirect lighting. A huge row of windows looked out onto Rhode Island's largest collection of yachts, most covered in decorative lights, reflected in the still water. The royal blue carpeting had a gold colored border of decorative signal flags and anchors. The other side of the bar had windows over the hotel's atrium, showing glimpses of a railing that looked as if it belonged on a cruise ship.

Still, it was just a bar and I was just the friendly bartender, holder of confidences and dispenser of non-advice. My patter was down to an art. "I'm not sure, sir, what do you think?" They'd compliment me on my wisdom. My tip jar would fill, and I would hobble to bed with sore feet.

I tossed the mixer cup up behind my back, caught it, slipped it over a glass, pushed down, twisted it, and shook the Tom Collins three times before adding a cherry. The gimlet and sour were ready when he returned from his first trip.

The customer getting his table's drinks worried Sarah, the waitress. She was new and thought she'd made a mistake. I smiled and shook my head. She smiled back and turned away, bending to another table, somehow without exposing herself in her short skirt.

I kept my attention on my customers, moving around enough to see the whole lounge. I listened for loud voices and watched for women edging away from men. Without thought, my eyes swept the entire room every few minutes, as well as looking up and down the bar for empty or nearly empty drinks. Whenever my glance met a customer's, I smiled.

I took a quick step towards a raised voice, until a woman's laughter started. An "instant couple" headed upstairs. His hand was well up her dress and one of hers rested on his thigh. I remembered the slippery feel of lingerie and smooth nylons under my palm in a distant way.

While I considered that sensation, slowly rubbing my hands together, a man at the far end slapped the bar for attention. Along with whistling, that entitled a customer to suffer a thirsty death. Still, I was paid and tipped for my manners, not his, so I ambled down to face him and check him out. With three Pearl Harbors inside of a half an hour, he needed checking.

"Yes, sir?" making a question of it, I moved just out of his view. His head started to turn, stopped and he pivoted his body to face me. "'Nother," and then he let out a peal of giggles. The waitress and a few of the customers glanced up. I was checking his eyes, watery blue and wandering from just below my chin to a point over my left shoulder, into the mirror, then back to my face. His rigid movements and lack of focus were clear warnings to any bartender. No more for this guy.

I hesitated and he reached over the bar and seized my sleeve, just above the cuff. Crossed my DMZ, and his own Rubicon, all in one motion. He shook it back and forth. "I said, I want another one," in the singsong voice of a nasty, teasing child. Then, he ordered, "Chop-fuckin'- chop." He scanned the room, as if expecting applause. He scowled at me, drawing his eyebrows down and in towards the middle, trying, I thought, for the appearance of resolve and authority. He looked peevish instead.

I twisted my wrist and pulled my left shoulder back to slip free, taking half a step away. I leaned closer, bending from the waist and beckoned to him to lean in. He had to support himself with both hands on the bar, and I could smell melon liqueur and cologne. His head swayed. "Sir," I murmured, "I think that it would be better if I fixed you a soft drink or a coffee, and ordered you something to eat."

"You're a fuckin' bartender," he said, loudly, "so tend the fuckin' bar and get me a fuckin' drink, you little prick. Otherwise, I'll have your fuckin' job."

I bit down on my back teeth and forced a smile, "Sir, I have to ask you to moderate your language since there are ladies present. You may feel free to speak to the manager, but I won't serve you anymore tonight."

"Do you know who I am?" he asked.

"No sir. I can ask around, or call the front desk for you if you've forgotten." He blinked a couple of times, and somebody laughed. He didn't like that.

"Fuck you, the manager, and that hot little waitress, waggling her titties at me and every man in this place. You doin' her? She any good? She a natural blonde? I'd give her a toss, but they always want more," with that giggle I was learning to hate. He gestured me closer, as if to confide a deep secret. "Y'know how you can tell if they're hot?" he asked. Then without waiting for an answer from me, "you check their nipples, and if they're bigger than a dime—" I put up my hand to stop him.

"That's it, sir." Formality, the bartender's ever-handy shield, kept me from grabbing his sloppy hair, and slamming his face into the bar two or three times. Formality kept me employed. Formality made sure I could pay the huge mortgage and tax bill.

"I'm a customer, I'm a shitpot more important than you think I am, and I want a fuckin' drink." He poked me in the chest with one finger.

I looked down and slowly brought my eyes back to his face. I wasn't smiling any more. He pulled his hand back and smirked.

"I'm afraid, sir, that I have to ask you to leave the bar, and not come back tonight," I said, no longer keeping my voice quiet. "Please allow me to get the door, and I'll be happy to serve you tomorrow or during your next stay." I slipped under the trap and stood on the customer side, careful to be close, but not crowding him. I turned slightly to one side, and had my hands loosely clasped in front of my chest.

Two of the three couples at table two were staring at us. The man facing away, the one with graying blonde hair, held a protective arm around his wife's shoulders. One woman brought her hand to her mouth, staring at Sarah with the understanding that women have and men should. No longer the confident and lovely young woman who'd started the shift, Sarah held her tray against her chest under her folded arms, like a shield. She had her back against a wall. Her cheeks and neck were flushed, with blotches starting to show on the skin of her chest.

"Fuck tomorrow, you little prick. Not going anywhere." He pressed his hand flat against my chest and tried to shove. I swayed back and reached across the back of his hand with my own. I held onto his wrist and twisted it behind him. When I stopped, he was leaning forward with his hand nearly between his shoulder blades. I had my free hand on his shoulder to keep him from turning. He was under control, but I'd wanted him to leave, quietly and quickly.

"Please don't touch me, sir. It's definitely time to go. You see that, sir?"

He nodded and mumbled. I lightened up and moved closer to his side. Except from behind, an observer would only see two men walking to the door.

At the door, I released him and stepped backwards into the bar. He turned to face me. His eyes were unfocused and he started to speak when the door closed in his face. I didn't expect to see him again. I was careful to stroll to the bar, smiling at the customers. I murmured apologies to those I passed. I slipped under the trap, and called Sarah over. "Sarah, let's start an order for a round on the house, and give them the hotel's apologies, et cetera. Right?"

"Paul?"

"Uh, huh," I mumbled, slicing a lemon.

"Did he say anything? At the door, I mean."

"I'm sure it was 'Farewell,' because he was starting the 'eff'' when the door closed."

She smiled uncertainly. "Yeah, 'Farewell'. Paul?"

"Yes?" I raised my eyes to show I was listening. "I'm sorry. It shouldn't have gone that far. My fault."

"It's okay,"

She took a deep breath. "When I first started here, I'd heard a little about you, but it was hard to picture. One second, the guy's being a jerk, the next he couldn't move."

She was a nice young woman, probably nicely brought up. I couldn't count the number of violent acts I'd seen, or taken part in. I doubted that she'd seen one before. "I messed up, trying to keep it quiet. He was too stupid to back down. Bar 101: If it starts, it has to end, right then, you know?"

She nodded. "Fun job, huh?"

"Usually."

"How about you, Paul? You okay?" she said over her shoulder as she walked away.

I shrugged, and wiped the bar down, emptied and wiped some ashtrays, busy work. In a few minutes, she came up with a full set of drink orders, so I tossed the knife and cutting board into the bin with the other dirty dishes and silverware.

We caught up to the bar's orders, and I slipped the voucher for the round into my drawer. Catching Sarah's eye, I gestured towards the men's room. She nodded. After I finished, I had an illegal cigarette, popped a breath mint and washed my hands. I stopped in the back room for a new bottle of gin, and returned to the bar.

A few minutes later, she came up to the gate, the waitress position at the bar, put down her tray and looked at me. I straightened from "the lean" against the back shelf and stepped towards her.

"Paul, I've been thinking about the talk."

"The talk?"

"The talk, the one you asked me to have with your daughter?"

I was raising Marisol alone. Sarah had agreed to help explain bras and leg shaving, makeup and high heels, and thank God, menstruation.

"Mike and I should come over this week and I'll sit down with her, while you two play backgammon." Mike was a fine chef, with lots of training, but the hotel wanted him to gain more experience. He worked ungodly hours, doing lots of the scut work in the hotel's kitchen. Sarah and he spent a lot of time apart, for newlyweds. "He'll bring some sweet something or other," she went on, as if I needed more enticement. I did. I wanted my little girl to stay a little girl. Forever would be almost long enough. Some of that must have shown on my face.

"Paul, I was her age."

"I know you're right."

"But?" she said.

"But," I said, smiling, "you're ready, she's ready; it's me who's the problem. Okay, find out when you and Mike can come over. I'll cook something, and we can have dinner. I'm no Mike Carpenter, of course."

"He loves that thing you make, what's it called?"

"Jag? Rice and beans with linguica? My grandfather used to call it 'poor portagee food.'"

"That's it, but I didn't think it was polite to say 'portagee,'" she said.

"It's an insult unless you are one."

She patted me on the back of my hand, and worked her way around the tables while I walked the bar, checking in with the customers.

For a Tuesday, we did pretty well, so smiling at customers as they left at closing time was natural. At the end of each of our shifts, she'd get the name of a drink from the book under the bar for me to mix. She rarely drank the entire cocktail.

"That old guy was a serious pig."

To her, anyone over thirty-five was "old." Whenever she was working, I caught myself checking myself for age spots.

In the "Novelty" section, she'd reached the letter "O." She asked for an Oreo, and sipped it slowly, enjoying the sweet vanilla schnapps and Crème de Cacao with milk. "This is delightful," she said, pulling off the high heels she wore for work and sliding her feet into a pair of battered running shoes. Her expression relaxed as if she were wiggling her toes. I didn't ask if the drink was delightful or the comfortable shoes. Never ask the question if you don't want to hear the answer, my wife used to say. Sarah sighed and got to her feet with a groan that sounded suspiciously as if she was mocking the noises I made when I straightened or bent over. Marisol did that sort of thing all of the time.

I cashed out, while Sarah started to clean up the table area. I worked the bar melting ice, restocking and wiping down. I put the perishables into the cooler, rinsed the ashtrays and loaded them into the glass washer. Sarah headed into the ladies' room to get it picked up for the housekeepers.

In the men's room, I started into one of the stalls and stopped with a tingle starting at the base of my spine, creeping into my crotch and up towards my stomach. It had been a long time or else I'd softened, but I barely made it to the toilet in time. Even emptied out, I still arched and collapsed on hands and knees, like a horse trying to buck a stubborn rider from its back. I felt weak and hot and cold. My throat burned from the vomit and roaring coughs.

He was lying on his right side, facing outwards from the stall, with his head on the base of the toilet and his legs crumpled under him. His right arm lay flat, palm up and barely visible. His left was draped behind him awkwardly. The mind plays tricks; I thought that he'd be cramped and sore when he woke up if he didn't roll over. The familiar handle of a fine bladed fruit knife stuck out of his left ear.

A tiny trickle of blood ran under his jaw, tributary to the small pool on the floor. He still smelled of melon liqueur, pineapple juice and cologne, but his bowels and bladder had emptied and he smelled of other things. His eyes were open, no longer glaring hate at me or anyone else. They seemed to be looking at something. Thoughtlessly, I followed his gaze. Nothing but the louvers at the bottom of the men's room door to be seen, and I was getting nauseated again.

When the door had closed in his face, I never expected to see him again. I was wrong; I'd be seeing him, just like this, every night.

Chapter 1

The night manager, the hotel manager and the hotel's lawyer were all in the bar with me. Sarah sat in a corner, still crying with her husband holding her hand, directing his flat gaze at me. She shouldn't have been part of a murder investigation. I'd already called the sitter to tell her I was going to be late, and she said she'd just sleep on the couch. Thank God for Mrs. Pina. I wondered if she could stay until I made bail or served my sentence.

There was fingerprint powder, yellow tape, footprints and lots of photos. There was the thermometer pushed into my late customer's torso through a small cut one of the coroner's men made. There were paper lunch bags taped over his hands, and the muffled complaining of a criminalist.

"A freakin' men's room, for chrissake, know how many pubes and fibers we're gonna have to put into the envelopes, and label, and mark locations, and log? And who gets to dust the toilets and handles? 'At's right, I do. Three-thirty ayem in the freakin' morning, am I getting laid? Am I asleep?" His voice droned on, but the words faded into the background.

Finally, there was the stretcher, and familiar body bag, covered with a sheet, and the night manager begging them to take the freight elevator.

Sarah and her husband got up to leave. They turned towards me with blank expressions and I wondered if there was a way to make it okay. They seemed to look at me as if they knew I was guilty of something. I didn't think that they'd be dropping by my house for Jag and backgammon. I wondered who was going to explain sanitary napkins to Marisol.

The night stretched into morning, and there was the "you-have-the-right" speech. I was brought to the bar's ladies room to take my clothes off. The criminalist held a paper bag for me to drop the tux and shoes, socks and shorts. He handed me a set of surgical scrubs and shower sandals to replace them. When I returned to the bar and we were all seated at one of the glass-topped tables, the detectives began asking question after question, then started again, sometimes changing the order, sometimes alternating with each other. I was tired and to keep my focus, as I had been taught, I started to pay attention to their appearance and manner, building stories and images from small clues.

The older detective was tall and slim, with a neat atoll of dark hair surrounding a lagoon of polished skin. He had steady gray eyes and didn't seem to blink as often as most people. His raw silk sport coat was better than his slacks and shoes. Maybe the jacket was a gift from a loving wife. When my neck and shoulders began to tense, I forced my mind from that thought and tried to concentrate. He wore a wedding band, a Timex watch, and when his jacket opened, a Smith and Wesson nine millimeter.

He leaned in to ask questions and back to hear the answers. I couldn't tell if it was habit or technique, but he was listening. He told his partner to "tone it down a bit." Good Cop, or maybe ready to make the switch at some point, pretending to lose patience and explode.

His partner was just as tall, but with a body-builder's physique. There was a badge-heavy swagger to him, and his short haircut gave him the look of a state trooper. He had all of the arrogance and surface toughness of mirrored sunglasses and polished boots. He was aggressive and openly skeptical, making me want to either defend each answer or slap him. He dressed better than his partner, with clothes cut to emphasize his inverted mountain peak shape. His jacket was full under his arms to allow for a shoulder holster, which turned out to be an undercover straight draw. He carried a Desert Eagle. Not standard issue, but a heavy, macho piece. Assuming magazine pouches under his right arm, he was toting almost eight pounds in gun and ammunition. Expensive hardware, and he wore no jewelry except a Piaget watch.

My bartender's eye told me: "No class." He leaned in to ask questions, like his partner, but never leaned away.

His partner called him "Dave," but I knew him as "Detective Petersen". The older guy was "Larry," but he was "Sergeant

DaSilva" to me. They had a gadget to take my finger and palm prints electronically.

I knew what would happen when they ran the prints. I knew what they'd think when they found mine on the fruit knife after they pulled it out.

Mostly, I wanted to go home and see my daughter again, then sleep, for a day or two. I was starving after all of that vomiting, and the thought of grilled English muffins and orange marmalade were a kind of torture. I could smell coffee and food cooking in the kitchen, making my mouth water, and I was swallowing constantly, making me look guilty as hell.

The managers greeted the police request to provide the names of the guests who were in the bar with undisguised horror. Both detectives waited, until the lawyer nodded at me. I reached for the sealed drop box with the receipts and told them that we needed the originals for billing. DaSilva countered, "Sorry, but they're evidence. We might need prints or get something from them that copies wouldn't give us. I can get a warrant, but it would take longer and cause a lot of hate and discontent." He offered to give us copies and a signed receipt.

"I'll talk with our merchant account carrier," said our lawyer, "I'm sure it can be worked out, Mr. Costa. I'll take the responsibility."

DaSilva took the box and all of its contents with him to the office downstairs. I was picturing the people from the bar and their interviews, sure to be fascinating to the detectives when they heard about the dead man and me. It was small consolation to picture the looks on the faces of any men and women interrupted in the wrong rooms.

"So after this guy, this Congressman Morley, started being an asshole and you tossed him, what happened?" asked Petersen. I realized that this was the first time I'd heard the guy's name, and learned that he was a congressman. He really was a shitpot more important than I thought he was, just as he said, and the butt-to-balls tingle started again. Things were getting worse, and I felt as if I was being sucked down some sort of huge toilet, circling the drain and spinning helplessly.

I had answered that question, in one form or another a half-dozen times. I took a breath, trying to be patient through the nicotine deprivation, fatigue and hunger. "As I told you, I offered the remaining customers—"

The night manager was interrupting. "He wasn't an 'asshole,' detective, and we don't want one of our valued customers referred to in that way." We all stared at him, including the lawyer, who hadn't said a word since Sergeant DaSilva left. He seemed to recognize his own non sequitur, but pressed on, "Even if he is dead, the poor man, we insist on treating our guests with courtesy, respect and style."

"Okay, so that includes stylishly and courteously driving a knife into his ear, too, I suppose," said Petersen, with a smirk. "Or maybe respectfully locking him up and heaving him out of the door?"

"No one has said that he was 'heaved out,' as you put it, and we don't know who drove the knife…" his words tapered off. His ill-timed sense of duty made him come up to look at the dead man as soon as I called him. He'd been even more violently ill than I had.

Petersen waited until it was clear that the interruption was over. He visibly enjoyed embarrassing the man. The young cop seemed to want to be disliked. He turned to face me, and leaned closer, "I have a question out to you, barkeep, care to answer it?"

I had been given time to collect myself. "Okay, again, I set up a courtesy round on the house, cut some limes, threw the knife into the dishpan, went to the men's room, checked the liquor stock to update our order, came back to the bar and finished the shift. I wasn't away from the bar for more than five or ten minutes at any point. Then Mrs. Carpenter and I started the light clean-up to get the bar ready for the housekeepers." Mentioning the cigarette would have given the hotel their excuse to fire me, even though all of the bartenders sneaked an occasional smoke.

"Mrs. Carpenter, the waitress?"

"Yes."

"Care to talk about your relationship with her?"

"She's kind of an innocent. We work here. Her husband is a good guy and works here, too. I like them in an 'older friend' way."

"Nothing beyond that?"

"Nothing."

"Ever want more than that?"

"No. She's young, in love with Mike, her husband. They were nice to my daughter. Both good with her, not condescending."

"You married?"

"Yes," I said, then realized he wouldn't understand. "No."

He hesitated. "So which is it, bartender? You married or not?"

For the first time, I was uneasy because of a guilty-sounding answer. I didn't like the feeling. Maybe I didn't want him to be talking about it or it still hurt or I just didn't like him or maybe I preferred "Mr. Costa" to "Bartender."

"Mr. Costa is a widower, detective," said the night manager. It had to be uncomfortable for him to speak after the detective's silent put-down, but he spoke for me.

The lawyer asked, "Detective Petersen, are these questions really helping your investigation? Hm? I'm sure that any personal background is easily found, if you need it. Hm?" If the looking-down-his-nose "Hm's" weren't a verbal tic, then they were meant to push a button or two.

Petersen nodded, and got back into his pattern, "Never saw the good congressman return?"

"No."

"Never saw anybody at all going into the men's room?"

"No."

"Never saw anybody go behind the bar and get the knife?"

"No."

He mumbled into his chest, "Never saw your dick when you were pissing, either, I suppose."

"Yes, I did," I answered, "I have to be careful, because that water is cold and deep. I don't shake it off; I bang it against the side of the urinal." He'd given me the opening to snap back at him, and break his rhythm. He'd had me automatically answering him, just as he wanted.

He tried to stare me down, but he had blown it by overdoing the coarseness and had to wait for his partner. The lawyer and the managers looked at us, from one to the other and back, as if watching a slow motion tennis match. I was tired, and had seen my first murder victim in a long time, I was hungry, still a little sick and I missed my daughter. Not to mention that I expected to get fired and I wanted to get that over with.

"Detective," said the lawyer, "I believe the hotel and its staff has been extremely cooperative, and we're entitled to know your intentions in this matter. Mr. Costa, for example, has stayed beyond his shift for well over three hours. I represent the hotel, but as an officer of the court, I think that you have more than enough information to decide whether or not further interviewing or other action is warranted." He didn't "Hm," that time. His voice was cold, and revealed no doubts.

The door opened, and DaSilva gestured Petersen over to the doorway where they whispered together. Petersen raised his head and turned to stare over at me. Everyone else followed his eyes and watched me, too. After a long moment, Sergeant DaSilva walked over, and made a little speech. "Gentlemen, it's been a long and trying evening, or morning, I guess, and I'm sure we could all use some rest. You're all free to go, but please make sure we know how to reach you." He was looking at me for that part. "We appreciate your cooperation in this matter. Get some sleep, and expect to hear back from us." Without another word, they were gone.

The lawyer was talking quietly with the hotel manager, shaking his head and they glanced over at me, as I paused at the door. "I guess you're on tonight," said the night manager,

"Yes, I am, six o'clock, I'll, um, be in for my shift then."

"Of course," he answered.

They watched me, in silence, with their eyes following me, like the barrels of guns.

Chapter 2

The door closed softly behind me, and there was a glow from the television set. Mrs. Pina's expensive nightlight was on, even though I had seen the sun rising as I drove to my duplex just on the Newport side of the Middletown line. I nudged her shoulder and her round face came to life, fully awake in an instant. "Paul! What happened? And your clothes? You must be starving, and Marisol was good. She did her homework, ate her dinner," She counted on her fingers to tick off all of the things my daughter did. I listened, and smiled without trying.

Mrs. Pina usually wore a bun, perched with architectural precision at the crown of her head. At night she released the bun, to wear graying braids hanging well below her shoulders. My grandmother had worn a single long braid at night, and the same bun during the day. Mrs. Pina was my upstairs tenant, and paid most of her rent by acting as a nanny and housekeeper. Her grandson mowed the lawn and kept the bushes from devouring the house, in return for another cut from her rent. I heard stirring in the kitchen and Marisol came out to provide her critique.

"You smell like the bar, daddy. Those pajamas are too small for you. The flip-flops look dumb. You've been smoking again, and you promised you wouldn't. You have big dark circles under your eyes, but I put on coffee and I sliced some English muffins for you. I have to get dressed for school." I opened my mouth to answer and closed it as she jogged away.

My daughter still had a childish roundness to her face, and huge dark eyes. Lately, in some lights, I'd seen the shape of her face as it would be, the curve of her lips and line of her jaw drawn tight as she turned her head. Her hair would sweep over part of her face, and she used the back of one hand to push it back into place, a chestnut curtain, in a way that was heartbreakingly familiar. She reminded me more and more of her mother.

She sat with me while I ate the English muffins and took sips of her ghastly coffee. How she got it to be so sweet with a stinging bitter aftertaste was a mystery. Her mom had made Cuban coffee, and 'Sol was trying to learn how. I hoped she'd get it before an ulcer kicked in. "Daddy?"

"Mmmmf, honey," swallowing. "What is it?"

"You look sad, daddy." She'd come a long way, to be able to say it. She sometimes still cried in her sleep, and whispered, "Mamacita," while dreaming. I was sure that she'd heard me calling for Isabel, too.

"Guess I'm tired, honey, it was a long night." Her eyes searched mine and just as I'd never been able to deceive her mother, she saw the evasion. She shook her head, postponing the talk she'd want later on.

"I gotta go," she said, "I have to do that stupid project for social studies, and Terri didn't do her share." As usual, she walked out to the curb just as the bus arrived.

I stood, looking down the street after her bus. The phone was on a table next to the picture window, and it felt heavy when I picked it up. No one to call. Nothing to say. No wonder it was heavy.

I had a pretty good idea of what was going on around me. By then, the fingerprint check had been blocked by the Department of Defense. I was sure that the DaSilva had transmitted them electronically, encountering the DOD match and block. That might frustrate him, but it wouldn't matter after they matched them against the knife, unless the killer had wiped it clean. Why choose a knife I'd handled, then wipe it? No, I was supposed to be blamed, and the incident at the bar provided a handy motive.

The victim was a U.S. Congressman, so they'd want this one closed right away. "Who gets my child while I'm doing hard time?" I asked out loud. Isabel's family was either dead or still in Cuba. I had no family left. Mrs. Pina was sixty-something and a wonderful nanny, but had no legal standing. I imagined a string of careless foster homes grinding away at the barely rekindled beauty and joy in my daughter's eyes, until it was all gone. I pictured an adult hopelessness in them before she started high school. Nope, I thought, not my kid.

I started a drinkable pot of coffee. It dripped with a groaning wheeze, while I tried to clear my mind.

Trust in the system had been ingrained in me as a second-generation American and Annapolis and my naval career fixed it in place. I wanted to believe that since I was innocent, the truth would out. Despite that desire, I had experienced the system's inertia and its tendency to go with what it got. There was enough to get me into a federal penitentiary, or strapped down with a needle in my arm.

"Initiative," a professor had said, years ago, "is an intangible, like pornography. You can't define it, but you know it when you see it. You know when you have it, and you know when your opponent has it. With initiative, you are unbeatable if all other things are equal. Without it, you can only struggle to regain it."

So Petersen and DaSilva were out there investigating their asses off, using limitless resources. They expected me to freeze and wait for their results. Who and what they were detecting was up to them. I had no way to be sure that the evidence they found reflected what I knew. I knew that I didn't kill the congressman.

It was a special case, a path to promotion and glory for them, but they had volumes of rules to follow. They were cops. To me, it was a battle. Battles are won when you find, fix and destroy your opponents, or put them in such a position that they flat ass surrender, much simpler than winning a war. Wars are won when politicians say they are.

Rather than sink into a funk, I escaped into my past. My grandparents were two individuals, who formed a new person as a couple. She deferred to him only for major decisions. If our family was a person, then she was the heart, while he was the muscle and balls.

I would never have left my country to go where I couldn't speak the language, with nothing but a willingness to work and the person I loved. They did, and in the few photos of that time, they looked happy, young and excited.

In my present, I was alone, trying to make this duplex home to Marisol. I rolled my shoulders, as if easing a long-carried load. Not good to find the past holding onto my thoughts, when the present needed them.

The phone brought me back. It was a reporter from the Providence newspaper, asking for comments on being a suspect in the Congressman's murder.

"If I'm a suspect, it's the first I'm hearing it. If I am a suspect, how in the hell did you find out? And last but not least, no comment."

There was another call five minutes later from the local television news, and the phone beeped with waiting calls during my "no comment" to them. I worried about Marisol or Mrs. Pina getting one of those calls. What if they started trailing around behind us?

I knew a little about using the system, so I got some of the law books I used to study for the Rhode Island Bar Exam. It took an hour to find the cases I'd vaguely remembered, before I drove to the local courthouse. Courthouses seem to be like old school buildings, the smells and sounds were familiar.

The clerk handed me the forms to fill out. The halls and waiting rooms were choked with an assortment of sad women looking for support, men trying to get visitation, witnesses, DWI's and job lots of the scared and angry, but I found a quiet corner. I wrote in the names of all of the news organizations I could remember. I cited the three cases I had found, signed here, dated there, initialed here and here, and filled in the blank as "Pro Se," giving it to the clerk.
Her eyes widened when she read it, but she made no comment. "Is everything in order?" I asked.

"Seems complete to me. His Honor will be going through cases in the order received, but this will come up pretty soon. Is the plaintiff here?"

"Plaintiffs, ma'am, plural. No, and under the guidelines," I gestured at the poster on the cinder block wall, "They don't have to be."

"Well. No," she said, "I mean, I guess not." There was the barest suggestion of a question in her hesitant agreement.

"I'm just a clerk, Mr.," she paused, "Mr. Costa. It'll be up to the judge, anyway, sir." She nodded to the next in line, a teenaged girl with a baby on her hip, and countless visible piercings.

I went into the courtroom, and waited my turn. "Mr. Paul Costa?"

I stood.

"This is typically a routine filing, but this is one regarding an unusual matter."

"Yes, your honor."

"Mr. Costa, there are constitutional issues here. I'm not unsympathetic, but it seems to me that First Amendment issues govern."

"Your honor, the First Amendment protects the press from government intervention, but does not guarantee unrestricted access to private citizens. The argument that the individual right to privacy doesn't interfere with the media's right to unfettered speech has been upheld in several cases. Both the Rhode Island Supreme Court and the United States District Court of Appeals upheld a citizen's right to privacy vis-à-vis the press. I cited three cases in support, and I would argue that you would be justified in issuing the order to protect my home, family and person from unreasonable intrusion."

"Mr. Costa, I have heard no countering arguments from the subjects of your restraining order, and I will need to review the cases you cited."

"I understand, judge."

"I will give you my decision after the morning recess."

The wait was interminable but I was back in the courtroom before the judge's entrance.

I stood, with familiar feelings of mixed fear and anticipation; standing in front of a judge.

"Mr. Costa, given the existing law and the lack of countering argument, I am granting you this order for a period of seven days. Defendants can file briefs or modification requests during that time. It will be your responsibility to provide service on all of the organizations named in the order, which will be done by constables or deputy sheriffs at your expense. Questions?"

"Thank you, judge. I'll speak to the clerk about how to get that done."

"That's correct, Mr. Costa. Please accept my best wishes." I took that as a dismissal.

I went to the clerk to get the order and directions on getting service. It was easy, with a check for a couple of hundred dollars. I'd have to tell 'Sol and Mrs. Pina about it, and how to enforce it, but that beat the hell out of the alternative. I also had to let 'Sol's school and the hotel know.

Once I got home, I found a legal pad and some pens in the desk I used to pay bills. The police had forensics and plenty of access to witnesses. I didn't, so I began with the victim. There was a reason to kill that man. Someone took huge risks to do it in that time, place and way.

I poured another cup of coffee and grabbed an ashtray. Isabel called my meanderings Attention Deficit Disorder. I called it thinking on my feet, and Isabel would give me a tolerant smile, tilting her head forward so her hair fell partly over her face. Marisol was going to let me have it about smoking in the house, but I needed them to concentrate. I checked the time to see how long it would be before 'Sol got home, and re-established the Internet connection that had been whimsically terminated by some switch, relay or microchip.

A long time later, I stopped. My eyes felt gritty and hot, and I knew enough of the public record of the public man. Congressman Richard Morley seemed to fit the definition of a politician, "One who makes the rare appearance of a statesman so clear to view by providing a backdrop of unremitting mediocrity."

The "Gentleman from Rhode Island" was a white bread blur, but the private man could generate dislike. Certainly, I had come to dislike him, during our five-minute acquaintance.

He was good at getting drunk, so I plugged into the network. Bartenders spoke often, particularly after serious problems. Customers to watch out for, stalkers, brawlers, addicts, prostitutes and scammers were all shared. You never knew where you might wind up working or with whom, so we cooperated. We might have uttered an unkind word or two about our employers. I was going through my address book, when the doorbell rang.

I looked at the clock. Too early for 'Sol or Mrs. Pina. I could hear Mrs. Pina upstairs, seeking out dirt that dared to defy her. My legal pad was covered with notes, arrows and circles and underlines. I flipped it over, and signed off of the computer before I went to the door.

Petersen and DaSilva had changed their clothes. DaSilva wore a three-piece suit, navy blue with light pink pinstripes, at least fifteen years out of style. He looked well rested, and bandbox clean and bright. The fact that the suit still fit him was a credit to his physical condition. Petersen wore a lightweight linen suit with the top two buttons fastened so his artillery showed as a noticeable bulge. It was comical or tragic, the way he just didn't get it. For some reason, he wore a canvas, broad brimmed hat.

"May we come in, Mr. Costa?" said a female voice. I hadn't seen her, standing behind Petersen, but I pulled the door open.

"My daughter will be home soon, and I have to get dinner going, and get ready for work," I said, "unless you're arresting me."

"No rush," said Petersen. "Plenty of time. We just want to introduce you to the lady who'll get to do that. We're holding her coat, this being a federal matter, now." There was anger in his voice, and I hoped that the woman standing to his right was the target. Solving a congressman's murder was a career maker, and it was being taken away from him.

DaSilva seemed resigned. "This is FBI Special Agent, Dana Kilroy, Mr. Costa, and she'll be leading the investigation. Detective Petersen and I will be part of a joint task force, providing mutual support." That was more information that I expected as a suspect. I smelled the effluvia of a jurisdiction battle and felt a stirring of hope. The more time they spent pissing on each other's shoes, the better for me.

"Commander Costa," she began, "is there somewhere we can sit and talk? There's a lot to clear up and not much time. As you may guess, there's a lot of publicity and pressure to get this wrapped up promptly." Her use of my old rank meant that she had my records from Defense, demonstrating her authority. "Wrapping things up," quickly would be much simpler if I was the killer.

I offered them coffee, and ushered them into the kitchen. It had been twenty hours and a bit since I'd slept, and I felt an ache between my shoulder blades that signaled extreme fatigue. Even if they didn't want coffee, I needed it badly.

"With respect, Mr., I mean, Commander, Costa, may I say that you look like warmed-up dogshit?"

"That is not necessary, Detective Petersen," the agent said. He smirked at her back, like a schoolboy taunting a teacher.

"With equal respect, Detective Petersen, I've never tried it, but I'll defer to your dining experiences," I said. DaSilva shook his head and kept walking.

I glanced at the mirror in the hallway and saw my reflection. He had a point. My face sagged and I wanted a shower and twelve hours of sleep. I hoped that I still had reserves to call on.

My light olive complexion was almost sallow. I saw muddy brown, bloodshot, tired looking eyes, a twice-broken nose with a few random scars, salt and pepper hair, and a thankfully slim build. I pulled myself more erect, forced my shoulders straight down and put a familiar arch into my back. I followed them into the kitchen. Dana Kilroy sat at the head of the table, my usual seat, Petersen stood, leaning against the kitchen counter behind her, and DaSilva had seated himself. I got mugs out, cream and sugar, being sure to hand Petersen the most effeminate mug I could find. He held it with his hands wrapped around it. I stood with my back to the stove, forcing Petersen to turn his head to look at me, while I could see Agent Kilroy's lovely profile. I stood in a nearly military "parade rest" and waited.

"Please sit down, Commander," she said.

"No, thank you, Agent Kilroy, I'm more comfortable standing, and if anyone wants anything, I can get it more easily from here." I said it pleasantly. "In a way you're my guests, and I'd like to be as good a host as I can."

Petersen straightened from his slouch by the sink, still holding onto his girlish coffee cup. He was doing his best to loom. "Siddown," he said.

"Agent Kilroy, since you're under the gun and I have a lot to do, would you like to start?"

"You think we give a single dead rat's ass what you have to do? Look at me, I'm talkin' to you!" Petersen said. I heard Mrs. Pina stop upstairs, and DaSilva looked at Petersen, slightly shaking his head. Petersen slouched back into my counter, looking at the ceiling and puffing his cheeks as he blew air out. He reached into his left armpit to scratch or play with his gun.

Dana Kilroy was about thirty-five or so, five-six, half a foot shorter than me, with the build and stride of an athlete rather than a model. She had ash blonde hair and even features. Her eyes were an incredible clear blue, with an incongruous Asiatic tilt at the corners. She wore a sensible skirt, no slit, nylons and shoes that could have had heels, but didn't. Her collarless blouse came to the base of her throat, sheer enough to show hints of lace where tricks of light worked through. Her jacket had no lapels at all, and it was cut full and long. I expected a holster at her right waist, rather than in a purse. I was annoyed at myself for noticing a hint of perfume when she turned, something that smelled like cinnamon.

I saw the holster where I expected it and the grips of a Beretta nine millimeter, similar to one I'd carried for a few years. Hers probably used seven round magazines, to keep the grips slimmer and more concealable. Extra magazines would be in pouches at her left waist.

Her blonde hair was pulled smoothly back, leaving no errant strands to fall into her face. It shone softly and captured the light with varying shades of gold. She aimed her exotic blue eyes at me, and reached into a small portfolio I hadn't noticed. "I've gotten Detective Petersen and Sergeant DaSilva cleared for this, and they'll be getting copies, Commander. Some of your records are still beyond my reach, for the moment." She paused, waiting for me to say something.

I tried to look pleasantly interested, but said nothing. I wanted them frustrated, but not angry. She shifted in her chair, careful of her skirt, showing a sign of discomfort.

She spoke again, "I know what the Newport police know, and we're still waiting for the coroner's report and autopsy. It won't surprise you to hear that we found a partial palm, index finger and thumb print on the knife matching your right hand." I noticed that she had a slight drawl, with no hint of New England in it. She spoke the way that career military people do.

"Also on the knife, besides Congressman Morley's blood; they found fruit traces, dishwashing detergent, some hair and brain tissue. The knife is sharp with a slight curve, a fine, narrow and flexible blade, approximately four inches long. Without further details, we are assuming that the knife penetrated the ear and brain to cause death. We are assuming that murder is the manner of death."

She paused to take a sip of her coffee. I wondered why she told me so much. I thought about interrogations, and how much of what went on was neither asked nor answered aloud. I assumed that she was trying to demonstrate how hopeless it was to try to hide anything.

She squirmed and her skirt pulled up slightly, revealing more. I wanted to show nothing but composure. Staring at her legs would not do.

"Lots of assuming there, wouldn't you agree, Agent Kilroy?" I said evenly. I felt Petersen's energy rise.

"You found the guy in a fuckin' men's room, with your fuckin' knife in his ear, two hours after you almost broke his arm and threw him out of your bar. The knife is covered with your prints, and you don't know a fuckin' thing about any of it. How the fuck much assumin' do you think we need to assume, here?

Both Kilroy and DaSilva were looking at me rather than Petersen, trying to make use of his hostility.

"Did anyone see Morley come back into the bar or the men's room?" I asked. "Can anyone put me in there at the same time as him? Is there any reason you wouldn't expect to find my prints on that knife? I'd used it at least twice during that shift, along with the mixing cups, lots of glasses and a spray bottle to clean the bar. Most of the bottles in the bar, the soft drink gun and ice scoop."

Agent Kilroy pushed herself back further in her chair and tugged at her skirt. "Commander," she began.

"Fuck that," interrupted Petersen. "He's just a fuckin' bartender, and a murder suspect, and this 'Commander' bullshit is just that, bullshit. Nobody got killed with a fuckin' mixing cup. He's got a lot to explain and now he's asking us questions? What exactly is this 'Commander' shit, anyway?"

Agent Kilroy said, "Commander, those are all questions we've been asking and will continue to ask until we have answers that satisfy us." Petersen might as well not have spoken. I was a long way from having control but so were they. I sneaked a glance at the kitchen clock over DaSilva's head. Not long before Marisol would be coming home and she would have to be told more if she got home before they left.

"While we're on the subject, could anyone tell me who gave my name to every journalist in the U.S. of A.? Anyone? I spent most of today in court, getting a restraining order, and it cost me an arm and a leg to get it served. Just curious about who should get that bill, because I intend to see the person who leaked that information in as deep a hole as I can put him," I paused, "or her."

"I don't know what you are talking about, Commander. I'm sure that no one in this room does, either. May I go on?" She said. I had been looking at Petersen as I spoke and he was rubbing the bridge of his nose, staring fixedly at DaSilva.

"For Detective Petersen and Sergeant DaSilva's benefit, I'm going to review some history." She began reading. "Paul Santos Costa, forty-two years old, orphaned at nine years old, only child of David and Catherine Costa, raised by paternal grandparents, Santos and Lourdes Costa, Fall River, Mass., deceased twelve and thirteen years ago, respectively, graduated United States Naval Academy, fifteenth in the class, commissioned Ensign." Petersen turned sharply in my direction.

"Various excellent fitness reports. Surface warfare, suitable for Executive Officer appointment. Leave of absence to attend Suffolk

Law School, transferred to Judge Advocate General Corps." She looked up, "Unusual, for someone on the command fast track." I couldn't think of a reason to say anything.

She went on, after a sip of coffee and clearing her throat, "Primarily a criminal prosecutor, various commendations, one for clearing an innocent man and prosecuting the actual rapist. After promotion to Lieutenant Commander and graduation from Command Curriculum, just down the road at the Naval War College, seconded to 'classified.' Anything you'd care to add to that? No? Why would a JAG attorney receive Command Training? All right. At thirty-six, resigned commission, without prejudice. Accepted into Naval Criminal Investigative Service. Resigned two and a half years ago, upon death of his wife, Isabel Costa, maiden name, 'Martel.' One daughter, aged eleven, Marisol Lourdes Costa. Currently employed as bartender. Resides here." She looked up. "Anything you'd care to add or change in all of that?"

I said, "An eclectic background, wouldn't you say?"

"I'd prefer 'checquered past,'" said DaSilva. Dana Kilroy smiled tightly, and put the folder back into the portfolio.

"Commander, those classified three years? My father was a naval officer, and I think I know what I'm going to find." Kilroy? I wondered if there was a connection. I'd served under an Admiral named "Kilroy."

"I'm not sure if murder fits your record. However, I don't see anything in your record to disprove that you're a bitter, angry man, deprived of his wife, struggling to raise a daughter alone and blaming the Navy for his problems."

Wrong, I thought, I blame myself

"It's not beyond imagining that you could kill. Those missing years in the Navy, the ones that are hidden behind a security block keep you from admittance to the bar, yes? They tell me you passed the exam on the first try but they want a complete background check prior to admission. The Navy won't give any accounting at all for that time, right? Plenty of reason for anger and frustration there, I'd say. You were a prosecutor; think you could make a case?"

We all turned to the kitchen door when we heard an angry whisper, "Daddy?" Marisol spun on her heel and walked stiffly away, like a marionette with an inept puppeteer.

I turned and left the room, not before staring at each of them in turn, daring anyone to follow. I found her curled up crying on her bed, where I bundled her in my arms, rocking her and humming old lullabies, until she sobbed down to hiccups. A soft knock on her door made us both look up. Two people stood in the doorway, Mrs. Pina, slightly ahead of Agent Kilroy. I wasn't sure if she came down because she heard the uproar, or if she was due to be there anyway.

Special Agent Dana Kilroy was leaning over Mrs. Pina. "I'm sorry," she said gently, "can I help?" The top of Mrs. Pina's bun came to the agent's chin, but she wheeled, pressing her square bosom forward like the ram on a Greek trireme.

Mrs. Pina was fluent in English, with a trace of an accent that became more obvious at moments of trial. She was whispering, but she could have been heard all the way in the kitchen. "Best for you now, police lady, is to leave my sweet girl alone with her Papa and me to try to fix this. Best to leave, now. If you need him, you call and make appointment, or you meet somewhere to do this. Helping is get out, now, and not to come back, ever. That will help." She was advancing and the Agent retreated.

"We'll be in touch, Commander," she said. I heard them leave, and later, I found three business cards on the table, hers with a note on the back, "I'm so sorry, DK." I held it in my right hand, tapping it on my left thumbnail. I needed a shower and shave before struggling with the damned studs on a tuxedo shirt, and then a full shift. I put my legal pad in my dresser drawer, off limits to Marisol and Mrs. Pina.

After supper, cleaned up and dressed, I kissed 'Sol goodnight. "I'm off tomorrow, and I'll talk to you then. I'm sorry I can't do it right now, sweetheart" She smiled bravely back at me, and her chin was firm. I wasn't sure how much she'd overheard, and what she'd made of that. If nothing else, she'd heard that I was "capable of killing," along with the "bitter, angry" part.

"They'll go away, right?"

"Right, muffin. Mrs. Pina's here, and I'll check on you when I get home."

Chapter 3

Wednesdays, I expected a different waitress, no bouncer and a quiet shift. The changeover routine took longer than normal because of the crowd. Diane, the waitress, looked harried. Once I had the bar, I saw whispered conversations and furtive glances in my direction.

The night manager stopped by, took a look around and left after nodding to me. Half an hour later, following the pianist, our best bouncer strolled in. When he reached the bar, he collected a glass of club soda and leaned on the trap. "So," he said, "you holding up okay?"

I liked the guy, despite his being a former Marine. "Good to see you. I'm okay, but I could sleep for a week or two."

"Yup, I can see that, Navy. Maybe Diane could keep you awake." He gave me an evil grin.

She was a few years younger than me and attractive. She had dark, curly hair, worn pulled back and up into a bushy ponytail. She had a fine figure and wonderful legs. Like me, she was a single parent, raising two teenaged boys by working two or three jobs. Her husband had died when her sons were young. Unlike me, she was socially active. When I started working at the hotel she made her interest clear. I found ways to avoid the issue and finally used my daughter as a shield.

She flirted with the male customers, flaunted her cleavage, her legs and lusty attitude. She had a knack for doing it without causing problems.

I looked up to see Diane looking directly into a male customer's eyes and slipping a ten-dollar bill into her bra. He was leaning forward trying to see more and she smiled, turned away and spoke to the people at the adjoining table. She looked over at me, winked slowly and licked her bright red lips. I must have had quite a look on my face because she broke up laughing and pointed at the table, gesturing for a round. I started mixing the drinks just as Teddy cleared his throat.

"Look, Paul," he began hesitantly, "I. Um, well, if you need me, or anything I can do or get done, you know." He was suddenly serious, and offering support. I had no idea what he could do, but he believed blindly that I was innocent and wanted to help. It gave me an itchy sense of embarrassment. Since Isabel died, people were accessories, labeled as co-workers, customers, employers, neighbors and acquaintances. I went through the motions, but was consumed by my own hurts and helping my daughter.

"You know that the night manager called me and the piano guy in because you're so busy tonight, right? You see the paper? Hotel's in it, you're in it, Sarah's in it and people are here to scope the place and you out. Diane said she chased two women out of the men's room, looking at the stalls and the floor. Probably trying to find blood or a souvenir. I'm tellin' you, Paul, if you were to start cutting up some lemons right now, they'd be popping flashbulbs, and asking you to sign their wine lists."

"Great," I said.

"Mind if I ask you something?" he said, with a different tone.

"Sure. If I don't like it, I'll let you know."

"You got an education and you sure as hell could have a better job, so why tend bar?"

"Guess I like the clothes."

It seemed pointless to tell him why I didn't mind tending bar. It paid the bills and kept me at a distance from people. It was occasionally interesting and sometimes enjoyable. What else could you want from a job? I got to spend more time than most guys get with their kids and it was a job you could leave at shift's end.

Busy shifts fly. I was tired at the end and the bar was a mess, but it seemed that last call arrived before I was ready. Teddy ushered the customers out, as smoothly as always. He didn't have to, but he always stayed to help clean and collect a drink before he left for home. He did the men's room while I was cleaning the bar. A true gentleman, he simply stepped in and kept me out of the room.

Diane got a Cosmopolitan and crossed her splendid legs, dangling one high heel from her toes as the foot rocked slowly up and down. "Teddy, dear, don't you have iron to pump or a brick to break?" she asked.

Teddy looked at me, with one eyebrow raised. He shrugged, handed me his empty and said good night.

"Thanks for your help tonight, " I called as he left.

"Semper Fi," he answered, just as the door closed behind him.

Diane was looking intently at me, still in the same pose. I wondered if I would need to fend her off. I was confused, because I didn't really want to. She could adopt an erotic position to count her change, with nothing on her mind except converting singles to twenties.

I was doing it again, using the image of her instead of the reality before me to hide. Earlier in the day, I'd felt my first interest in a woman since Isabel had died, so I was open to Diane's appeal. I assumed that she'd picked up on that. For the first time, I wasn't thinking about gentle rejection, but the boundaries of lace and silk and skin. Fighting an erection, I thought about the psychology of death and change and its affect on people. My libido awoke after a death, the threat of arrest, and my attraction to an FBI agent who was willing to imprison me. None of it seemed healthy.

About a year earlier, Mrs. Pina, of all people, had raised the subject. "Paul," she had said while dusting, her back to me, "if you ever need me to stay overnight with Marisol, I can do that."

"Why?" I asked. "Why would I stay away overnight?"

"You are a man, Paul, and not bad looking. A little skinny, maybe, but not bad. Good brown eyes and face, not pale and not pretty. Just right for a man's face." To Mrs. Pina, anyone who could make his knees touch was a little skinny. "I know that you have lost, and I know that you try and try to make 'Sol a happy little girl again. I know that you are letting part of being a man sleep, you understand." She was blushing, because in her world, no woman said things like this aloud to a man.

"Paul, in time, a woman to wake you will come to you. There are such women. Sometimes, even a good, married man needs such a woman." She was crying.

I had patted her on the back, until she turned and fell into my arms to be held and to cry her memories back into the past. Finally, she put both hands on my chest and pressed herself away. "I know the time will come." She went back to stalking cobwebs, saying no more.

"Paul?" Diane was asking, by her tone, probably for the second or third time.

"Sorry, Diane, preoccupied, I guess."

"Who's the lucky girl?"

I looked back at her, without answering.

"Honey, I was just kidding, to lighten it up, you know? Nobody here thinks—" she stopped. "I've seen you deal with things, and you never did it harder than you had to. Except that one guy who got grabby with me. Did he ever complain?"

"No, I explained things to him."

"'Explained?'"

"I'm a reasonable guy, Diane. I got him to understand."

"Oh. Right. Okay. Anyway, nobody thinks that you couldn't do it, but nobody here believes you would. Paul, are you listening, or still trying to look down my dress?" she said, then, seeing my embarrassment, "I don't think that you're interested, but it would take the edge off, right?" She looked down at the top of the bar, and then raised her eyes.

I turned my hand over and took hers. "You don't use friends that way."

She turned away and nodded, squeezing my hand. I freed it after a moment.

After I walked her to her car, I looked over at my old silver Saab. The body was sound, the engine ran well, and I stayed off the gas to keep the turbocharger from kicking in. Marisol loved the convertible top. I'd been holding onto it for "one more year" for the past three years. Isabel had told me that I was too sentimental about cars.

I drove home thinking about blondes and brunettes, and legs and breasts, high heels and sleep. I should have been thinking about motive, method and opportunity, but I let my mind drift. I was lucky to have a short drive, because I was nearly stumbling when I made it home. Mrs. Pina yawned. "Sol had trouble sleeping, but she's down for the night." She stretched onto her toes and kissed me on the cheek. "Sometimes," she said, "even grown men need a smooch from a grandma."

Marisol was asleep on her back, with both arms over her face. I saw tearstains, and felt a hollow spot forming in my stomach. In my room I looked at my bed with something like lust. I put my clothes onto hangers or into the hotel's laundry bag, before I finally got myself under the covers. I expected to lie awake, but I was asleep before I sank into the mattress.

Chapter 4

I woke, confused. My eyes opened wide as I felt around on the sheets and my shorts. At my age, I'd had a wet dream. I guess after almost three years, I shouldn't have been surprised, with the thoughts I'd been having all day. No way was Mrs. Pina going to find out about it, so I stripped and made the bed back up with fresh sheets. I threw it all into the washer, with some towels to make it look like a regular load.

I took a shower, but skipped shaving. I told myself all kinds of things. I was careful not to tell myself I was afraid, or that I'd somehow betrayed my dead wife.

I was home alone, a note from Marisol, telling me not to worry. She was supposed to be a little girl, and I admired her courage and resilience, hating the need for them. I was looking at a day off and the chance to get some work done, if I could focus. I pulled out my address book and started to make some calls. I kept what might be the last residential landline in Rhode Island for Mrs. Pina and my daughter, and used it while my mobile was charging.

The congressman favored Pearl Harbors, Blue Hawaiians, white and black Russians, with an occasional Rumrunner. They were all potent drinks without a strong taste of alcohol. He could get hammered, but not have to deal with the taste? *Don't think too hard,* I thought. He liked strip clubs, bars with hookers and "sophisticated singles" bars. The latter were places for married people to escape from their spouses. Bartenders in Newport, Providence and Warwick remembered him well.

Bouncers knew him. Waitresses tried not to be alone with him. The maitre d' at another hotel's restaurant knew a guy. He called him, and called me back with the number. When I called, the bartender asked me to drop by and talk. "It'll be worth it to you, and so help me, I think I'll feel better, too," he'd said.

It was a tough drive to get to the "gentlemen's club" where he worked. I'd never worked at a strip joint, a different kind of job. Customers simmering from a combination of overpriced beer and frustrated lust didn't sound like fun, but it paid pretty well. Even though it was early when I arrived, they had girls working on the stage.

There are two kinds of bars: a shotgun being straight, usually with a mirror behind it, and a horseshoe, a complete or partial ring. If you have more than one bartender working, a horseshoe is better. Otherwise, I preferred the shotgun, keeping customers in front of me, and the mirror helped when I was faced away from the room. The "club" had a circular bar, with the stage filling the center. Steps were cut into the bar to allow them to walk up to the stage. Two brass poles marked the north and south of that world. With no windows and muted lights, it looked like midnight. There was a solitary customer at the bar, leaning on it, gazing up at the dancer, who listlessly gyrated to some hip-hop thuds and shouting.

After the shock of seeing my first bare breasts in over two years, the dancer's slack expression was so dispiriting that I had no thought of sex. Her high heels, with lacy ankle socks seemed like an odd combination I wondered about the woman inside of the expertly displayed body. I saw nothing behind her eyes. Besides making the women more visible, the elevated stage put the dancers in a superior, controlling position. To the men, they were presented with no secrets left. There was a sad mutual dislike in the arrangement.

Tim Foley was built like a boulder at Stonehenge, with the same skin texture. "Davy says you're okay," he said.

"So." He took a deep breath and began, "It's about this girl. Not the one on stage, another one. She used to work here. Lois is her real name. A nice girl. Thinks the guys are mostly lonely. In here, that's safe, because we watch. Out there," he pointed with his chin to the door, "they're on their own. Lois danced as 'Lolita,' started out in kind of a Catholic School outfit. She'd strap in tight for her Lolita thing, and they'd kind of spring out, when she popped the bra."

"Anyhow, that Senator, or whatever, Morley? He was in once or twice a week, usually during quiet times, like now. Most of the dancers would get a few bucks off of him, put up with him copping a feel when they come down to the bar but blew him off for anything outside. They smelled money but something warned them off."

I interrupted, "The girls, Tim, are they straight, or do some of them work?" He answered with a back and forth waggle of one hand, palm down.

"They keep it cozy if they do. Lois is just a pretty girl, trying to make the living she can with what she has. Not a hooker, or college girl. She's a soft touch for guys with sad eyes and a good line of shit, though. You'd do okay."

I blinked. "The money in the game, is it pretty good for the straight ones?"

"Depends on how good they are at getting into the guys' heads. If they can make the guys think that each one is getting her turned on up there? Two or three grand a week, cash, easy. A guy thinks she's half naked and it's all for him, and the money goes into that g-string as fast as he can get it out of his pocket. You'd think he'd notice that other guys are giving her money. Course, when they do notice, we get fights going. When three guys are all buying her splits of champagne at twenty per, you have to wonder."

"So, Lois?" I said.

"Sure. So he comes in, place is empty and Lois does Lolita for him. All by himself, like that guy back there. It got to him, you could see it. The little plaid skirt, the knee socks, then those great, big, standing-right-out-there knockers. He's panting and blowing, flinging money up onto the stage like it was on fire in his pockets."

"Liked her?"

He paused, searching for words. "Tell you what, guys like him don't 'like,' they fuckin' well 'want.'" The venom in his voice caught at me. "We get them in here. It gets so you can see them." How about you? I wanted to ask. Do you like her? Do you more than like her? Instinct, experience and training won out. He had to do this his way, so I waited quietly.

"Anyhow, she finishes her dance, and comes out, dressed in a sexy outfit, the way they do, and hustles a couple of champagne cocktails, you know?"

I nodded.

He continued, "He's sitting there, talking. Not laying a hand on her. I'm talking this sincere look and nodding as he listened to her, like she's interesting as hell. I fish, and you go to where they like to be and offer them what they want. Only you put a sharp fuckin' hook in the middle of it. That's what he was like."

I could almost see it going on at the table he'd pointed out.

"So time passes, the boys start to come in, and more of the girls start coming in, and Lois is going off. Our guy offers her a ride. She drove this SUV that spent more time in the shop than on the road. That day, she was gonna cab it. She says okay, they leave together." He started to shake his head, stopped and looked up. His eyes were looking far away.

"Time goes by, a week or two, and Lois is bore-assing all of us about the senator, or congressman, whatever. He takes her places, he 'listens,' 'shares,' gifts, just an all around great guy. His wife is in D.C. and their marriage is for shit, just political, wife's cold, has boy toys, fucks the pool man and the paper boy, his kids hate him, he's lonely, and like that."

Tim paused to catch his breath. "The other girls tried to warn her. She got mad, so I bit my tongue. That's that. She switches her act, getting away from 'Lolita,' starts keeping more on. After about another month or two, she's starting to show."

"Show?"

"Yeah," he made a big rounding gesture over his abdomen, "show. I caught her crying in the dressing room, when the manager fired her. By then, she ain't seen him in a month. He's down in D.C. for 'the session.'"

In this day and age? I thought.

Tim spoke, as if he heard my thinking. "She just lost her head. Supposedly he's fixed and can't make a kid." He paused, and took a couple of breaths. "So there I am, offering to help, and I wind up taking her to a woman's clinic, and they take care of it. No more baby. No more problem, right?" He paused, looked over his shoulder at the stripper. Looked into the mirror at the only customer. "Shit," he said softly. "So I took her home, tucked her into bed and left. I should have stayed. I think she wanted me to. I was too pissed to offer."

"Something went wrong, because a few mornings later she calls; she's still bleeding and it smells funny. I take her to the hospital, and this is 'septic' and that's 'toxic' and when they finish cutting away the bad parts— she's twenty-four, and taking hormones." It was tough watching him.

"Tim—"

"Nah, I'm okay. I'm okay. Feels better to tell it. So now, finally, she's mad. Finally. She catches a Southwest flight to D.C. on my credit card. A week goes by, maybe two and I ain't heard nothing. I'm about to get a ticket to go down there." He was talking faster and I needed him to stay with it, so I interrupted, holding my mug out for a refill.

As he leaned under the bar to the coffee pot he went on, "Finally, she comes in here while I'm working and she's wearing dark glasses and a turtleneck. Not her style. I pull the collar down and there're bruises all around her neck. Not hickeys— bruises, green and yellow. And when I take off her sunglasses, there's a shiner. Cut lip, some old swelling around her mouth, a serious ass kicking. She's so fuckin' pretty, though. No, she didn't bump into the Senator; she got mugged, blah, blah. I got mad, not at her but she might have thought so; I don't know." He paused to hand me my mug of old, black coffee.

He was talking faster, as if trying to dump it in a rush. To avoid looking at him, I glanced up at the stage, and saw another set of bare breasts. They belonged to a freckled redhead, and barely protruded from her chest, except for the long, purplish nipples that tipped them. Her legs were long and lovely. She looked like somebody's teenaged daughter.

"She came to thank me and pay me back for the tickets. I told her to keep the money, and walked her out to her car. It wasn't her old SUV, but a brand new red Miata convertible, Maryland tags, with lots of luggage. 'Timmy,' she called me, 'Timmy, I have to go. I was stupid. Now I have to go for awhile. Wish I'd been smart about you, and things, sooner' she said. She kissed me on the lips, once, and got into her car and drove off. I wanted to stop her, but it was like she wasn't even here. It was like talking with a ghost." He stopped.

"Can you reach her?" I asked.

He looked at me, and I saw what I'd already heard. His face was cold and still, and any vulnerability was gone. His voice was different. "She's out of this, Paul."

The smells and sights and sounds of the day so far had done nothing but make me sad. I handed a five to the dancer sitting next to the guy at the bar. She held out a strap for me to slip it under, and I placed it directly into her hand. One less guy to paw her, one less to try to hunt her into bed as a notch on his belt.

Her eyes opened wider, and she looked me fully in the face. With animation in her eyes, she was astonishingly lovely and young.

It was almost noon when I got home, so I got back onto the phone.

Everyone had questions, from "How are you?" to the one they all wanted to ask, "So, didja kill him?" before providing the answers I needed. Extracting promises to keep the calls private was touchy, but dissembling is second nature to bartenders.

Washington is a long way from Newport but I had a few names. "A gentleman, nice guy, good tips, well-mannered, moderate drinker, scotch and water," was what I got. Seen either with his wife or with appropriate people. Morley was not a nice man close to home. Apparently, when he got close to work or in front of more powerful people, he got nice or at least under control. The world has lots of not-nice people, though, and most make it to a ripe old age.

His wife and family resided in Washington year-round, although he maintained a residence in Rhode Island, where the rest of his family visited for vacations. I thought the media lived for this kind of thing. The Congressman played dirty up north, and clean in Washington.

He had some kind of cover, if he had done the damage to Lois himself. He had money that wasn't accountable to anyone to buy her silence. So she was dumb enough to get involved, to get pregnant. Dumb enough to confront him but smart enough to be content with the money he'd offered and run.

Tim was no idiot. He saw something in her. He was hanging on, loving a woman who couldn't return it. I could understand that. The woman I loved wasn't available, either.

'Sol came home, boiling over with the day's events. I mentioned my plan for the afternoon and she jumped at it.

People came from all over to Newport for summers. It was the tail end of the season, but we headed north to Bristol, bringing a kite to the state park. For her entire life, I had been trying to find a kite that I could get airborne and keep there. This latest version was absolutely guaranteed to fly in the lightest winds.

Marisol thought that was hysterically funny and kept humming the Air Force Anthem. When we got to the park, she played with an old couple's dog while I assembled it. She'd been hinting about a dog, and I was finding it harder to ignore her. This one was some kind of fluffy, dust mop looking thing, with a shrill bark and a mountain of attitude.

Then I flung the contraption into the air, where it drew the string tight and climbed. It climbed until it exhausted the supply of string, and hung in the sky, barely visible except for its neon color.

'Sol held the reel and gazing up at the kite, asked, "Daddy?" I hesitated for too long. "Daddy, please? Mrs. Pina said that it's your place to tell me, and I can trust you. Some of the kids," she stopped and started to bite at the cuticle of her index finger. She did it with enough aggression that I put my hand gently on hers until she stopped. I tried not to let my anger come through. Whatever her classmates had said must have come from the adults at dinner.

"Honey, people say things that they should never say, and probably wouldn't if they thought about it for a minute." I tried to give her an honest, but carefully edited version of events, and what it meant to us. I told her that I wasn't going to wait for the truth to come out. I was going to act on my own.

"Daddy?"

"Yes, sweets?"

"Mamacita said that you're the smartest and bravest man in the world. She used to say that you were like the men on TV, the good guys. She said that you could do anything you wanted to."

"Mamacita said that about me?"

"Yes." She looked down for a moment, "Sometimes I still talk to her, you know."

"Me too, honey."

When she looked back up, she was smiling. "Daddy, you got a kite to fly."

After we reeled in our new kite, I stashed it in the trunk of "the tank," as Isabel had named my Saab. We found a place that made pretty good chowder and reeked of hot grease. Something about the smell of frying made Marisol feel comfortable. Whenever we went out, if she smelled it, she liked the place. We laughed at silly things and held hands on our way home.

Later that afternoon, she finished her homework and dozed off, looking a little wind burned, with a small secret smile around her eyes.

The phone rang, moments before the computer modem would have dialed, and I picked it up. It was a woman's voice, speaking softly and quickly. She started out like someone calling a business. "I'm looking for Mr. Paul Costa?"

"Speaking," I answered, "who's calling?"

"I'm trying to reach the Paul Costa who spoke with Timmy Foley, earlier today."

"Timmy," I was sure was tolerated from one person in the world. "Lois?"

There was a pause and for a second I thought she'd hung up. "It is you. Good," she said.

"Lois, Tim made it clear that he doesn't want you in the middle of this."

"Timmy told me, but I need to talk to you myself. Can I call you Paul? Paul," she began, without waiting for an answer, "Do you know Timmy loves kids? Coaches Little League and all. The boys worship him. Wouldn't get kids from me. Nope. He tell you about that? Did he tell you that I was too stupid to protect myself? Did he tell you that?"

I started to interrupt her, but decided that my grandfather had been right. Long before, he had counted my ears, then my mouth, "Two ears, one mouth. Listen to two words before you speak one. Listen twice before you speak once."

I had a whole speech ready, about love, and hope, and pity, and protection and how tangled up they could get. I knew that she was already protecting him. She knew Tim. She knew that her pain would become his. She was twenty-four, or five, at the most, though, and had no idea how fast time passes and how its pace increases like a runner finding his stride.

"Lois," I said, and stopped. "I was going to give you free advice, but it's worth exactly what you pay for it."

"Timmy said you're smart, but I think I know what you'd say. So instead, promise not to tell Timmy any more than he knows."

"I promise." The silence dragged on. "Lois, if you can't talk to me, that's okay." I could hear her breathing, and my own.

"He called me, before he talked to you. I told him to tell you the whole story, all of it. Then afterwards, he told me about you. He said you're smart, and you might have been a cop, because you made him think of cops when you talked to him, but a nicer sort of."

I wasn't sure if that was a compliment.

"I'm not Morley's first, or the last. It's like this club, you know? The initiation really, really sucks. It's a big club, not hard to get into, I guess."

The life was starting to leave her voice. She was animated by anger, but she seemed to be unable to hold onto it. I liked her for that. She had every right to be in a rage, but didn't have the nature to nurse it. "His standards weren't that high, I guess."

"Lois, I'm no one to give you advice, but pushing yourself down won't help. You said it was a big club, right? He was an expert hunter and I doubt that you'd ever been prey before."

She paused again, "How much do you know about men like that? Is Timmy right? Are you a cop? Or do you just know about them? Timmy knew, and so did some of the other dancers; is that how you know?"

"Little of both, I guess. I was a cop, sort of, and I have to know about people to do my job. Nowadays I'm a bartender, like Tim."

"Not like him; he said that. He said that talking to you is easy but that there's something really hard in you. He said you're sadder than hell, too."

God save us from smart people.

"You didn't kill him," she said, as if it was a fact. There will be two tides tomorrow, you didn't kill the congressman. "Timmy says you could, but he doesn't think you did, and I don't either."

"Why not?" I asked.

She didn't answer.

If they were picking that up somehow, then DaSilva might, and maybe it would get through to Agent Kilroy, she of the pretty legs and nice underwear.

"Unless he did something to somebody you care about, I don't think you'd get mad enough. I don't think that you care much otherwise."

Just beautiful. They were sure of my innocence because I didn't give a damn about anybody. The hell of it was that they were right.

"I didn't kill him. I threw him out of the bar earlier because he had a foul mouth and he was drunk. He was dead, under a toilet when I found him after I closed." I failed to think of more to say.

"I have some things to do before I come home." It wasn't a response, just her reaction to the change.

There was wisdom in her, and courage. I heard resolution in her voice. For that moment, I was jealous of Tim Foley. "I'm still trying to find all of the women like me. So far, anyone who made him look at what he did got a warning. Those warnings could get rough. Timmy told you?"

"About the bruises?"

"Yes, but I didn't tell him what happened. That would have sent him off into all kinds of trouble." She waited. I really didn't want to know. Maybe for a change, I'd think of her first; it would be good practice for me. She wouldn't tell me unless I asked. I believed that she really needed to. Bartenders are supposed to know things like that.

"Do you want to tell me?"

"No, but I have to. You. Somebody." She stopped for a moment and when she started again, her voice was a little different, as if she was telling a story about a stranger.

"When I called his office, he made arrangements to meet me at my motel." I could hear the pitch of her voice rise.

"And he showed up?"

"Yeah, he showed up. With his son and some other guy. I was ready. I was ready. I had a video camera set up, in the closet, focused so you could see the whole room. I turned it on when they knocked on the door. I got it all recorded, sound, too. The three of them taking turns. All of it."

"Jesus Christ," I said quietly, not blasphemy, but a prayer.

She was crying, finally. I had been hoping she would. Crying healed. Isabel believed in crying if there was pain. "I can still smell the carpet, and see that gray bedspread, with flowers on it, all rumpled. I can feel them on me, and in me, holding me down. I fought so that they'd hurt me, because I wanted to be hurt. Is that sick? I don't know."

The words were coming, faster and louder. I wanted them to stop, but she needed to say it all. The words probably tasted like vomit, and getting it all out would be far better. "When I think about it, I can hear them, too. Dick was applauding his son, like he'd hit a home run in little league. The other guy was the worst though. Just cold. Didn't talk, except, 'don't move,' or 'spread your legs,' 'open your mouth,' like he needed me to move my head to cut my hair, or like a dentist says 'open wider.'"

"I may have to stop for a minute." I heard her breathing, like a runner at the end of the race, "No, no, I'm okay. Anyway, I got it on recorded, clear, and you can hear it, too. Them, me begging them to stop."

"And you sent the congressman a copy?"

"Damned right, Personal and Confidential to his office, in a box from one of his porno videos tapes. He loved porn, and he'd send the tapes or DVD's or even flash drives to my apartment for us to watch together. He always needed to see something before—"

"And he paid?"

"I got a big check and a receipt from some lawyer. I saved the envelope and made copies of everything for my safe deposit box. The receipt said it was for 'videography and miscellaneous services' and said 'Paid in full,' like a warning, you know? I knew what would happen if I said anything, after the money. He knew I had a copy of the flash drive in a safe deposit box, along with all of my medical reports. Timmy doesn't know that he can open the box, too. I gave a letter to a lawyer to be opened if anything happened to me. That letter would have told Timmy what to do. I guess it's blackmail, but it's less than I'd have gotten if I'd sued him."

She had a point. Lawyers get settlements, but if you do it yourself, it's extortion. Sometimes I was glad I didn't practice law.

"Do you know who killed him?"

"Nope. Wasn't me, wasn't Timmy, wasn't you. That's what I know." Then she hung up, without another word.

I cradled the phone, walked over to the picture window and stared at the Japanese maple in the front yard. Maybe it would live, despite my best efforts. Mrs. Pina's grandson was trying hard to keep it alive. It looked a little better I thought.

So, she was so scared that she arranged a "Dead Man's Switch." The name came from the controls on a railroad engine. If the engineer took his hand off the controls, the switch would open and the train would stop. More than one spy was walking around free because of a Dead Man's Switch.

If Lois was harmed in any way, the "Gentleman from Rhode Island," would be exposed as a sexually dysfunctional rapist and serial cheater with a seriously ill son. The Dead Man's Switch only worked if the target was aware of it, with no ability to prevent its activation. It worked if the target was afraid of the consequences. Hers was simple and deadly.

Now the target was dead. No, there were two others. Did both of them know about it? Was there a way to short circuit the switch? If they felt threatened, but were unaware of the switch, Lois was possibly in danger.

Tim was off and I didn't have a home number for him. The automatic call back was blocked so I couldn't go directly back to Lois.
I wished that I'd asked. I had been a pretty good interrogator in my time, a good investigator, a decent attorney but I hadn't gotten enough clarity or specifics. Or was it that I didn't think of her as a "subject"? I didn't know if she knew the possible sources of danger, and I should have made sure. She knew about the Congressman and I felt my dislike for the dead man starting to rise.

After I tried and failed to find Tim Foley's number, I started scribbling on a legal pad, laying out a time line. Most of the details were concentrated in the time leading up to closing time a couple of nights in the past, the rest being vague notations, with a gap before his death. I had Lois noted.

I called the strip joint, and was told that "we ain't an answering service, pal." I didn't like the "pal," but he hung up before I could tell him so. If I sat and waited, then things would happen to me. Before I had time to change my mind, I picked up the embossed business card and dialed a Boston number.

"Federal Bureau of Investigation, how may I direct your call?" said a real, live receptionist. My tax dollars at work. I asked for Special Agent Dana Kilroy, and was told that she wasn't available.

"I'm sorry, sir, but unless it's an emergency, I have instructions to send callers into her voice mail." She did so, without waiting for my answer.

Agent Kilroy's voice in the recording was clear and professional, her greeting brief. The cool neutrality sent me into a high school state of nerves. Just like the combination of a business-like attire and attractive lingerie, it seemed to be a mixture of the professional and the sexy. Of course, erotic thoughts made me think that I was being unfaithful to Isabel, so guilt was close by. I took a deep breath and asked her to call, leaving my home phone number, one I was sure she already had. "We should talk, but I'd prefer some sort of neutral ground."

The phone rang a half hour later, "Commander Costa?"

"Yes, Agent Kilroy."

“I’d prefer that you come here to the office to talk, or that we meet at the Newport Police Headquarters.”

“Nope. Not unless you take me into custody, and if you wanted to do that, you would have.”

Her sigh was exasperated, but her voice was controlled, “Commander, do you enjoy goading us? What if I tell you that I’m aware of your ‘investigation’? What if I tell you that I spoke with my father, and that he spoke to some old friends but I’m keeping that confidential for the time being?”

Kilroy. Her father. My old boss. No wonder she’d been able to get past the obstacles surrounding my records. Vice Admiral Thomas Reilly Kilroy. He probably still had lots of old friends. He had to be retired, but his reach would still be long, and capable of parting bureaucratic obstacles.

“I’m sure the admiral was a big help, Agent Kilroy, but I have no idea what it gained you. Regardless,” I spoke right through her attempt to interrupt, “I won’t be interviewed in Boston, or with DaSilva and Petersen unless I’m in custody. I will be glad to speak privately and unofficially with you.”

After a long wait, she took a breath and named a restaurant about halfway between Providence and Boston. She told me to meet her there at nine o’clock. There was no “goodbye,” just a silent phone. For the first time since the hotel hired me, I called in sick.

Marisol woke from her nap, and I fixed her a sandwich. We chatted until Mrs. Pina came down. ‘Sol and I went to her room to check her homework. When I returned to the living room, her plump protectoress was carrying a laundry basket from the cellar. I checked a couple of cable news channels. No surprises, full investigation, no information released, just the updates about Morley’s official memorial service, showing a clip of his wife and children. The family’s private funeral would be conducted after the autopsy.

I watched the well-groomed, preppy son, the impeccable wife and grave, shy daughter. Whatever I was looking for, I didn’t see. The son looked as he was supposed to, arm around his mother’s waist, and holding his sister’s hand. The man of the family. They were a political family, and they knew how to work a visual image. The local papers would have that picture of the three of them. I turned it off, and got a cup of old coffee.

My daughter walked into the living room and sat next to me on the couch. We had an unspoken agreement not to mention the murder. When I looked at the kitchen clock, it was already seven-thirty. "I have to go out," I said to her and Mrs. Pina, "but not to work. I'll be home as early as I can."

I dressed in the "Newport Uniform," khakis and a blue jacket, with a blue oxford cloth shirt, and no tie. I finished shaving, and was rubbing on some cologne, when I realized that I was taking a lot of care with my appearance.

It isn't a date.

Mrs. Pina sniffed as I walked by and made an approving face. Marisol looked me up and down. "Oh, yeah," she said, "you're slamming." I made a mental note to find out if "slamming" was a good thing, and if so, how she knew. I kissed her on the forehead, and got into my car. It seemed safe, looking at the sky, so I put the top down and pulled out.

I drove up Route 24 onto 95, and fought my way through the usual build up at the interchange to get into a useable lane when the light dawned. She knew about my investigation, she'd said. Assuming that nobody had called the police or her, then I'd been under surveillance. My phone was tapped, too. I said, "Shit," aloud. By law, anyone who spoke on that phone would eventually have to be told about it. Any of Marisol's friends, as well as all of the people who'd thought we'd spoken in confidence would get an official letter from the Newport Police.

I was relieved to think that I must have seemed like an innocent man, but I'd dropped Lois and Tim squarely into the mess. They had motive and there was the question of possible extortion. I was angry with myself and the intrusion. Of course they'd put me under surveillance and tapped my phone. They left me on the loose to see what I'd do. Basic stuff, Cop 101, and I had blithely worked the phone and wandered around. It was called "situational awareness," and I'd blown it.

"It isn't a chess game," I'd been told years before, "the opposition isn't obliged to wait their turn to move, nor are you."

I said, "shit," quietly, one more time, and tried to adjust.

Lois's phone call would have given them enough to work on.

Chapter 5

The decorations in the restaurant were supposed to call coaches, carriages and country inns to mind. I nodded to the bartender when I saw him. He looked surprised, but nodded back. I watched his eyes when he had no orders. They swept the lounge, and when he caught me looking, he smiled and nodded. He leaned against the back shelf with his arms folded, providing privacy to his customers, yet ready to serve them on short notice. I knew the position well, and knew that he'd shift sometimes, to get the shelf away from the back of his thighs and ease his back.

I smelled grilling beef, and decided that whatever happened, I was going to finish supper. I looked at my watch to see that I was four minutes early. The hostess seated me, handed me a menu the size of a wall map, and I told her that I was expecting a guest, just in time to see her.

Agent Kilroy strode up to the table. I should have been thinking about what she was going to ask. I shouldn't have noticed her short wine-red dress and black stockings. Or that she was wearing heels. I shouldn't have noticed that her hair was loose with reflected golden light or that she was beautiful. She looked like a woman, not the enemy. I was thinking of satin sheets and a sex-scented bedroom. I should have been thinking of a daughter and a wife who still seemed to be within reach.

Remembering the stinging slap on the back of my head from my grandfather, his "manners reminder," I smiled and stood until she sat. Her walk was smooth, still athletic and graceful. The heels added an entrancing sway to it. Nothing provocative about it, I'd have said. Except that it was. She stroked the back of her skirt down and tightened it across her rear as she sat. I was careful to be looking directly into her face when she swung her legs under the table.

I glanced over her shoulder and noticed that a couple of the men who had seen her come in found her attractive, too. What the hell should

I care? Except that I did. I smelled cinnamon, and saw her tan, where her watch had slipped a bit. I heard the slither and rasp of nylons as she crossed her legs under the table. I might have imagined that sound. Except that I didn't.

She had tapped my phone, had me followed, broken open records that were supposed to be unbreakable, and I was as hard as a bar of iron. Along with that, I was comparing her to Isabel. Those are bigger, she's a bit taller and her legs are just as nice, but maybe slimmer and that's different; wonder if it would feel different?

"Something from the bar?" said the motherly waitress.

"Chardonnay for me," said Dana Kilroy.

I was surprised, but it was okay with me. I ordered a light beer, and the waitress trundled away.

"So," we said together. I laughed, but she only smiled. When she smiled, there was a slight curl to her upper lip.

Focus, dumbass, I thought. You aren't a kid. "You look very nice," I said.

"I had plans to go to a show tonight, but this was more important. I didn't have time to change."

"Oh."

"Yes, oh." She paused, "But thank you, anyway."

"Commander—"

"Agent Kilroy, it's been 'Mister' for some time."

"Mr. Costa, you apparently know that you've been under surveillance."

"No, Agent Kilroy, I didn't until I was halfway here. I figured it out. Too late, but I did figure it out. My phone, too?"

She nodded. "I wanted to tell you again how sorry I am about your daughter being exposed to that interview. She's what? Twelve?"

"Eleven."

"She didn't deserve that, and I really do regret it."

I looked at her, carefully. I believed her. "Thank you, Agent Kilroy."

"You know, I think this 'Agent Kilroy' and 'Mr. Costa' business is slowing things down. Dana?"

"Sure, Dana, please call me Paul."

"Detective Petersen had surveillance and said you lost him in Warwick, so you must have known about it." I thought about that for a minute. I hadn't seen any surveillance, and the only place I'd gone was the 'gentleman's club' to meet Tim Foley.

"Your phone tap should tell you who I spoke with and where I went, so it's time for cards to come onto the table."

"I certainly agree," Dana said, leaning forward. I looked into her neckline enjoying the low cut black bra that forced up a smooth curve of creamy skin. I pulled my eyes back up to meet hers. She was smiling a bit, but it turned off abruptly.

"Excuse me," I said, knowing she'd caught me.

She smiled again. "This once." That sounded a lot like flirting as I remembered it, so I smiled back at her. "Cards on the table?"

I nodded. "Petersen," I said.

"Detective Petersen is newly appointed as a detective, and we rely on Sergeant DaSilva to guide him. He had surveillance on you and said you deliberately lost him in Warwick."

"Any doubt that he said 'deliberately'?"

"None." Seeing her concentrate on something that wasn't my arrest was a relief.

"I'll get to him in a second or two. Let's start with what I know. First, I did not murder the Congressman. Second, he was scum, and lots of women are apparently in his wake, damaged, if not destroyed. Somehow, he's been able to cover that up."

"And he's a murder victim, possibly yours."

I ignored her and continued. "Not only is 'Detective' Petersen inexperienced, and an arrogant, abrasive jerk, who doesn't know a good interrogation when he sees one going on, but he's a liar."

"I know you don't like him, and I know you deliberately provoke him, but this isn't helpful."

"Oh, I don't like him, but that isn't it. He's lying. I didn't go anywhere near Warwick. If you check my phone logs, you'll know where I went and when. It won't take you long to find out. Warwick would have taken me a good half hour out of my way in nasty traffic. He's lying. I didn't do any counter-surveillance because I didn't know he was there. Maybe he lost me, I don't know, but I didn't shake him off in Warwick or anywhere else. I think he was with me until I got home."

"Why would he lie?"

"Great question, isn't it? I don't know. He knows where I went, and he isn't bright enough to come up with anything better. There's a reason he doesn't want you looking at that strip joint. I don't know if it's important, but he must think so. Did he call in and tell anyone as soon as he supposedly lost the tail? Was there a delay of about an hour? "

"Yes," she said after a moment's pause. It sounded as if she was thinking aloud. "He reported that he had been trying to pick you up again. You know, anything, any evidence or sign that isn't directly pointing at you seems to be 'bullshit' as far as he's concerned. Detective DaSilva and I believed it's because he doesn't like you."

I thought about how delightful it was, hearing her force "bullshit" through lips I was fantasizing about.

"Petersen said that he was looking for me?' Alone? Warwick?"

"That's what he said."

"Not in this lifetime. Warwick's a maze, one-way streets, divided highways, heavy traffic. He should have reported immediately when he 'lost' me, right?"

"Yes, but Sergeant DaSilva passed it off as inexperience."

"Dana, when you were a green agent, did you ever blow off procedure? Didn't you rely on it to keep you out of trouble?"

She nodded.

The waitress returned with our drinks.

"Let's order," I said. I heaved the huge menu up into view, moving it around to see it, and finally fished my half glasses out of my shirt pocket.

"I only need them to see," I said.

"Contacts," she answered, gesturing toward her eyes while studying the menu.

"Please tell me they're not tinted and that's really the shade of blue your eyes are."

"What shade is that?" asked Dana, with a smile.

"Cerulean," I said, wondering what made me say that.

"No tint. Transparent, like you." That required either a lot of conversation or none at all. I chose the latter. I might have been blushing a little, too.

The waitress came back, and took our order. It was silly, but I was careful to avoid garlic or onions. "Thought FBI agents had to have perfect vision," I said, trying to avoid the subject of the murder. I managed to avoid murder, but fell right into dumb.

"Nope, just correctable." She plunged a fork into her salad, and began to eat. "Sorry to just dive in, but I'm starved. It's been a long time since breakfast." The cherry tomato on her fork waved in the air as she thought of something. "Mm, wait." I took a bite of my salad, and waited.

"Tomorrow," she said, "I'll have a private talk with DaSilva. In the meantime, could we talk about you?"

I opened my mouth to speak, and closed it as the waitress arrived with the main course. "Your cologne is nice by the way, no musk," said Dana. Never, not once in hundreds of interrogations, had I ever complimented a subject on a choice of cologne or perfume. Not even Isabel.

"I don't like musk; the smell might make a rhino charge."

"Lots of rhinos here on the South Shore, I don't blame you." It was tempting to enjoy more of that sort of exchange, and I got the impression that she wanted to. Instead, I went back to her request.

"What is it you want to talk about?"

"I guess you know who my father is and what he got for me. He said you were a comer, until you jumped off track. Then you were gone. You tend bar, and you're a murder suspect. You've managed to alienate twelve and a half percent of Newport's detective bureau, and I guess I'd like to understand."

My reflex was to tell her that it was none of her damned business. I took a deep breath. "Your father is Admiral Kilroy? Commander Atlantic Naval Operations?"

She nodded, "Yes. Past tense. He's retired."

"Where do you need me to begin?"

She cut into her haddock with the side of her fork, lifted it partway to her mouth and asked for the beginning.

I told her about my parents. How my father would blow pipe smoke into my ear to soothe my earaches. It always felt good, and smelled like home. Pipe smoke still made me feel comfortable and drowsy. His huge hands, thick and rough, that held and touched me gently. I couldn't remember a word that my father ever said to me, but he always seemed happy to have me with him.

I went on, trying to decide what to say and what to leave out. When it came to the accident that took my mother and father, I hesitated.

There was no snow, but it was cold and raw outside. To celebrate an anniversary, they left for their night out, planning to go all the way to Boston for dinner, and dancing at a nightclub. I smelled my mother's perfume when she left; something called "Windsong." My father smelled like pipe tobacco and Old Spice. He waved as he helped her into the car. They were smiling at each other when he started the car. *Not the worst of last images.*

I described the struggle with the state to allow my grandparents to keep me. I told her about school, and the things that made a difference to me.

"Your father could probably tell you about Annapolis, but let's just say you endure it, and get on with your career."

I didn't try to explain how restive I became and how I began to resent her father's interest in my career. I did tell her that I had disappointed the Commander, Atlantic Fleet.

"CommLant," she interrupted.

"Your Dad."

"Small world," she said, smiling.

When I started out as a Navy lawyer, I was older than most of the more experienced attorneys. Anyway, time went on and I was a good prosecutor. I had a good record, and I had faith in the system.

"Until you reviewed an old, dead case, for some reason," said Dana.

"No reason, just an accident. Seaman Frobisher was nineteen. He may have been marginally mentally challenged. He was a nice enough kid, willing, you know. No initiative, but given orders, he'd carry them out. Not much potential, but easy to lead and command.

At the time, the standards weren't as high as they are now, and the navy had lots of Frobisher's."

It just looked wrong, a quick and dirty railroad job. It took about six months, but Frobisher was free, with rank, back pay and benefits restored, just in time to get out of the navy. The guilty Petty Officer was busted and went to prison. The prosecutor and defense attorney in the case were reprimanded, with notations made in their files.

Frobisher went to work as a cook in a restaurant in Portland, married the boss's daughter, and is the father to two girls. I get a Christmas card with a photo every year.

"Justice done, and a happy ending," said Dana.

"The commendation got some attention, good and bad. The first prosecutor still had friends and no one wants waves. I wound up prosecuting some security violations and espionage. The cases went well and I found myself training at the special school in Virginia."

"And you worked in the Office of Naval Intelligence?"

"You got that from your Dad, right?"

"He only said you did time as a spook, some sort of spy."

"I was Counter Intelligence, more like a sneaky cop."

She paused for a time, reached across the table and took my hand. That was an un-FBI thing to do. I liked her firm grasp and soft skin. I felt the tension from talking about my past. She looked straight into my eyes, smiled, and said, "And then you met your wife?"

She had come across the Florida Straights in a leaky motorboat, and the FBI tied her to a Cuban agent who'd been targeting us in Florida. They wanted a naval expert to interrogate her. The navy sent me.

"And you married her," Dana said, smiling.

"Good summary," I answered. "I like that, no extra details."

Isabel had crossed one of the busiest shipping channels in the world, with nothing but her clothes and credentials as a psychologist. She was greeted with fences and guards, looking an awful lot like Cuba. Her file photo captured the strain she'd been through and the anger that was starting to simmer.

The CIA still had officers obsessing over Castro and the imaginary appalling danger he presented. One of them had done Isabel's initial intake.

The woman who waited for me in the makeshift interrogation room did match her picture. I recognized her from the photo, but no picture could show how luminous she was. The force in her look and the warmth that glowed from her wasn't on film either.

My idea of a long-term relationship was one that outlasted a weekend. I couldn't talk about my work. Most of the world didn't even know that I was a Lieutenant Commander in the Navy.

"Career over all?" said Dana.

"I'm not sure. Maybe, or maybe it was an excuse. No one got near, so I never lost anyone."

"Being orphaned, that's not surprising."

I looked up, sharply. "Maybe, or maybe not," I was surprised by how much her words angered me.

She withdrew her hand, and apologized.

We paused. Then, slowly, I reached across the table and put my hand over hers. I watched my hand on its long voyage, and when her hand stayed in place, I raised my eyes to meet hers. "I get touchy over things that I shouldn't. Sometimes, I try to push people away," I said as softly as I could. "And Dana, you can put me into prison. I'm innocent, but I know how things can happen when the pressure comes on. I don't understand why I'm feeling," I hesitated, "like this."

"Like what?"

My mouth was too dry for this conversation. I decided to continue, but held onto her hand. It turned over, and her fingers enfolded mine.

"Can I get you some coffee and dessert?" said our waitress.

"Just coffee, black," we both said at once.

I smiled, she smiled and the waitress smiled. I wished that this were a date. On the other hand, it was miles from interrogation. I had no idea what we were doing. I looked at Dana, and she smiled. My hand and hers were still together. She was an FBI agent, investigating the murder of a United States Congressman, and I was probably her best suspect. She was holding my hand and listening to my story as if it was fascinating. She was wearing a date outfit.

The waitress returned with our coffees, and left the pot on the table.

As if she'd read my mind, Dana said, "I might be tossing my career away. I'll be in Bismarck, North, or is it South Dakota?"

"What about your tickets to the show?"

"Ticket, singular. I was going to go alone."

I grinned. It appeared that I could talk with a beautiful woman and let her know that I enjoyed her company, found her attractive, and liked to talk with her. Talking to her about my wife made it guilt-free somehow, and I was beginning to relax. I reminded myself that she was still the opposition until she proved otherwise. The conversation had slowed, so I took a sip of coffee.

"I cleared Isabel at the end of the interview."

The CIA officer who originally interviewed her asked me, "What the fuck was that? An interrogation? An interview? A date? What? She batted her big brown eyes, and she played you. Since when do we tell them they're cleared until the committee decides they're clear? Fucking squid. She would have spread out on the table for you to get out of there."

He wound up curled in a ball on the floor. When he could breathe and talk he spoke with a hiss, "You fucking swab-jockey. You just assaulted a federal agent in front of a witness, right jarhead?" He was speaking to the marine guard who was posted just outside of the interview room.

"With respect sir," said the lance corporal, "members of the Corps do not appreciate being referred to in that manner. This Marine wasn't watching. This Marine was visually scanning the corridor, as ordered. Sir." No one is better at telling a superior to go to hell in a proper way than a Marine.

"You may think I'm done, squid, but believe me, it ain't over. You too, jarhead." The agent limped off, but I had Isabel's file and my clearance for her in my hands when he left.

Isabel Martel was given a temporary visa, along with an application for asylum. She had sponsors in Miami. When she left the internment facility, I was waiting at the gate, in a rental car. She got in without a word, and I took her to her sponsors' home to be introduced for the first time. I handed her a booklet, outlining the requirements for licensing of psychologists and social workers in Florida, along with the correct application forms. I also gave her my mailing address. I asked her if I could call her, just got it out as she got out of the car. "I was interned for four weeks, one day, and seven hours," she said. "I wish to be free for at least that long. You will have your chance." Her smile lit up, finally.

I found myself on shuttle runs, from Washington to Key West to San Diego, with infrequent stops in Fall River to visit my grandparents. My grandfather told me to marry the woman immediately and he could meet her afterwards. My grandmother glared at him, and hissed in Portuguese. He laughed until she started to smile and then giggle, covering her mouth.

I was in a motel in Key West, when Isabel's time limit was reached. I picked up the phone in my room and punched in the number. She picked it up as soon as the second ring started.

"Hello, Commander," she said, before I could speak, and we laughed together for the first time. We were married a few months later, with her sponsor pulling some strings to get us through the Catholic preliminaries. I bribed the sneakiest yeoman in the Navy to get my paperwork through. We spent our honeymoon on Martha's Vineyard after an overnight in Fall River. My grandfather was smitten, my grandmother asked her about grandchildren before she hugged her. Then she warned me to treat my new wife well. Isabel pronounced my grandparents to be just like her own.

Since I had no real address, there was no home to bring her to. There was quite a bit of money in my savings though. I hadn't spent much for most of my career, except for necessities, so it was a matter of finding a fixed location that wouldn't upset my superiors. We wound up in Virginia. I had already finished a pointless investigation at the Naval War College in Rhode Island, looking for a mole. Since I had to be there as a student, I completed the Command Course.

"Anyway, when I got back to our headquarters, I was told that my marriage to Isabel had 'compromised my ability to remain impartial,' I had no business 'establishing a relationship with a vetting subject,' et cetera. On the other hand, she was absolutely clean, and aside from falling in love and marrying her, I was clear. There was a question of possible assault charges, affecting my second shot at full Commander. Long story short, I was invited out."

They told me, unofficially of course, that the rest of the Navy didn't want me. Forcing me out completely wasn't justified, so they gave me an option, and I resigned my commission to enter the Naval Criminal Investigative Service.

So after training, I was headquartered in New London, with a home for the first time since I entered the Naval Academy. Isabel took the license exams for Connecticut, passed them with her routine flying colors and started making us a home. She found an office and began seeing patients. My grandparents were aging and not as healthy as I wanted them to be and we both wanted them to see their first great grandchild.

Our first was lost in the eighth week, the second in the tenth. We had been told it was unlikely that she could carry a child to term, assuming she could get pregnant again. Isabel was inconsolable and I was at a loss, so I took her for a visit to my grandparents. My grandfather and I sat in the living room, supposedly so we couldn't hear the women talking. My grandmother held her like a child for a long time, sitting in her kitchen. I heard Portuguese, and even the lullabies she sang to me as a sick, scared or lonely little boy.

They came to the living room to sit with my grandfather and me, and we were all quiet. I could smell coffee and soup. I watched my grandfather doze, smiling, as he held my grandmother's hand. A couple of years later, they were both gone, in their sleep, months apart, she first, then him. They had arrangements made and were buried, side-by-side on a hill facing the rising sun. Isabel was pregnant with a lot of time in bed, bored out of her mind. She swore it was with my grandmother's help that she gave birth to Marisol. I was there, I cut the cord, and I held her and cried, looking from her to my wife.

Isabel and I began spoiling 'Sol. We read books. We had three baby carriages, used a diaper service and had to move a mountain of dolls and stuffed animals out of her crib before we put her to bed. Isabel nursed 'Sol, for a long time. She loved it. I loved to watch over them as they rocked and the child suckled. I'd never seen an act more beautiful, loving and pure.

I worked and was away, often. The nastiness and dangers of my job never really touched me. At night, I would call and read stories to our child over the phone, not worrying about the cost. When I was home, we spent our time together. I was married to the most beautiful and brilliant woman I could have imagined. I had a little girl who was loving and well loved. I had a job that gave me a lot of satisfaction and I was good at it.

Isabel would sometimes get a sitter and come to visit with me if I was within driving distance, for what she called a "Jintera night." Jinteras were good time girls in Cuba. People would look at us as we left my motel room because of the noise we made all night long.

It was right before Christmas, and we hoped to do some shopping, but I was called away to Newport. Nothing serious. Isabel called and left a message at the hotel, telling me to expect her by nine that night. I should have called and told her to stay home. I should have told her how tired I was. I missed her, so I let her come.

At nine I was in the hotel room, showered and shaved, with a bottle of her favorite wine on ice. At nine-thirty, I was irritated. By ten I was worried. At eleven, I called home, and got the sitter. At midnight, things came together. The police reached the sitter, who called me, sobbing. I called the state police and drove to the hospital. By two that morning, she was gone, massive chest and head trauma. Her car, not "the tank" like the Saab I still drove, but a cute little Honda, was crushed into abstract art, with metallic tears and pulls where she was cut from the wreckage. It was awful to see the little Hula doll that I'd given her as a joke, still stuck firmly onto the back sill. Of all of the images from that night, that grinning and swaying little figure remains vivid. It was such a tacky little thing, so "not her" in its garish poor taste, that we both laughed and occasionally played with it, making it sway. 'Sol thought it was cute.

Later, I had the car crushed by a junkyard. I made it a point to be sure that the little hula girl was crushed with it.

I talked about trying to drink it away for the first two weeks, then the Intervention, and the ongoing therapy that 'Sol and I worked so hard at. My realization that I couldn't remain an investigator, if I was going to be father and mother both, about applications to the bar and the turndowns because of my dead-ended records. I resented that, since the Navy only had to account for the time, not give specifics. I hadn't left on the best of terms, but I had served well and the rigid refusal spoke of some bureaucratic vendetta.

I told her about using the last of my savings to buy the house in Newport, and going to the six-week bartending classes, my early jobs in biker bars, neighborhood bars, restaurant bars and finally at the hotel. I told her about how much better things had become, and how well my daughter was doing. Finally, I wound down and stopped, almost in the middle of a sentence.

The coffee pot was empty, and both of our cups were drained

"We have to leave, Dana, they're ready to close here."

"I have some things to say, and some questions to ask."

"I know a place, can you follow me?" I thought about that for a second and laughed.

"Your car is pretty easy to pick out."

"Okay, so follow me."

We argued over the check, until Uncle Sam won out. I was not unaware that we were holding hands, until we got to the door. She slid free.

Chapter 6

I led her south until I reached a small municipal airport, where we parked. The air was summer warm, so we sat down at a picnic table under a streetlight, with the shadows of moths tumbling over us. She started without preamble. She was a navy brat, and had moved from one station to another as her father climbed the slippery rungs upward to his own flag. He wanted her to attend Annapolis, since women were considered admissible by then. She elected a liberal arts school, majoring in psychology and criminal justice.

She joined the FBI, hoping to become one of the "profilers." She was gaining experience as a field agent. She didn't mention her mother at all. I remembered that I had never seen the woman at any of the social functions where she would have been expected.

I listened without interrupting her, wondering if this was still a prelude to questioning me. I learned how and where she lost her virginity. Back seat of a car, at seventeen, to a guy she convinced herself she loved. How she cried over the loss, later.

Her first arrest had involved a gunfight, and she tried to describe the fierce joy she felt when it was over and the let down hours later. Finally, she stopped. "Here I am, with the best suspect I have, in the biggest case I've ever been handed. I have to be losing my mind."

"I didn't kill him, Dana. I just flat didn't. I don't think that what killed him, or who, had anything to do with me." She had a decision to make. She stood, as quickly as a short skirt and picnic bench would allow, and I rose with her. The physics of the thing brought us face to face, and I was glad that I'd avoided garlic and onions.

I could see that my breath was stirring a few of the long blonde hairs that had slipped into her face. I felt her hand curl around my neck, and she drew herself up taller. She had a hand to my chest and felt my wedding ring on its chain. We were almost there.

I saw blonde hair, instead of inky black, tilted blue eyes instead of brown, and it felt strange suddenly. I found myself standing with my hands at my side. I was within easy reach of a beautiful woman. She was stopped by her job or me or maybe good sense. As I gazed at her, speechless, she reached up to pull the chain around my neck out of my shirt. Along with my confirmation medal, she touched the wedding ring that was strung on it. She tapped me on my chest with the heel of her fist, looking down at the ring.

I thought of all the things I should say, all of the things I could do. I thought about wrapping her in my arms, bending her onto the picnic table and just letting go. Letting her that close, letting myself take a chance at hurting.

She stepped back. That's all she did. She might as well have turned and run, because it was the same thing. She turned and started walking towards her car.

I opened my mouth to say something. I couldn't think of a thing and closed it. I watched her walk, with that enticing stride and sway. I admired her figure. I liked her intelligence and insight. I couldn't imagine what I could want that she didn't have. I wanted to call out to her, for her to try to have patience. She closed her door firmly. The engine started, and she backed smoothly out, shifted and drove away. I saw her brake lights flare, and then dim, before she drove out of sight.

I had a long drive to make, and the beer I'd had with dinner made me sleepy. The open convertible top helped keep me awake. Whenever I started to relax, the night's happenings made my heart beat faster, and embarrassment tingle up my neck and across my cheeks. I found my way to the second-rate highway that took me through the last of Massachusetts, and into Rhode Island.

It was one of those trips where you don't remember the drive.

I woke Mrs. Pina. She looked at me, searching my eyes. She patted my arm, said goodnight and headed upstairs. My clothes wound up on the floor of my bedroom, and I flopped onto my bed in my shorts.

Tossing and turning for what seemed like forever, I suddenly sat up. "Shit," I said out loud. I rose and got my legal pad, wrote a couple of quick notes to myself and went back to bed. The bed rose to meet me like a true lover would, and I sank into it. And I slept.

Chapter 7

I dreamed of my last night with Isabel, felt her touch on my cheek and woke up. Marisol was there. “Daddy, I have to go to school, but you were talking to Mamacita. You weren’t calling her, but just talking, like you used to at the kitchen table.”

“Must have been some dream,” I said, as casually as I could. “I don’t remember it.” I smiled at her, hating myself for the lie. However good my intentions were, it wasn’t a good thing.

Either she believed me or let it go, because she kissed me, told me that coffee was made and that she had to run. “Have a good day, sweetheart,” I called after her. I was awake for good, and I remembered that I’d written some notes to myself. I got up and poured the coffee, doctored it up and sipped it.

My notes said a couple of things; “Petersen lied. Why? Washington, Son, Daughter, Wife? DaSilva, what’s up with him? Dana, apologize, asshole.” The final one, I was sure, was what allowed me to sleep. First things first. I called Dana’s office, and didn’t leave a voice mail for her. I left a verbal message with the receptionist to call me at home.

I lit my first cigarette of the day, picked up the phone and called DaSilva’s direct line from his business card. It was time to work my way into the enemy camp. I had a good feeling about DaSilva, and some unsavory ideas about Petersen. I had no illusions about DaSilva telling me much. He wasn’t the kind of cop to go easy on me for helping him out.

I believed that he‘d want to know about Petersen’s lie. I believed that he’d find out what was behind it. I didn’t think he’d ever tell me directly. I was a murder suspect; he was investigating the murder. He was under enormous pressure to make an arrest, and I was an easy target. I hoped he could stand up under the load. I wasn’t sure about liking him, and I was damned sure that he had no liking for me, or dislike for me, either. It was all guess and gut, but it was what I had.

"Newport Police, Sergeant DaSilva," he answered.

"Sergeant, Paul Costa," and a silence followed.

"Yes?"

"We need to talk, Sergeant; it's important, and should be unofficial, at least to start with."

"I don't want anything unofficial. Murder is as official as it gets. You've been evasive, and you've created friction within the team. I don't trust you, and you must know that you're my best suspect right now."

"Sergeant—"

"Okay, now let's try to understand each other, here. You shook a tail, you've been asking questions and talking to people. You've been working this since it started. You've blinded my partner to anything and anyone except you, and there's an FBI agent who's resisting bringing you in. We have whole new areas to check out because of you. I have everyone from the President of the United States to the editor of the *Providence Journal* yelling for an arrest. You're beginning to piss me off."

"I didn't shake a tail, DaSilva," I said, leaving his rank out on purpose because I wanted his attention. "No counter-surveillance, because I didn't see the obvious. I didn't try to lose Petersen, didn't know he was there, and I wasn't in Warwick, where he claimed to lose me."

"How did you know?" There was a pause that turned into a wait. I let him think it through. "Okay, when and where?" he finally said.

I named a doughnut shop in Middletown, just over the line. He agreed to meet me there in an hour. He said he'd worry about the tap on my phone and any surveillance and we hung up. I took a long, deep breath and headed for the shower. The phone rang while I was in there, and I had no idea how many rings I'd missed, but thinking it could be her, I stumbled and with a towel half wrapped around my waist, I heard her leaving the message that, "Agent Kilroy returned your call." I listened to it a few times, listening for signs of her feelings. I should have known better. She sounded cool, professional and provocative.

I was dry, so I shaved, dressed and fired up the Saab, leaving the top up. I thought about calling her back, but decided that there either wasn't time, or that I couldn't think of how to tell her any of it. I hoped to come up with something brilliant soon. I wasn't feeling brilliant, and DaSilva was formidable enough.

He was waiting for me when I walked in. He'd ordered me a cup of coffee, black, as I liked it. He remembered that detail from the interview at my house. There was a message there, that this man was a serious observer, with a memory that could assemble details into a coherent picture. I warned myself to be careful, as I sat down. "Thanks for the coffee," was all I said.

"'Welcome. You start."

"Good to see you, too, Sergeant."

"You aren't intimidated. I get it. You start."

"Petersen was lying. I didn't lose him. I didn't go anywhere near Warwick. However I know what he told you, I know it. Okay? He was slow to report it. He was slow enough to wait for me and follow me home and get clear before he called in. He claimed I lost him deliberately. False." I told DaSilva where I went, but not Tim Foley's name. I left Lois out, even though he already had to know about her. "He claimed I lost him in Warwick. False. I told you where I went, and you can corroborate that with your phone logs and tapes. I'm guessing that you have my cell phone monitored, and you can pick up GPS from that, too. You can time it. I was there for about an hour. There's something about the strip club. He tried to isolate himself from it. Question is why? Maybe it's personal, maybe it's related to the investigation."

"You've been muddying the water since you found Morley's body, and you're still doing it."

I had no response to that. "I have to leave town this week," I said, "Is that okay?"

"No, Costa, it isn't okay. I need to know where you are; I need to talk with you after I check things out."

"I didn't kill him."

"Probably not, but I want to be able to reach you on short notice. I want you to stop your amateur investigation and contaminating witnesses or potential witnesses. I want you to stop running down leads, or having small private ideas about this. I want you to let us do our jobs."

"You mean like Petersen?" I asked with raised eyebrows.

"Leave Petersen to me. He's my partner, and he's a brother officer."

"So he's sacrosanct."

"He is my problem to resolve, and we'll leave it that before you make me mad."

"I'm going to trust you on that. I think you're straight. I could be wrong, but I've known a lot of cops. Besides, I'm a bartender, I'm supposed to know things."

"You're supposed to know how to mix drinks and keep your mouth shut."

"That too. Unless you plan to arrest me, I'll go. I can do things that you aren't allowed to."

"Which will seriously foul up my case."

"Mix drinks, hearing and seeing all, saying nothing, remember?"

He stopped and thought for a moment. "Shit. You know about the surveillance and phone tap. You can lose somebody if you want to, right?"

"Depends, you know, one car, maybe two, no problem. You and the Bureau won't be throwing parallels and tailing from ahead and helicopters and all of that. I go old school and ditch my cell, and it gets a bit easier, too."

He looked directly at me and seemed to be trying to see behind my eyes into my brain. "We never had this conversation?"

"What conversation are you referring to?"

"Nice. Washington, right?"

I said nothing, looking into his eyes.

"Right. I can't pull the surveillance, and your phone is still going to be covered."

"Petersen's your problem, those other details will have to be mine."

"You get nothing from us. You're still the best suspect we have."

"No bullshit from you at all, Sarge. That's why I love you."

“Too late for sweet talk. You and everyone else. I can sure feel all the love.” Finally he smiled.

“I’ll stay in touch, Sergeant,”

“I would if I were you.”

Before I returned home, I called the hotel to put in for my vacation on an emergency basis. I thought about the other bartenders, and how they’d been eyeing my shifts. I’d worked for a long time to get them. I could find myself working days, having to go through it all again. Assuming I was able to stay out of jail and hang on to my job.

I called Mrs. Pina to tell her that I’d need her full time for the next week, and gave her an additional rent discount. That may have insulted her, based on her tone, but she agreed. So far, so good. I had to tell Marisol, and I could make my reservations on the Internet. No travel agent, and by the time they found the transaction on my credit card, I’d be gone.

I also had to figure out what to do about Dana Kilroy, and get it done privately. Perhaps I could find a way to keep my mind clear when I thought about her. Probably not. Just try not to think of incredible eyes, soft hands and like that. Try to think of your daughter, and maybe saving a life for her. I pictured my daughter’s face, and imagined her the adult I thought she’d be. Lately that had been getting too easy to do. Since I was imagining her as a beautiful young lady, I put a dazzling smile on her face and a wedding gown on her, as I walked her down the aisle towards the fabulously wealthy, loving man of her dreams. She would, of course, remain a virgin until that day.

Then came the tough part. I got home just before Marisol, and was sipping a cup of my own coffee, when she came in. I started out on the wrong foot, referring to myself as “Daddy,” as if she was a toddler. Big mistake. It took at least two apologies to get past that, along with acknowledging that she really was “almost a teenager.” She sulked for a minute or two, and then asked me what I had been going to say.

I almost slipped and called myself “Daddy” again, but caught it and said, “Some of what I need to do isn’t in Newport.” She looked gravely at me with huge brown eyes. She was as unreadable as her mother had been, when listening intently. I took a deep breath, "I have to go away, probably for less than a week."

"Where?"

"I can't tell you. But I'll call you every day, sweetheart."

"Why is it a secret?"

"Honey, it just has to be, I'm sorry," thinking how awful it felt. I had an image of Petersen, or worse, Agent Dana Kilroy asking her where I was.

"Mrs. Pina will be able to reach me after I get there, sweetie."

"Daddy, will this go on forever? I mean will they always think you killed that man?"

"They're smart, honey, and they have a lot of ways to find things out. They'll find the real guy, but I'm just going to help a little."

"Like when you used to be gone a lot?"

"Just like that, 'Sol."

"Mrs. Pina and I will keep things safe and stuff."

My throat got tight. "I'll call soon."

"Okay. I have lots of homework to do, and I have to call Terri." She headed for her room in a swirl of dark hair and expensive sneakers.

"Paul," began Mrs. Pina, "Is this wise?"

"I don't think I have much of a choice. They'll look no farther than they have to, and they're being pressed to make an arrest. I trust a couple of them, and one knows what I'm up to, so it should be okay."

"I meant leaving 'Sol," she said, the reprimand clear in her voice.

"No, Mrs. Pina, I don't think it's wise, but I have to be out from under. She has to be out of it."

"The police are to be trusted, aren't they?"

There were millions of words to be said about that, or none at all. I had to pack and go, so I chose to say nothing. I packed two suits, a couple of dress shirts and dress shoes. I managed a couple of more casual outfits and dressed in a suit and tie. I threw my legal pad, a calculator, an old pocket tape recorder, with some spare tapes and batteries and a few other odds and ends into a briefcase. Now I really had to go to Warwick, and I really did have to lose a follower.

She was lying on her stomach with a book open in front of her. I recognized it as her Social Studies book, with an assignment from this year's nemesis, Emmett Davis. He was a fine teacher from what I saw, with an eye for bright kids and the imagination to challenge them. He was peculiar looking, with a nightmarish comb over. Marisol had a love-hate relationship with him but kept going back for more.

She wasn't reading, if the body language I knew so well meant anything. I thought that if she was crying, I wouldn't be able to go. She wasn't crying. She was furious.

"Sometimes, you get into your car to go to work or just shopping and I get scared. This is worse. You're going somewhere you can't tell me."

"'Sol," I said, wondering how to explain about grownups "just doing their jobs," as if that were an excuse. Then I decided that she deserved better. "I have to do what I can do to be sure that this is over. Nobody, nothing, anywhere is more important to me than you. And I'm a little selfish, because I hate any time that we're apart. D'you understand?"

"I'm not stupid, Daddy, and I'm not a baby. Of course I understand. I don't have to like it, do I?"

"Nope."

She giggled, finally. "I'm pissed off about it," she said, looking at me from under her hair.

"Pissed off," was not supposed to be in her vocabulary and I looked up sharply to see her grinning at me.

"Now that I have your attention," she said, and giggled again. "I won't say it again, Daddy. Promise. But I am, you know."

"Okay, daughter mine, last time I hear that kind of language from you, right? You can slide, this one time. I'll call you soon, honey." I kissed her on her forehead, smelling shampoo from her hair. She flung her arms around me, and I sagged, thinking "Daddy heaven." The last time we'd been apart overnight was the night her mother died.

Up until then, I'd been away frequently, and sometimes for extended times. She didn't like sleepovers yet. Our counselor said to be patient and let her work out her own limits, not to force it. So, here I was, "forcing it." That congressman had a lot to answer for. He could have gotten his sorry ass murdered anywhere and based on what I already knew, probably should have, long before.

Chapter 8

It wasn't hard to spot the car, a Crown Victoria. Did anybody in the world drive them except cops? One head in the car. I hoped it was Petersen. I opened the garage door and pulled out, turning down the street so he would have to turn around, unless they were using multiple cars. DaSilva had to make it look good, but I doubted that he'd have more than one car on me.
Staying within the speed limit, I turned and headed for I-95. He was three cars back, as I pulled up the ramp some time later. Like riding a bicycle, I thought, remembering training exercises and the times I'd had to do it for real. Give him time, make it last, lull his inexperienced imagination. Picture him going back and telling them he'd lost me again, almost as good as a Red Sox World Series win. DaSilva would know. He might have told Dana. If not, she'd guess. Knowing DaSilva, it would be Petersen in the car behind me, in the center lane, cooking along just over the limit.

I turned the radio on, listening to the usual complaints about the Red Sox from a listener in Medford. Or was it Malden? Wherever. They droned on, as if a powerful offense and limited bullpen was a new development. I'd been hearing it for forty years, and I expected to hear it on my deathbed. I made a mental note to take 'Sol to a game pretty soon. She loved Fenway Park, and she was developing a taste for baseball and hot dogs and stupid souvenirs that cost stupider amounts of money. I automatically made the shift over onto Route 4, saw the Ford slip in a few cars behind me and I continued to drive at moderate speed in the center lane.

My exit was coming up, and I checked the traffic on both sides. I pulled into the left lane and wound up the RPM's to kick in the turbocharger. I felt the boost and saw the speed climbing. The Crown Vic had to pick up speed and pull to the left to stay on me. I watched for the exit, and checked for gaps to my right.

I kept looking into my mirror, checking the gaps, watching speed, distance, then twisted the wheel to the right, tapping brakes and clutch, to slow into the center lane, downshifting as quickly as double-clutching would allow. I was all the way across the right lane and onto the exit ramp in one continuous curve, braking heavily, not skidding, downshifting again and letting the engine decelerate the car. There were squealing tires and horns braying at me from behind. I hoped no one got hurt, except maybe for a certain cop, as I exploded from the ramp into traffic, cutting across two lanes onto Route 2 and diving further left as if headed to East Greenwich. More horns blaring, lots of tires squealing, and I knew, creative cursing directed at me.

The speedometer was showing forty-five just before I braked again, without a directional, pulled into a gas station, then behind it and into a car wash, paying five bucks to wash my car. I got out and stood in the glassed-in alleyway, watching traffic and passers-by. He'd have had to be much further away from me and aware of what I was thinking to make it onto the exit ramp, much less follow me here. I gave it the full treatment, including "Royal Wax" for seven dollars more.

I checked my watch. When my car was done, I drove to the business district. Warwick really doesn't have a center, so I parked at a public garage right near the police station and hopped a cab to the airport. I mentally added up the cost to park, thinking of how many tips it was going to take to make it up. No sign of a big Ford. I checked no luggage, pulled an electronic ticket and after a reasonable wait, went through security, bought a book and headed to the gate.

Did I notice DaSilva at the food court watching the security checkpoint? Would anyone watching notice that we saw or knew each other? I don't think so. He was a pro, and I'd been one myself. I was sure, then, that it had been Petersen on my tail, and I imagined his embarrassment and anger. That was just fine with me. I boarded, found my seat, and even found room for my bag and briefcase within shouting distance.

I would loved to have heard the conversation when I lost Petersen on Route 4. I had to call Dana at some point, and Marisol. Our home phone was probably still tapped, but they would only hear how much I missed her. I closed my eyes and slept.

The plane was slipping from side to side when I woke up, probably fighting a crosswind on final approach to Baltimore-Washington. The small commuter jet landed on one wheel, then another, finally settling onto all three. When we got to the gate, I waited until most of the plane emptied before getting my bags and heading out. I didn't expect to recognize anyone I saw, at least on the first viewing.

I took a cab into Baltimore, got out and looked around for a few minutes. Then I took another back to the airport, where I rented a car. My motel was on Washington's outskirts, on the Virginia side, and I checked in using my real name. If they were on me that tightly, a false name wasn't going to help.

Once I was in the room, with my clothes hanging up, I flipped on the television and had a short wait before the update on "Congressman Morley's Killing: The Search." I hit the mute button and picked up the phone, took a deep breath, and dialed a number that I'd never forgotten. "NCIS, Beaman speaking." I didn't know the name.

"Is Al Williams there?" I asked.

"Agent Williams is off today, can I help you?"

"This isn't an emergency, just an old friend trying to get in touch."

"Oh." Retirees are the bane of government employees, and his tone made his feelings clear. The voice on the message sounded like Al, and I spoke my name and the hotel number into it. I also said that it was urgent, and off the books. I hoped that the obligation he'd felt remained with him.

I spoke with Marisol, talking about her evening, and what a great cook Mrs. Pina was. That made me sure that at least one sugar-laden treat had been made. She asked me how things were and I told her fine, but I really, really missed her. Really. I pictured a cop or agent listening to this, rolling his eyes and yawning.

We traded "I love yous" and argued over who should hang up first, with her finally winning, so I softly cradled the phone. I picked up the phone one more time, and dialed the number I had for Dana Kilroy.

"Agent Kilroy," she answered.

"Paul, Paul Costa."

"Yes? How can I help you?" My name wasn't mentioned, so I suspected that she had an audience.

"We should probably talk when you have some privacy," I said, all in a rush.

"Definitely. Can you give me a number and time to get in touch?"

I tried not to hesitate, and gave her the number. "I have to rely on your discretion."

"I understand,"

"Talk with you soon."

"Oh, yes, give me an hour, okay?"

I looked at my watch, "Okay, an hour."

I hung up, and the phone rang immediately. "Long time," said Al Williams.

"I need to call in a marker."

"You need more than that, my man; you need Clarence fucking Darrow. Word is that they have you."

"So how did I get down here if I'm in the bag?"

"Good question, but we're not talking about that."

"Right, you're not giving me the addresses and phone numbers for all of the surviving Morleys, and you aren't going to give me the name and number of a reporter I can trust, right?"

"That's right. Got a pen?" He rattled off two addresses and three phone numbers. "Daughter still lives with mommy, the son has his own place. The third number is a TV lady. She's pretty straight. I'd only trust her so far, though."

"Thanks for not telling me any of this, Al."

"Paul, you need to watch your six. There's one more number." He read it off. "His name is Peter Viater, and he can supply needful things."

"We're even, Al."

"Nah, not even close. Remember, this conversation never happened."

"Needful things," he'd said. Once we'd had to bust in on some guys selling small arms out of an armory. They were supposed to be armed to the teeth and dangerous. Out of sheer nerves, we'd dubbed our pistols, shotguns and MP-5's "needful things." I wondered what sort of rumors he'd heard.

I lay back on the generic bed spread, looking at the generic art on the walls, and thought back to all of the motel rooms, hotel rooms and efficiencies that I'd lived in for all of those years. The air conditioner stirred the heavy drapes, and the television kept scrolling repetitive bulletins across the bottom. I waited for the phone to ring again.

While I waited, I thought about a gun. An armed man walks differently. It can add that swagger that some young cops possess. I kept the number, but decided against using it. I stared at the ceiling, wondering if sleep would ever come.

The phone's chirp startled me out of sleep. I wondered what had happened to bells. A phone should ring, I thought, as I picked it up.

"Paul?" Her tone was incredulous, and she laughed. "Sorry to wake you."

"What did I say?"

"I don't think I could imitate it," she responded.

"Sorry, I was really out I guess."

"And now you're in a D.C. suburb. Great." She divided "Great," into two syllables. "Petersen is livid. You lost him again."

"Really?"

"That's what DaSilva was saying, not a half hour ago."

"He stays too close, and doesn't anticipate."

"I'll pass that along." There was a pause.

"Paul, about the other night," she began.

I cleared my throat artificially.

"Okay, you first," she said.

"I guess I messed up."

"I just thought I'd made a fool of myself, coming on to you like some lush at the bar."

"No, I was the fool."

"So when will you give up, let us do our jobs and come home?"

"One way or another, I'll be back by Friday."

"Not an answer. There have been some developments and you need to know about them."

"How safe is the phone you're on?"

"It's clean."

"Okay, tell me."

And she began. "It's not likely that the Congressman was murdered in the men's room," she said, "And the knife was an afterthought. He was probably dead or nearly so when that went in."

I thought about how cold-blooded or sick with rage someone would have to be to drive a knife into a dead or dying man's ear.

"So what killed him?"

"Myocardial Infarction," she said, slowly as if reading it.

"Heart attack?"

"Kind of. The Medical Examiner is still working on all of that. Pretty much puts you in the clear."

"That's nice," I said, "But."

"There has to be a but with you, doesn't there?"

"I'm not in the clear, really, am I? There's still pressure on to have someone take the fall."

"Neither DaSilva nor I are worried about it."

"How about the Assistant U.S. Attorney and the local D.A.?" There was a pause. "That's what I thought," I said. "Something in his secret life got him killed, if he was murdered. Or at least got the knife into him after he died. There's nothing of the public man to make him a target. It wasn't random. So, it has to be his private life."

"Paul, you have no authority, no support; you should just come home."

I thought about how tempting that idea was. I missed Marisol, and the hints at more time with Dana sounded good.

This was sitting over my head, and in the background was a young stripper who maybe earned an effort from me. I honest to God felt good. I was carrying my weight on the balls of my feet. My arms were swinging. Maybe it wasn't worthwhile to anybody but me, and that was just fine. I felt like I did just before a fencing or boxing match, as if I was unbeatable.

Realistically, my record as a boxer and fencer should have given me pause. Still. I felt as if there was nobody faster, smarter, tougher or better. There was a certain "fuck you," in me that I'd missed.

There was a line from a bad movie that I'd always liked, "I'm here to kick ass and chew bubblegum; and I'm all out of bubblegum." It was the only part of the movie that I remembered.

"Dana, I expect to be back by the end of the week but it's still something I have to do. I intend to piss a few important people off, if you'll pardon the expression. You need to be able to deny any knowledge of my actions."

"DaSilva knew about this, didn't he?"

"Of course not."

"If he didn't, he wouldn't be so relaxed about it."

"I'll call him tomorrow. You too, if you'd like."

"I'd like, but maybe we could be a bit less, um, businesslike?"

"Maybe a lot less."

"Oh, good," and she gave me her home and cell numbers. I felt pretty juvenile, and allowed myself a minute of that. I was lying on the bed and I dozed off.

***

I woke up, ready to call the lady reporter. Al had called her, so she was expecting me. It helped. She explained "background, deep background, off the record," and told me about the lengths she had gone to protect sources. She gave me an address in Washington, and told me to meet her in an hour. I'd left my cell at home, so the desk clerk did some digging and found a map. I got into my rental and wandered up and down one-way streets, into and out of ghettos, down streets with picture postcard buildings and finally found the restaurant.

She knew what I'd be wearing, and right on time, a very thin woman came to the table. Supposedly, television adds weight. I mentally added ten pounds and decided she'd look a lot better. Her facial skin was deplorable, probably from too many hours in heavy make up and her hair was lacquered into rigid order. She sat, held out a painfully thin hand and shook mine, looking directly into my eyes. She had luminous green eyes that would look good on screen.

She dropped an immense black handbag on the table, pulled out a pack of cigarettes and lit one, drawing deeply. "Will this bother you?" she asked, too late.

"No, it's fine," I answered and lit one of mine.

"Thank God. I'm so tired of that bullshit. I pack on weight when I try to quit, and that's death in my business."

"I'm sure you become morbidly obese."

"Laugh all you want. Men get gravitas, women get pudgy. Mostly it sucks. I only have an hour or so, then I have to get to the studio."

"Sandra. May I call you Sandra?"

She nodded, spiking me with a suggestive glance and then she sat back, crossing her legs.

"My name is Gerald, and I'll be your server," said the effeminate young man standing at my elbow. "May I get you anything?"

"Coffee for me, black, please," I answered, and gestured towards her.

"Same, and a bagel, toasted, cream cheese."

"I'll be right back," Gerald smiled and glided away.

We sat silently until he arrived. He poured, passed the bagel and cream cheese to her and left. By then she had lit, smoked and stubbed out three cigarettes. I was putting my first one out.

She turned sideways in her chair, so that her legs were out from under the table. While slender, they were nice. She was a woman who was aware of herself, but something about her made her more pitiable than attractive. I couldn't define it, or explain it. "Sandra," I began again, "What did Al tell you?"

"He said I could trust you, that he'd worked with you for quite awhile, maybe you saved his life. Men always say stuff like that, but Al's pretty low key. He said that if I helped you, maybe it would be worth an exclusive. He said you're not bad looking, and that I'd like you. He was right about that, anyway."

"Thanks, " I said and smiled. "Maybe you could tell me what you know about Congressman Dick Morley, off the record?" Her lazy smile faded, and she brought her legs back under the table.

"That prick Al said something about it, but you have exactly two minutes to convince me you're real, or I'm out of here," I still felt sorry for her. Anywhere I went I opened someone's healing wounds.

After I told her about Lois, she said, "A club. With a shitty initiation. Good line. She hit it on the head. You're sure he's dead?

Maybe someone should dig him up and drive a stake through his fucking heart, just to be sure."

"Definitely dead, and with a fruit knife in his ear, instead of a stake through his heart." Something about it resonated. It might mean nothing at all, or the knife might have been a kind of punctuation mark.

"It fits. He was a shark, or maybe one of those fish that hides on the bottom with this weird growth. It dangles it over its mouth like a lure, and the little fish come up to eat it, and he explodes out of the mud and eats them."

"Angler fish?" I said, to slow her down a bit.

"Yup, that was him." She was silent for what seemed a long time. "Anyhow, a lot of women in the business, political or news, warned me. Unfortunately, they warned me too late. A few of them were club members. Never in DC, always out of town, always someplace else. Rhode fucking Island, for chrissake."

"He kept it clean here?"

She nodded.

"How about his family?" I asked.

"Wife, perfect congressman's spouse. Drinks a little, smokes secretly. Any extramarital stuff is discreet. No sense of how attached she was to him, or what she knew about him. For all I knew, it might have been okay with her. Son is the kind of pig that looks great and popular with some women. I think he's his father's son." She stopped for a sip of coffee and a pull on her latest cigarette.

"Dangerous little shithead, I think," she went on. "Daughter, pretty, blonde, perfect congressman's daughter. Shy, but handles herself well. Mousy attitude, not looks. They have a houseboy, 'Adam.' I'm not sure what he does, really, but he sounds like the guy Lois described. You know, the third in the hotel?" She reached into her purse and pulled out a file. "Here's what I know. There's a section in there about me." She looked down and picked at some lint on the tablecloth.

I wrote the motel name and my phone number there along with the room number on a napkin and handed it to her. "If you think of anything, or if you just need to talk, I'll be there for a few more days."

"Wait a minute," she said, "There's a quid pro quo, here, Paul Costa. I need your word that you won't talk to anyone without talking to me."

"You mean news or media?"

She nodded as if there was no one else to talk with.

"Agreed. Any story, you get, before anyone else. At least a day. Okay?"

"Okay, thanks." She put the napkin into her purse, after folding it neatly. "What's your plan?"

"Plan? Oh, you think I have a plan. I have some vague ideas, that's about it."

"And you won't share with me?" She was smiling and now attractive. She wasn't hunting, she was talking and listening. I liked her better this way.

"This is all deep background, right?"

She nodded, smiling.

"The cops can be systematic and follow clues. They get to harvest carefully, making sure that each item is clean and fresh and useful. I just shake the shit out of the trees and hope something ripe falls out."

"Remember what I said about driving a stake through Morley's heart. Even a dead bee can sting." She swallowed the last of her coffee, and put out her cigarette. I lit one more for her and watched her walk out. She possessed no butt at all and nice legs, shown to advantage in a dress and shoes that were chosen for her by someone who knew how. I thought about how lonely and desperate she must have been to be open to Morley.

I finished my coffee, over-tipped Gerald, and left, walking out into the humidity.

***

Since I was running on an entire night's sleep, I pulled out the map and picked a route to the Morley family home.

The map didn't account for construction and three unexplained traffic blockages. The townhouse looked as I'd expected. Probably worth a million or two, with a security pad outside.

I walked up to it and pressed the white button. The male voice said, "Yes?"

"Paul Costa, to see Mrs. Morley, please."

"Do you have an appointment?"

"No, but if I need one, I'll speak to her assistant."

"Please wait there, sir," said the voice.

It seemed like a long time until I was buzzed in. The man who met me at the door was taller than me, maybe six-two or three. He had dirty blonde hair, pulled back from his forehead, heavy brows and a body builder's physique. He was wearing a golf shirt; about two sizes too small, blue slacks and running shoes. "Good afternoon, Adam." He blinked and resumed the basilisk stare he'd greeted me with. "Good afternoon, Mr. Costa. This way."

I followed him through a light green alcove and hallway. Stairs to the left. There was a phone on a small table in the hall, and mirrors, photos and paintings. Elegant and tasteful, including the small chandelier overhead. There was a drink cart, beautiful seating and a butler's table. On a love seat upholstered in some blue damask sat a lovely woman, whose picture I had seen. In most of those pictures, she had been seated gazing up at her husband, Dick Morley. She wore a dark green pantsuit that harmonized with the room. She sat perfectly erect, head up, with her legs turned slightly to the side, crossed at the ankles. She held a glass in one hand, and an unlit cigarette in the other.

"That will be all, Adam," she said.

I pulled out my lighter and she leaned forward, taking the light.

She looked up to see that Adam had left. "You've got nerve," she said, "Coming here, I mean."

"First, may I express my condolences for your loss?"

"Thank you. Since you're here, please make me an extra dry martini, lemon twist, straight up. You'll find everything you need over there on the cart."

After a quick surge of irritation, I figured, okay, let's do it, but like a gentleman who's a guest, not a damned servant. She had Boodles gin, and a cute little ice bucket. I mixed her drink, adding a twist of lemon peel, a classic martini.

I poured myself a healthy glass of Glenlivet. I handed her the martini, and walked across to another chair and sat. I crossed my knees and looked over at her as she sipped her drink. She looked up sharply. "That is a perfect martini, like a cold cloud on my tongue."

"It isn't the first I've made"

"No, I don't suppose it is."

"Mrs. Morley, I didn't murder your husband."

"He died of a heart attack of some kind, I'm told. Why did you push a knife into his ear?" She was calm and spoke slowly.

"Didn't do that, either."

She took a drag from her cigarette, pulling so hard that the tip grew extra long and hot, then took a large sip of her drink. "One of the joys of being the widow, instead of his wife, I can smoke and drink again. I really missed that. Always in moderation, never smoking. It was ghastly. Wonderful perks, though."

"I'm sure. I don't mean to intrude on your grief, but I do need your help to clear myself."

"Paul, my husband was a leader, an outstanding legislator, and well liked by his colleagues. Each election got him a higher percentage of votes. He had only a few enemies, and they aren't killers.

"You, on the other hand, had already beaten him up and ejected him from a bar where he was peaceably minding his own business."

"Not exactly."

"Perhaps you could elucidate," she said and smiled at using the word. There was the slightest slurring of her sibilants. If I hadn't seen her drinking, I might have thought she had a lisp.

"Of course. He was in the bar, and had been drinking. I declined service and offered some alternatives. He got loud and abusive and I escorted him out, after he tried to manhandle me."

Her eyebrows rose. "He tried to hit you?"

"No, ma'am, he just grabbed me."

"Please don't call me 'ma'am,' Paul. It makes me feel old and unattractive."

"Anyway, I had to control him as I walked him out. Once a customer grabs you—"

"Yes, I understand."

"If this is too painful, we can stop," I said, meaning exactly the opposite.

"You mix a nice numbing drink. He loved power and his job."

"Mrs. Morley, I'm under suspicion and I did not kill him. I found his body, that's all. I can't just sit and hope for the best. I need to know as much as I can, and you might be able to help."

She stopped to consider, then looked me up and down. "What is it you need?"

I realized that this would be my only chance at her; that she was slightly drunk and somehow receptive, whether grieving or relieved. "I still think your husband was murdered, Mrs. Morley. I need to know how it was done, and who would want to do it."

She continued to sip her martini, and take long drags from her cigarette, considering my speech. "I have a friend; he's with the government. It's possible that he can help."

"Could you introduce me to your friend?"

"I'll call him as soon as you leave."

I wrote down the name and number of my motel, and gave her my room number. "I appreciate it."

"Dick was a good Congressman, but he had his failings, I suppose."

"How about your son, Jason, I believe?"

"Chip off the old block, fruit doesn't fall far from the tree. He's his father's son, one hundred percent."

"Same kind of integrity surrounding his job?"

"Job? He was my husband's aide, working for a dollar a year. He lives off of his father and me. Has an apartment, but the rent comes from my checkbook."

I was wondering how close he really was to his father. I opened my mouth to ask.

"What the fuck are you doing here?" said a male voice.

"Jason, your language," she said mildly.

"Mom, this man killed my father, and he's sitting here, drinking our liquor and chatting with you like a—."

"Jason, I know no such thing, and neither do you. He's a guest in our house and I won't have him spoken to in that manner."

He glared at us. He looked just like his pictures. His hair was perfectly cut and styled, and he was dressed in gray slacks and a designer shirt. He was perspiring freely, so he had just come in from the heat. Adam stood next to him, with a pretty young lady. The daughter. Adam's bearing screamed that he was carrying a gun. I looked at his arms and hands and decided it was probably at the small of his back.

"Adam," said Jason Morley, "Mr. Costa was just leaving. Perhaps you could show him the door?"

"Certainly, Mr. Morley." I stood and put my drink carefully onto the coaster.

"Mrs. Morley, I appreciate your hospitality and graciousness, under the circumstances."

"Nothing," she said, "'S'nothing at all." With only the slightest ladylike slur.

I felt the sudden power shift in the room. From her to her son, as sudden as the drop of an axe blade.

Adam approached from the side. "Don't need the rough stuff, Adam," I said turning so that we faced each other squarely.

"Jason, please stop this." A girl's voice, soft and hesitant. The sister.

I glanced at the siblings. He had a wolfish leer on his face. The sister, Charlene, as I remembered, had a hand to her mouth and a mixed look of fascination and fear. Their mother lit another cigarette, and her martini glass was empty except for a lemon peel. I had a feeling that if I'd mixed her another drink, she'd have taken it from me with the same sang-froid.

"Please come with me, Mr. Costa," said Adam, quite calmly. Then he grabbed my wrist in his left hand, keeping his gun hand free. He had it half right. I took my own hand, the one he was gripping, in my free hand and twisted and pulled at the same time. My bent arm snapped free as I twisted away. I paused for a split second and spun back towards the houseboy.

The torsion and drive from my hips concentrated at my elbow as it met Adam's face. His head snapped away and he clawed at his back with his right hand.

I stepped forward and grabbed his short ponytail with one hand, his chin with the other, turning his face upward, pulling his head downward. That spun him to the floor, on his stomach. Since I had a fistful of hair, I pushed it into the nape of his neck as hard as I could, dropping one knee onto the back of his thigh. I pulled the Glock from his holster, ejected the magazine, and jacked out the chambered round.

"Adam," I said, "You should never carry a round in the chamber, it's dangerous. You could blow your ass off that way."

"Mrs. Morley, you are a gracious hostess. Thank you. Jason, I'm sure I'll see you again."

"Bet on it, asshole," he said. Adam was dazed, but still stared at the empty pistol. The sister hadn't moved.

"Pierced by your rapier wit," I said, walking back down the sterile, elegant hallway and closing the door softly behind me.

I was back at my motel in half the time it took me to get into the city. Between the quick drive, and the atavistic joy from hitting back, I was feeling pretty good. I hadn't solved the real problem, but Adam probably took part in assaulting Lois, and the primitive in me rejoiced in the once-removed payback. It made a point and I had gained some insight into Morley's family.

Chapter 9

I struggled with the little plastic keycard to get my door open, then sat down to read Sandra's file. Her research started with Morley's personal details, birth, education, military service, marriage and children.

Camille, his wife, was the middle daughter of a Newport old money family of declining wealth. From the marriage she gained income and prestige, and he locked into a whole new league of funding and support networks. He also acquired a decorative and decorous ornament for campaigning. His first known step off the line was with a colleague's aide during his first term. They parted amicably, but off the record, she described him as twisted. He had allowed his ten-year-old son to watch them having sex, and told her about it afterwards.

There were others, where videos were recorded and given to the son. In one case, drugs were used to allow the fourteen-year-old boy to have his first sexual experience while the father watched and taped it. After a few pages, it was numbing and I felt awful about my growing detachment. I set it aside and lit a cigarette. There was a small coffee maker in the washroom area, so I started a pot.

Someone knocked at the door. I looked over at the file, figured it was best kept private and started in that direction. "Who is it?" I asked. There was an indecipherable male voice on the other side of the door. I closed the file, and for no particular reason, slipped it into the plastic laundry bag hanging from the rod. I wanted it hidden and that was the quickest spot.

I slipped the security bar back and turned the lever handle. The door exploded inward, and there they were. Jason and Adam faced me; Adam with his Glock pointed at my face. Jason was behind him as they walked into the room. The entire left side of Adam's face was swollen, and his eye was nearly closed. That felt nice, until I remembered the gun, and that there were two of them and that I was alone.

Jason was smiling, and there was something small, but apparently heavy dangling from his right wrist. He stepped forward and swung it towards me. There was a peculiar sensation and smell, and the room seemed to flow down and away. I saw his arm go back again, maybe I saw it come forward, or maybe I just knew that it did.

Chapter 10

When I opened my eyes, the room was dim. There was a long time where I lay still. It took some time to realize I was on the floor. When I did, it was baffling. How did I get down there? Slowly, things started coming back to me and I started to rise, first one hand under one shoulder, then the other. I tried to do a slow, agonizing push-up. I collapsed to the floor. The flare of pain in my ribs radiated to my shoulders and down to my crotch. On the fourth try, I got myself onto my hands and knees.

I was still there, swaying, waiting for the nausea to pass, when Sandra was magically kneeling at my side, with an ice bag and some towels. She got me into a chair somehow and was unbuttoning my shirt. She held an ice pack against the left side of my forehead and hissed when she saw my chest. I looked down slowly, and waited for the blurring and random clouds to clear.

They had kicked the cheerful shit out of my ribs and crotch while I was out. I felt lucky that they hadn't gang-raped me, for good measure. "They searched the room, too, it looks like," she said. "My file?"

"File?" There was a time where it was dark, and then I could see. "Paul? Paul, my file."

I remembered a file. "Hid. Gimme a second." I could remember things from the day before. "Time is it?" I heard myself ask.

"Three in the morning," she answered slowly. "I finished work and I thought we could talk, I was so wired, but when I came to your door, it was partway open, so I walked in and found you. I unplugged the coffee pot, it was burning up."

"Out long, then." The coffee pot. When did I start it? I had to think for a long time, about reading the file, and then somebody knocked on the door and I put it— over there. "Okay, laundry bag." My clothes were still on the hangers, but looked rumpled. She returned

with the file in her hands, flipped through it and sagged back into her chair.
"It's all here, but out of order."

With my head clearing, I became aware of pain. My ribs felt bruised, at least, cracked maybe in a couple of places and my crotch felt swollen and I was sick to my stomach. She looked hard at me and helped me to bed, packing more ice around my head, ribs, and handing me a bag for the nether regions. She kicked off her shoes and curled up on the chair next to the worktable. She rested her hands on one high arm, laid her head on her hands, and left her eyes open to watch.

Once in awhile she woke me, shined a cigarette lighter in front of each eye, then let me go back to sleep. It was full morning before I woke. I couldn't find anything that didn't hurt, including my tongue where I must have bitten it.

"Interesting life you lead, Paul Costa."

"You mean getting beaten up?"

"You talk in your sleep. All women's names, 'Isabel,' 'Marisol,' 'Dana.' You must keep busy. It makes me wonder what's wrong with me. At the restaurant, you gave out the 'Thanks but no thanks' pretty clearly."
"Isn't you, Sandra."

"You already let me down gently, so you don't have to say anything about that."
Thank God, I thought. The phone rang and we both started. She didn't attempt to get it. That told me something, too. She'd been in rooms or apartments where a woman answering the phone wasn't safe. The loneliness in her brought on a wave of pity on one hand, and a bit of anger as well.
"Hello?" I said.

"Paul," said Mrs. Pina, sounding angry and I hoped, relieved. Mrs. Pina was not a person I wanted to be angry. "You didn't call last night."
"Mrs. Pina, I'll explain when I come back. There's a lot happening here. Can you put 'Sol on the phone?"

Even the silence that followed sounded angry, but eventually I heard her voice, "Daddy?" There was both question and fear in it.

"Honey, I'm so sorry. I was out until late, and I couldn't use a phone. Everything's okay, though."

"Daddy, I was so scared. I thought all kinds of things."

The pang I felt at the eighth part of truth I'd just told her got worse. I was furious, too. I was angry with myself, the people I was involved with, and the whole damned situation.

"'Sol, it's okay. I have a little more to do down here, but I'll be home soon. Okay, sweetheart?"

"Promise, Daddy?"

"Promise. Just as soon as I can. I miss you too much to stay away."

"Mrs. Pina's pretty mad, Daddy."

"Can you fix that for me?"

She giggled. "Maybe, we'll see."

"I love you, little one."

"Love you, too, Daddy." She was upset enough to she let me get away with calling her "little one." She thought it was a baby name. When I turned from the nightstand, Sandra was looking at me. "Nice," she said. "Was that your kid?"

"Marisol, my daughter."

"How old?"

"Eleven, gorgeous, of course."

"Of course. I have to go pull myself together and go to work. You need the hospital. I think you might have some broken ribs. You definitely have a concussion, and that cut over your eye needs a stitch or two. I didn't take you earlier because I didn't think I could get you into my car, and you didn't want an ambulance. I can drop you at the E.R. on my way to work, and call housekeeping to get the blood out of the carpet."

I looked down and saw a stain on the carpet. I hadn't noticed that I'd been cut. I knew that I was pretty well done, in terms of mobility and so forth, but I could make a few calls, gather a bit more information and then go home. The hospital would cost me a day, but she was right.

"And you should make a police report."

"The people I call will probably tell the DC cops."

"There had better be one hell of a story at the end of this, or I swear, I'm gonna make this beating look like a day at the beach. By the way, who did it, anyway? Do you know?"

"Jason and his boy Adam. At gunpoint, to start with."

She inhaled audibly. "I hope you've read my part of the file. I don't think I can talk about it." She seemed to like being tough, so that admission made me understand how bad it had been for her.

I changed the subject. "You seem to be pretty handy at first aid and all of that."

"In the army, I was a field medic."

"Army, now TV news? Anything else you'd care to share?"

"I usually save that for pillow talk, and you messed that up."

"Sandra—"

"Before you try to be all kind and flattered, it would be better if we were friends. I have a feeling that once you get going, you'd be a little too intense for me. I'd be too flighty for you, but I think we could become good friends. It makes me wish you were gay."

I must have flinched.

"Lots of women find gay men to be the best friends, no sexual tension, but the male vantage point. On the other hand, a good male friend with a little sexual tension would be nice. You could use a woman's viewpoint now and again, I bet. Let's get you checked in to the Emergency Room."

"Do I have time for a quick phone call?"

"Quick, please."

I called DaSilva's number, got his voice mail and left a message to call me at my motel with a time to reach him. I asked for four hours from the time of my call. When I staggered on the way to the elevator, a surprisingly strong, thin arm caught me around the waist. She stopped at the desk and told them lies about the bloodstain, and led me to her car. She drove a luxurious Japanese car and I asked her about blood on the seats. She laughed and locked the doors from her side. We whirred and purred, until she pulled up to the emergency room entrance. I walked in on my own.

There was the ritual about the insurance card and co-pay, and all of the potentially horrifying side effects of their treatments, and interminable waits. One to get into a curtained area, then another until the doctor appeared. Finally, taped, wrapped and tied, they told me what to do about pain. I'd been in the johnny that covered my upper abdomen, but not much else, for the whole time.

I would have signed anything for clothes and some dignity. Not too bad though, on the whole. No hernia, some swelling, "edema" they called it, two bruised ribs, three stitches and warnings about concussions and signs of worse. Then I was wheeled out to meet the cab to bring me back to my motel. The painkiller had kicked in.

In my room, the message light on the phone was flashing. There were two calls; one from DaSilva and one from Dana. I kicked that around for a bit, and called DaSilva first.

"Newport Police, Detective Bureau, Sergeant DaSilva."

"Hey, Sarge."

"Hello, there."

"Privacy?"

"That's it."

"Call me back in twenty, you still have the number?"

"I have it. Make it an hour, though."

We hung up, and I dialed Dana's number. She'd called in sick. I called her home number and got her machine. I left a message to call me and left the number. I turned the TV on, and saw that housekeeping had been here. The carpet looked clean and damp and the mess from the careless search had been picked up. There was a note to call the front desk. I ignored it and sat up on the left hand bed. I called Al's friend about a gun.

A little while later, he called from the lobby. He was on the low side of thirty, with a military bearing, but a strange ponytail that came from the crown of his head. "Al called," was all he said. I wondered what the relationship was, but it was better to leave that alone. An investigator, Al would have lots of strange contacts. It wasn't as if finding a gun in DC would have been hard, but this was a lot more convenient.

Outside in the parking lot, we stood near the trunk of his car. I counted out his money and he handed me a Beretta, nine millimeter, fourteen round version, two spare magazines, a box of shells and a holster that could clip to either side of my belt. He had no pouches for the magazines, but that was okay. I could pick up a cleaning kit later on. No numbers on the gun. The action felt crisp and solid. I wondered if there was someplace to practice.

"Three miles up the road, to the right as you leave is a gravel pit. It has a chain, no guard, and nobody cares if you shoot there," he said. "Lots of guys go there to shoot, and as long as it ain't autogetem, nobody cares."

"Autogetem," Ranger slang for full automatic, machine gun-style firing. He carried himself like a soldier and sounded like one. Strange what happens to some guys when they get out. Some of them tend bar, some sell guns. We shook hands, and he told me to feel free to call him anytime.

I tucked my purchase into the brown grocery bag he had given me. No one suspects grocery bags. When I got back to my room, I sat on the bed and field stripped it. I remembered the smell of gun oil fondly. I loaded all three magazines and slapped them against my thigh to seat the rounds. I tried the holster and a couple of draws. I settled on my favorite, butt forward, on my right hand side because I could reach it left handed, and it provided the only way to draw a weapon seated at a table or in a car.

Right on time, the phone rang. "DaSilva," he said.

"Hi. Free to talk?"

"Yup, so tell me."

I went through it, leaving the gun but nothing else out, including jamming Adam to the floor. I wanted to read the rest of that file as soon as I took my medicine and got my head to stop hurting.

"Sounds like you struck a nerve, Costa."

"I think so. There's something nasty there, Larry. Oops. Can I call you 'Larry'?"

"Just did."

I told him more, about Lois, and Sandra's file, and the Dead Man's Switch. I left out names and he noticed. "I'll want names at some point, you know."

"I'm sure you will."

"What kind of shape are you in? You described a good ass-kicking."

"I'm okay for what I still need to do."

"And you found yourself a piece?" This guy was frightening. He seemed to know whatever the hell he needed to. "Don't answer that. About Petersen. He's got some strange connections, and had lots of juice pushing him into the office, and we're trying to pin that down. It isn't a happy thing, but you helped out by putting us onto him. We're trying to find out what's up with that strip joint too."

"How about the Congressman's autopsy results?"

"Interestinger and interestinger," he answered. "Even over a clean phone, I'm not happy discussing it. Bring me a copy of that file. Sterilize it if you want, but I need to see it. Write down a summary of what you got from the young woman and the bartender at the strip joint. We have it on tape, but your statement will help us."

I remembered the thousand and one exceptions to the "hearsay rule," and knew that he was already thinking about a trial. I'd bet that the District Attorney loved the guy.

"Get whatever you have to do, done, then get your ass back here. Between Mrs. Pina, and Agent Kilroy, I don't know who's going to drive me bughouse first."

"Agent Kilroy?"

"Cut the shit, Paul, okay? We aren't friends, but don't jerk me off, okay? She's a good cop, for a fed, but she can't lie for shit, and she lights up whenever you're mentioned. She asks about you before she asks for case specifics, and whatever you two have going on isn't hurting anything. For the record, you're clear."

"You're a piss-poor cupid, Larry."

"You're all grown up, Paul. You got yourself under suspicion for murder, fucked up a perfectly simple investigation. You've been around the block, you're sitting in Washington, fucking, DC, with the shit beaten out of you and a gun on your hip."

"So, what are you saying?"
"Aren't you kind of ashamed to need a cupid?"
"Screw you."
"Not, now, I have a headache."
"Got it."
"And do something about Kilroy and Mrs. Pina."
"Got it."

We hung up. If the murder was a murder, and the murder wasn't solved, at least the investigation wasn't looking at me. If it hadn't hurt so much, I would have heaved a sigh of relief. My daughter had a future. I dozed off, dreaming of dead men under toilets, and cells and handcuffs, and flighty women in elegant drawing rooms.

It was hot and stuffy when I woke up, startled. It took a moment to realize that the phone had been ringing. I lit a cigarette and answered it.

"Hello?" said an unfamiliar male voice, "This is Paul Costa?"

"Who's calling?" I said, putting the cigarette out as if I needed my hands free.

"I'm a friend of the lady you visited, yesterday. She called and suggested that we should speak. I confess I'm a bit nonplused by that. On the other hand, the fact that she made the suggestion impelled me to call. I'm really not comfortable speaking over the phone, but I have some time today. Can we meet?"

His old-fashioned speech was contagious, I guess. "I think we ought."

He mentioned a hotel, not far from where I was, and gave me a room number. "Is there a more public forum at the hotel?" I asked.

"I would be happy to meet you in the lounge, if you'd find that more comfortable."

We agreed to a half hour, and I took a few minutes to clean up a bit. I found the place, and walked into the lounge. There was one man, sitting at the bar alone, with a glass of wine in front of him. So help me, I swear it was port. That had to be him.

I sat next to him, and ordered a muddled Old Fashioned. The bartender looked baffled, so I rattled off the recipe and turned to the man next to me. Navy blue pinstriped suit, tailored, single needle, wingtip shoes and a silver tie complemented a trim build and utterly distinguished looking man. His blonde hair was graying. He was old money aristocratic, and tough as nails. I'd met men like him. Camille Morley had chosen well. "I'm Paul Costa."

"Yes, I took the liberty of pulling your records. Quite impressive, although you tend to be a bit of a loose cannon. You seem to have provoked a bit of heavy-handedness."

He paused, as if waiting for a response before he spoke, "May I assume that Camille's son was responsible?"

"Him and their pet ape, Adam."

"May I also assume that it has something to do with Camille's late husband? His murder and your role in that?"

"I'm not sure. Neither one of them said anything, just got right down to business. There's doubt that Congressman Morley was murdered."

"If you agreed, you'd be home with your daughter by now." Suddenly the old world courtliness was gone. His tone had gone harder, and his blue eyes, under white brows were leveled at me. "You wouldn't be carrying that gun at your right waist, and you wouldn't have insisted on a public meeting."

"All true. By the way, what would you like me to call you?"

"Please call me Rob. May I call you Paul?"

"Certainly, Rob. Short for Robert?"

"It's Friedrich."

I decided not waste time on the question that his answer begged.

"Camille is a lovely woman, and we've been friends for several years. Ever since my wife passed away," he said.

"She is lovely. She's also tough, smart and resourceful."

"Yes. And fragile in some ways, and vulnerable in others. Her husband was trash, and her son is worse."

"How about the daughter?"

"She's a lovely young girl, under Jason's thumb. Before that, she was under her father's."

"Must be tough to watch."

"I'm sure that it's tougher to live through."

I paused to consider. "I'm going to put a hypothetical situation to you. Please be patient with me, but be honest, as well."

"I lie for a living, Paul, that may be difficult."

"I'm a bartender; we lie too."

He smiled. "Of course you do. Put your hypothesis. I promise that if I can't talk, that I'll tell you so."

"Fair enough. A man in late middle age has to die. He has to die within a ten-minute window. Ideally, it should look like a heart attack. The man drinks heavily, and associates with women he doesn't know well. He's a guest at a hotel and drunk. Can it be accomplished?"

He looked at me through those level blue eyes. "Easily."

"Would there be any traces?"

"Only if one knew exactly what to look for."

"How difficult would it be for a layperson like me to obtain the services and materials needed?"

"With sufficient funds, not hard at all."

"If I were the person doing the post-mortem, what would I be looking for and where would I expect to find it?"

"Do you have an e-mail address? I don't have that information, like a lot of technical matters. I can have someone e-mail you that information to pass along to the coroner. I can't be seen to be involved and I can't help officially."

I hadn't touched my drink, nor had he, since I'd sat down. We seemed to think of it at the same time and each paused to sip them. Mine was awful. I set the glass down. "Mixing drinks properly is becoming a lost art," said Rob.

I nodded.

We rose to leave. "Paul, be a bit circumspect, and you may find things go more easily for you."

"Good advice."

"It was well meant."

I thanked him, trying to sound sincere, shook his hand and left.

I still needed to speak to young Ms. Morley. Most of the family's sickness could be pointed directly at the Congressman, but his wife and children had tolerated it, and in the case of the son, taken an active part. People trying to raise happy, healthy adults had produced mass murderers. Morley's games had been dangerous. He'd been playing with fire.

I made a note on my legal pad to ask Dana about that, and about what could turn the father and son against each other, or what would happen to the son's mental state when the father died. I thought about that, and Jason Morley's assertive control of the household, before I made the phone call to the Morley townhouse.

"Morley residence," said Adam's voice.

"Miss Charlene Morley, please," I said.

"Miss Charlene will be with you in a moment, whom should I say is calling?"

"How's your eye?"

"About the same as yours, dickhead."

"Miss Charlene, boy. Chop-Chop, you go run get Missy Charlene, make quick fast. I need speak her on magic box. You go run her, tell her, same-same. You number one good boy." I heard voices in the background.

"Why are you calling?" she asked, without a greeting.

"We need to meet," I said, being careful to say, "we," "I know things you need to know, and you may know things that I need too."

"Suppose I said that I know what I need to, Mr. Costa?"

"I'd say that perhaps you could still see your way clear to helping me."

"Mr. Costa, you may well be my father's murderer, you assaulted our houseboy, and my brother—"

"Miss Morley."

"Charlene."

"Charlene, I didn't assault Adam, I protected myself from him, and stopped when he stopped trying to hurt me. Your brother appeared at my motel and he and Adam beat me at gunpoint. I can't understand why, unless they just enjoy it. I didn't kill your father, and I believe that we need to meet, and sooner rather than later." I left out the part about wanting to go home.

There was a long silence before she gave me an address in Arlington. We agreed to meet there in three quarters of an hour and

hung up. I was partly afraid, and partly hoping that her brother and houseboy would come with her.
I eased my way to the elevator and car, favoring my ribs and head, and aiming my crotch away from any potential threats.

Chapter 11

My map got me to the health club right on time. There were brightly polished chrome dumbbells, free weights and racks to hold them, on the far side of a tall glass wall. Lots of people, men and women, were on stair climbers and treadmills and stationary bikes and complicated weight machines. All of them were dressed in workout outfits that probably cost more than my best suit.

I was seated at a juice bar, waiting over a peach smoothie when she walked in. Like the "bartender" at the juice bar, she was wearing white shorts and a golf shirt, looking as though she was going to teach an aerobics class. She turned some heads when she sat next to me.

She seemed withdrawn and shy but I sensed a lot of anger from her. She didn't show it, but if she'd come into my bar, I'd have been watching her intake carefully. I'd have checked her I.D. as well, even though from my research, I knew she was twenty-two.

"Mr. Costa," she said, "Why am I here?"

"I'm trying to be tactful, Charlene, and it's going to be hard to do that and to be factual, too."

"Hard to be tactful about my father, so let me help you. He was a pig in his private life. He made sure that Jason grew up to be just like him. He mistreated my mother, he abused any woman he could and kept it secret." The hatred was physical in its affect on her; her color and face changed.

"Including you?" It was a shot in the dark, but it seemed to me that the Congressman abusing his daughter would fit the pattern. She understood. In today's world, it was discussed openly.

"You're wrong. You think he was sexually abusing me, and he didn't. He had other ways to degrade a person." She was emphatic, but not convincing.

"You don't have to tell me, Charlene," as gently as I could manage it.

"You must be a great bartender. Isn't that what drunks do? Tell their problems to their bartender?"

"I think that's more in the movies and on television, and you aren't drunk."

"No, I'm not drunk. Still, spilling your guts to your friendly bartender must have some basis in reality. Anyway, are you a friendly bartender? Could you be my friendly bartender for just a little while?"

She was looking upwards, as though searching her own mind. I couldn't think of anything to help, so I kept my mouth shut. I often thought that I should do that more. It worked well for my father and grandfather.

"When I was a freshman in college, I was an innocent, you understand?"

I nodded, thinking I didn't, but she had to be kept going.

"I went to an all-women's school in New England. Graduated Magna Cum Laude, but that first year was hard for me." She grimaced.

I wondered if there was anytime that wasn't hard for her.

"I doubted my orientation, I guess. Anyway, I fell in love with a sophomore, and we became lovers. Another woman, I mean."

I nodded, hoping that my expression was neutral.

"Later on, I realized that I'm not gay, but she was gentle and caring and understanding. I'd never been close to someone who wanted me to be more and better than I was. Can you understand how that felt?"

I nodded.

"Somehow, Adam or Jason or my father found out. Doesn't matter, it amounts to the same thing. My father."

"One night, when he was drunk, he showed me a professionally edited video, with fades and background music and all. First Heather and me, then Heather with Jason. I think for the one with Jason she was drugged, or drunk. Jason was pretty rough," She was talking fast and quietly, looking straight down at the bar. "Being the frightened little nothing that I was, I was afraid to confront him, or Jason, so I went to my mother. Then I went to Heather and blamed the whole thing on her. My mother just held me and cried and had a couple of drinks. Heather sat and stared. I just kept shouting at her, telling her about all of the hurt that was done to me. To me." She smirked a little.

"She dropped out, and I never heard from her again. My father still had the DVD when he died. I finally got up my nerve a couple of days ago, and threw it in the trash, after I broke it in two." She was petering out after all of that, uttered in a fast monotone, like a poorly rehearsed recital. But she wasn't quite done.

"Maybe I'm my father's daughter," she said softly.

I started to speak, but she kept shaking her head.

"No, you don't understand. My father has a whole closet full of videotapes, DVD's and flash drives; floor to ceiling. I only took the ones of Heather and me. I left all of the rest. They're all in his house up north. I drove up and got rid of the ones that concerned me. All of the rest, all of the people he screwed up are still there."

I thought about that, and all of the potential suspects on those recordings. I wondered if DaSilva and Dana had seen them.

"The closet is hidden in the basement. If you don't know how, you'd never find it."

"How do you open the closet?" I asked, hoping I wasn't pushing too hard.

She gave me detailed instructions, "I need your word that those videos won't hurt anyone else. I want them to hurt no one but my father."

I thought he was beyond being hurt."I promise to do all I can to protect the people on those tapes. I hope that's good enough."

"It will have to be." She handed me a key and a card with the Congressman's address on it. On the back of the card, she scribbled a note giving me permission to enter. No wonder she'd graduated Magna.

It wasn't happy, but there was some animation on her face. "I hope that those tapes really screw my father. I really hope so. I want you to find a way to destroy what's left of him. Can you do that? Can you?" She was talking like a small child, begging to be taken someplace nice. Her forehead was shiny, and she tossed her head.

There was an unhealthy heat coming from her, like a low-grade fever, and she was smiling and crying all at once.

"I can't wait to see what those tapes do to his precious legacy. I want to see whatever nice things people had to say about him just blasted away. I want to get even for me and Heather. Is that wrong? Is it? Can you do it?" She was crying, but there was a grin on her face she couldn't control.

"Easy, we need to slow down here," I said with my throat as open as I could make it. Voice deeper than usual, and calm, slow, and gently commanding. The shy young woman who came in might never have existed. "First things first, Charlene, okay?"

She nodded, as if I said something profound.

I remembered seeing something like this before. After interrogation, a Marine who'd killed a superior officer confessed, and all of the anger, hate and energy that went into killing him surfaced. It was as if he was still driving the bayonet into the second lieutenant, over and over again. She was like that. She was living a moment that she hoped for. Part of her knew that the moment wouldn't come, but she still wanted it so badly that it seemed real to her.

It took a half hour to get her calmed down and on her way home. She left looking as she had arriving.

I drove to my motel and past it, about three miles to a gravel pit.

I found a lot of well-ventilated cans of various sizes, lots of brass, and quite a few spent bullets. I had half a dozen cans up, each smaller than a human head. I paced off seven yards, and fired single shots at one of the targets, then pairs, then emptied the pistol, all fourteen shots into a can, making it dance.

I backed off to ten yards, chose another can, and repeated the exercise, firing from eye level, with a Weaver grip, then from chest level, shotgun style, with both eyes open. At twenty-five yards, I was still hitting the target. I emptied one box of cartridges. It felt good to shoot and that the draw, fire and reload was comfortable and familiar. I tried a few one-handed, right then left, at seven yards, five hits out of five right handed, four out of five with the left.

At the motel, I sat down with one of their towels laid out on the work surface. Between bites of fast food, I stripped and cleaned my pistol, laying the components on the towel, and thought about my next steps. I had to keep pushing, but it was time for Rhode Island.

I would have loved to ask Isabel about the Morleys. Then I thought of Dana, with the same expertise.

I jotted down some notes on my legal pad, so I could speak more intelligently with her about it and wrote a long report on what had happened in Washington. It surprised me that none of the local police had been in touch. I'd expected DaSilva to put them onto me.

Unless I slowed down, I had some freedom of movement, but I didn't like being a target for the Morley ménage. Stopping would present more danger than the reckless charge I'd been making. I called Sandra's office and left a voicemail telling her how to reach me in Rhode Island. It was getting late, but I called home.

I caught myself gripping the phone while I talked with 'Sol. It was a little hard hearing her, since my ears still rang from gunfire. I was delighted that her social studies teacher had given her a special project, forcing her to use the library rather than the pre-digested pap in her text. "No internet," she said, "can you imagine?" She was going to have to think. Mrs. Pina told me to hurry home. I hung up after a half hour, smiling for the first time that day, because I was going home soon.

Dana was next. I took a deep breath, looked at my notes, and carefully turned them face down. Then I dialed. Eight for long distance, then one, six-one-seven, and her number. It rang twice before she picked up. Her voice was the same. She sounded cool and non-committal when she answered.

"Dana? Hi, it's Paul."

"Paul!" it was almost a shout, then she quieted, "Paul, how are you? I spoke with DaSilva."

"Which is not the conversation I hoped for."

I could hear the pause, and her voice seemed a bit deeper, and lighter, all at once. "So have at me, Paul. I would love a less professional talk with you."

"I'm kind of rusty."

"You're damned near seized up, But I'm the soul of patience."

I laughed, and started with what popped into my mind. "Are you aware of the affect you have on me?"

"Yup."

"Until you came along, I hadn't thought of a woman since my wife died. I mean as a woman, you know? You have touched me."

"Oh, that's nice. See, you aren't all that rusty, after all. Now, please get your ass home? I hope to take this conversation into some kind of concrete, hard reality."

"Dana, my reality is just fine, right now."

"It's going to waste then. Unless the TV person that DaSilva mentioned is around?"

"I'm kind of limited, I guess. One at a time, that's me."

"I knew that. Otherwise, it would have shown before she slithered onto the scene."

"Slithered?"

"Get home, Paul. Bring your information and all of that. Bring an appetite for me. Did I mention I'm a pretty good cook?"

I was struggling to keep up, but I managed to remark on having an appetite already, and we hung up, laughing together. I missed laughing and talking with a woman. I felt fresh, despite the pain pills and beating that I'd taken. I called the airline and changed my reservation, and lay down to try to sleep. It took an educational program about the iguanas of some island in the South Pacific to put me under. I was glad that they didn't talk about their mating habits.

***

I showered, shaved, dressed and packed, putting Sandra's file into my briefcase to finish on the flight. I figured I'd surprise Marisol, and maybe Dana. I was feeling rested and only a little sore. Even my tongue felt better. My first stop was a bus station. I had to get my new pistol home. It had been expensive and it had provided some comfort. I expected to need comfort again. Bus company freight was reliable and they did little examination.

I spent some money on bubble wrap, and box and tape, went to the men's room and packed the whole thing up, including the cleaning kit. I used their label and they weighed it for me. I'd pick it up at the bus station in Providence the next day.

I turned my car in, picked up my tickets and checked one bag, keeping the briefcase with me. I was whistling when I got to my gate.

Unless they were simply sadistic assholes, why had Jason and Adam gone to my motel to take the insane risk of beating me up? Why would they do that, and how could they be sure I wouldn't file a complaint? Even with all of the political shelter in the world, they should have been worried. Why not wait until I was in New England? Why not set up an alibi? Charlene knew I'd taken the ass kicking, so would Camille. Some famous dead guy had said, "A secret shared by two is a secret no more."

There were people I cared about close to home. They had lots of ways to keep me quiet without coming near me. I had to control those thoughts, so I pulled out Sandra's file and began to read what had happened to her four years before.

New to the station, she had obtained an interview with the Congressman. Afterwards, he offered her dinner. I remembered how provocative she could be, and pictured her putting herself on offer for Morley. Not hard to see "a man of appetites" taking advantage of the opportunity.

At first, with all of the sneaking around and sudden trips to Rhode Island, she thought that she was in love. The tone of her writing was self-mocking, but her feelings at the time came through. There was some rough sex and porn to help him along. There were even viewings of him having sex with other partners. She admitted to finding some of it intriguing at first, until she realized that he was watching it for himself. It started to dawn on her that she was an appliance to him.

By then, she would leap out of bed, afterwards, to shower and cry. Often she found herself curled in the corner of the tub, with the shower beating hot water onto her. He alternated kindness with the rough power games that gave him more pleasure than sex. She couldn't bring herself to end it. She described herself as sick, enjoying the treatment as if she deserved it.

Apparently, it took him over a month to lose interest. I was impressed by her ability to hold him for that long. She had done a good job of degrading herself, and that made me sadder than I already was. The bond held, until she found herself with gonorrhea.

When she told him about it, he blamed her and hung up. Her doctor prescribed antibiotics and warned her about her partners. Using her journalist's contacts, she found out that he'd infected at least three other women, and hadn't bothered to tell them or the woman who'd infected him. She didn't explain how she found out, and there were no names mentioned.

The woman who'd infected him was found next to a bicycle path in a park near Washington, alive, with broken elbows and knees, and a bottle of penicillin. She never saw her assailants. In the three years since her attack, she had recovered to the point of no longer needing a wheelchair for short walks.

Sandra had to do something. She was a journalist and a researcher. She did research and compiled the file she gave me. She said nothing to anyone until she gave it to me. I wondered why I was the guy, until I found a note clipped to the end of her section. It was written on motel stationery. She must have done it while I was asleep or unconscious.

"Dear Paul," it said, "This may or may not be useful to you, but it's been sitting in my desk at home. I still catch myself reviewing it. It really pisses me off that after all of this time, he is still fucking with my mind. It pisses me off that I hadn't done anything to stop him.

DO something about all of this. I thought about using it to ruin Morley, but it would have hurt other people. Would have made a hell of a story, though." There was a happy face kind of drawing, only it was leering and winking, instead of showing the inane seventies smile. "I think that being your friend will be fun, but I think of you at night. Take care of yourself, Sandra. P.S., don't forget that I get a twenty-four hour exclusive. S."

Smart woman, and smart to try to let go of her anger and hate and guilt. I stopped short. Time for me to get smart, too. The plane landed shortly after that liberating thought. Easier said than done, I supposed, but not the same as impossible.

Chapter 12

Baggage claim at T. F. Green is nicer than Logan, or any of the majors, and I was out, in a cab, less than twenty minutes after we arrived. After my ride into town, I paid my garage bill in Warwick. On my way home, I looked into my mirror a lot but didn't see anything more than once. I didn't care anyway, as long as I was going home.

Then I was at the door with my luggage and my daughter flung herself at me. I dropped the bags and caught her up, swinging in a circle. There was no way to describe how much that hurt, but it didn't matter. We were together and I couldn't manage a word. I was kissing her cheek and her hair and holding her. I managed to tell her how much I missed her before she was off and running at the mouth. I heard about school, and her trials and tribulations. I heard about Mrs. Pina's cooking and how early she made 'Sol go to bed, and she missed all of her favorite shows. Finally, she got around to how much she missed me and how bad I looked. She braced herself on one foot with a hip cocked, folded her arms and reminded me that she wasn't a baby anymore and I had to tell her.

Mrs. Pina was standing in the door. "Paul, why don't you come in. 'Sol, you need to let your Papa come in and sit down. He will tell us all about it." Marisol nodded and ran into the kitchen. I carried my bags to my room and dropped them on my bed. When I came out, I smelled coffee brewing and recent baking.

The coffee was awful, but the blueberry muffins made up for it. Mrs. Pina told me that 'Sol had made them with no help at all. I ate three, with butter, figuring that cholesterol wasn't as tough as me, anyway. I got a cup of Café a la Marisol down, without making faces, but Mrs. Pina was drinking milk. When I sat back in my chair, there was my daughter, beautiful, intelligent and insightful. She was looking me over, "Daddy, you're sitting like you hurt, your face is a mess, and you keep moving your mouth like it feels funny." She wasn't missing a thing. I edited it, but she got the gist of it.

"Did the men who did this kill that other man?" she asked.

"Maybe, honey, or he might have just kind of died."

"That isn't what the papers and most of the kids at school think."

"He might have just died and he might not. I don't think the men who roughed me up killed him."

"Why not, Daddy? If they could do this, why not kill him?"

"It's partly just a feeling, or maybe I know things that I haven't really put together, yet. That happens, you know?"

She nodded.

"So if he just died, or somebody else did it, is everything okay?"

"It's fine, sweetie." She smiled at me, and asked me about the coffee. I told her it was delicious.

There was a knock at the door that made us all jump. "Hello Sergeant DaSilva," I said, when I opened the door. He was alone, wearing a pair of dress slacks and a tee shirt with a picture of Porky Pig in a policeman's uniform on it. Porky was smiling, cradling a nightstick, the caption read: "Pigs are cool."

I tried not to laugh, but Marisol couldn't help it. It was impossible to contain it when she started, and shortly all of us were in the kitchen, letting the last few chuckles die out.

"I don't have much of a casual wardrobe," said DaSilva.

"Sergeant," I said, "what you do have is in the way of being 'classic.'"

"Classic," said Marisol, and started to giggle.

"You should see what I wear surfing." Marisol got him some coffee.

"'Sol makes Cuban coffee for me," I said quickly, to warn the detective. She handed him a muffin and the butter dish, while Mrs. Pina bustled around, pulling a dinner together.

"Larry," she said, quite casually, "are you staying for dinner?"

"Please," said Marisol. "We hardly ever have company."

He nodded. He was munching happily on a blueberry muffin, after sipping some coffee. How did she make it, he asked.

"My Mamacita taught me," she answered, smiling, and started to rattle it off to him. I thought it was nice having a guest. It would be better with more guests, and I started a list in my mind. Would this place be more of a home if I started to treat it like one?

"Your dad and I need to talk privately for a few minutes," he said to her after waiting for her to finish. "I hate to take up your time together, but it's important." She and Mrs. Pina left and sat down in the living room, while I smelled baking cod and simmering chowder. "Paul, I have a couple of things for you. First of all, you can't be wandering around illegally carrying a firearm. Here." He handed me a card with my picture and an endorsement to carry a concealed pistol. It sure as hell looked like my signature, too.

"I know a guy who did some time for forging checks," he answered, before I got the question out. "If you got rid of the piece, you can legally buy and wear another."

"It's coming up in a bus shipment."

"We really do have to do something about them. It's way too easy to move all kinds of stuff by bus. I had to pull some strings, but it may help." He handed me another laminated card that showed I was licensed as a private investigator and bail bondsman recovery agent. That would have been even tougher with the gap in my records that the Navy insisted on maintaining. The gap that kept me from practicing law should have prevented me from getting that license.

"I have something for you, too." I went to my room and got my report out of my briefcase and handed it to him. "Sorry about my handwriting, but it should be pretty comprehensive."

"Not to mention, interesting." He leafed through it quickly. "What's next?"

"After a shower and a change of clothes, and dinner, and some time with my daughter you mean?"

"Yes, after all of that."

"After that, and some rest, I have to visit some old acquaintances about some of theirs."

He handed me a file. "Coroner's protocol, M.E's report, including toxicology. You never got this stuff from me, okay?"

"What stuff is that?"

"Stuff?" he answered, and smiled. The smile faded.

"Petersen," he said.

I waited him out.

"He's off of the investigation, and doing robbery and stuff like that."

"Thanks for letting me know."

"You should have heard him on the radio when you lost him, by the way. He sounded like he'd wet his pants. He knew he had to tell, but he hated to do it. I have to admit I enjoyed it."

After DaSilva called his wife to tell her he was having dinner with us, we sat down to eat. Seafood, corn on the cob, and a flaky sweet pastry for dessert. As an act of kindness, Mrs. Pina made regular coffee, telling Marisol to "sit and enjoy your papa."

DaSilva left, explaining that he'd get Dana, calling her "Agent Kilroy," a copy of all that I'd given him. Marisol said goodnight to him, and kissed him on the cheek. He was delighted, and laughed all the way out when she waved to him and said, "Surf's up!"

We sat in the living room, after we did the dishes, watching T.V. and talking about a trip to Washington to be tourists. Mrs. Pina said goodnight and headed upstairs. Marisol and I sat on the couch together holding hands. She went to bed, with only a small argument, when she found that I'd be home all day the next day.

I dialed Dana's home number, got her machine, and left her a message. I had a moment of jealousy, wondering where she was and with whom. She was a federal agent, I reminded myself; they didn't work nine to five. I felt young and unsure of myself. I felt stupid, too. I was suddenly tired and sore. I took a painkiller, staggered to my room and undressed. I barely made it under the covers before sleep took over, and I was dreaming.

It was one of those dreams that take you into your past, with incidents that happened, and incidents that couldn't. People I knew drifted in and out of it, along with people who were faceless. The face that kept coming up was a familiar one, and I woke with a start, as if falling in my sleep. I pulled out my legal pad and wrote the name that went with the face. I fell back to sleep and didn't dream again.

Chapter 13

When I woke, I looked at my legal pad. I'd scribbled "Dennis Pereira." It was a real name. He came from my past. In the present, we remained friends even though we probably shouldn't. I had visited him in prison, sent him Christmas cards and stayed in contact.

We grew up together in Fall River. He was the only absolutely fearless man that I knew. Dennis never refused a dare, never backed down. We used to say that he had more balls than brains. That wasn't true. Had he given school the effort that he put into everything else, he would have graduated near the top of our class. He wasn't lazy and worked for a landscaper to save money for the car he wanted. He got it two days after he got his license. At sixteen and a-half, he was driving a two-year-old muscle car that he owned outright.

He bootlegged tapes, hustled pool, made outrageous bets and almost always won them.

After high school, he'd embarked on several extralegal enterprises. He wasn't caught until after I was at the Academy. When I was home on liberty, I visited him at the penitentiary in Bridgewater. The undercover cop that bought the truckload of hijacked cigarettes couldn't help liking Dennis. Not many people escaped his rakish charm. When he got out, he did well enough to buy a condo in the new high-rise near Battleship Cove. I visited him there and found him hosting a party. Among the guests was a girl I'd been madly in love with in high school, newly married. She was flirting outrageously with Dennis, who laughed it off, handing her back to her husband.

In the present, I found him living in Taunton, up in Massachusetts. At that hour, he'd probably be asleep, if not in his apartment, then at some woman's place.

After Marisol went to school, I gassed up the Saab and headed north. Dennis had a phone, but I probably still had a tap on mine.

Taunton had been a prosperous town, forty or fifty years ago. It was ninety percent dead now, with all of the ills of a city and few of the good parts. I used my road atlas to find Dennis' address and walked up to the second floor of a three-story building. My cell phone remained at home on the charger. Just in case, I couldn't bring the law to him. I'd worked at a bar around the corner not long before. Not a nice neighborhood, and certainly nothing like the condo he'd owned in Fall River.

When he opened his door, he hadn't changed much. Still built like a brick standing on end, with massive arms and a goatee. Brown eyes, dark curly hair and a daring grin with startling white teeth offset bowed legs when women met him. The smile got broader when he saw me.

Dennis was wearing a pair of basketball shorts that came below his knees and a tank top. Muscles bunched and slackened as he walked. When he turned and led me into his apartment, I could see part of a scar from a prison fight. He headed straight into the kitchen. The place was clean, if worn. In the kitchen he reached up to the top of the refrigerator, needing a stepstool, and brought down a cookie jar shaped like a cupcake. "My girlfriend made it in ceramics class," he said.

"So how much do you need?" lifting off the lid, where I saw lots of money. I didn't bother to ask where it had come from.

"Jesus, Dennis, I didn't come to tap you for money."

"You'd do it for me."

"What I need, you might not be able to help with. I need a name." He looked at me from under his eyebrows.

"You still some kind of cop?"

I sat down at the kitchen table. "Let me tell you a story. Got coffee?"

He put the ceramic cupcake down in front of me and started a pot of coffee. We were comfortably silent while we waited. He drank his extra light, with lots of sugar. He had to get all of that energy from someplace.

"First of all, I'm not a cop anymore."

He nodded.

"I need a name, someone I can trust and talk to, off the record."

"What kind of name?"

"I need a professional killer, the best you can find."

"You can kill anybody you want yourself. Hell, if you're in trouble, the two of us can do it."

"No, thanks. I need to know how to do something. I need to know how something was done, I think." I realized how stupid I must have sounded.

So I told him.

"The kind of guy you're talking about, they're the best of the best of the best, you know? They don't wind up in jail. They wind up in the south of France, on a white beach, screwing rich, tan women. Sure as shit not going to find one in Walpole."

"Probably not, but you always have favors going on, right?"

He nodded, with that wild man grin of his. "True enough."

"Okay, so somebody knows somebody else, right?"

"I get it. I'll try, but it's gonna take some time."

"Careful on the phone, Dennis, it has extra ears."

"Always careful on the phone. Ever since a tap got me three to six at Walpole."

We finished our coffee. "You hear that Kathy Sousa is divorced?"

"Sorry to hear that."

He gave me a wicked smirk, "She'd love to hear from her very first knight in shining armor." He handed me a slip of paper with her phone number on it. "Maybe you need to have a little fun, too."

I left that whole conversation alone.

"Hey," he said, now serious, "A man's business is his own—"

"Yeah?"

"But can I ask you something?"

"Sure."

"You're in the clear, even the papers are starting to say so. Papers get it right eventually, right?"

I nodded.

"So why the fuck are you chasing it? There's nothing in it for you but trouble, more than likely. You have a kid, and you have a life you should be getting on with. You should be tending bar like a fish should be riding a motorcycle. You could be doing lots of other jobs. You're after this thing like it matters to you. Why?"

I started to tell him it wasn't his business. Then I remembered him going to his money without hesitation. I remembered flashes of thousands of moments from childhood to manhood.

"Dennis," I started to say, but stopped.

He waited.

"This killing may fix a few people's lives, and may fuck up a few others. It's definitely screwed my family over. That's not really it. It's as if I've been waiting to do something that matters, but being afraid of it at the same time. I'm pissed."

"You bastard," he said, smiling again, and leveling a forefinger at me like the barrel of a six-shooter, "You don't even know why, yourself. You're full of shit, you know; you're doing it because you fucking well feel like it, right? Admit it, Paul. You're doing it because you want to. Nothing wrong with that, you know. Sometimes you should do something for the hell of it. Sometimes you think too hard. Always did."

I started to answer, but he interrupted, "When your wife died, and you visited me in prison, you weren't really there. You weren't anywhere, man. Just going through the motions. Look, somebody beat the piss out of you, but you're up, you're moving, and you are one intense son of a bitch right now. You want to run around righting wrongs, that's cool. I'll do what I can."

As I drove towards home, I tore the phone number into pieces and scattered it into the car's slipstream.

Chapter 14

I got home before 'Sol was due, so I called Dana at the office. I had to leave another message on her voicemail. I was starting to feel frustrated. I missed her voice and her laugh. I missed the cinnamon scent of her cologne. I missed her.

I picked up the phone, and started calling some of the other bad boys I knew, putting out the word that I needed help and asking for call backs. Finally, I made one more call.

Debbie Fugazzi was the smartest person I knew. I met her in kindergarten, and went all the way through high school with her. Her homeliness had gotten her some ugly remarks and bad treatment, and I'd exacted some revenge for her sake a time or two. It never seemed to bother her, and she was nice about tutoring her fellow students. She was particularly nice to a guy who wanted to go to the Naval Academy, and nursed him through chemistry with a decent grade. She was a much better teacher than the guy who got paid for it. She was valedictorian of our class, and went on to become a doctor. I never went to her as a patient. The thought of her probing my nether regions was chilling.

It took a couple of tries to break through her receptionist's screening, but finally, I got her on the phone. "Paul Costa, now there's a blast from the past," she said. "You're my brush with fame right now, or is it notoriety?"

"Can you explain the difference between a covalent and an ionic bond?"

I heard the smile in her voice at the memory, "Sure, but you still won't get it. Long time."

"I could use some help."

"I'll bet you could, but I'm not sure what I can do."

"Have you got a few minutes?"

"Try me."

"What do you know about heart attacks, 'myocardial infarctions,' if I said that right."

"You said it just fine. And before I answer, I need two honest answers from you."

"Fair enough, I guess, Deb, shoot."

"Did you kill him?"

"No."

"Did you know that I had a major crush on you, from seventh grade until after we graduated?"

I was startled, then thought about some of the time we'd spent together. "I didn't at the time, but I guess I should have. I just thought you were nice and trying to help me out."

She sighed. "My mother thought you were a hoodlum. You stood up for me. Not much kindness to be found at that age, and you were kind to me."

"So," she said, more briskly, "How can I help you?"

"A guy's having a heart attack, what happens and what does he do?"

"Depends. Usually, he gets a lot of pressure, pain in his left arm, maybe wrist, sometimes both arms or wrists. The pressure might be in his chest, maybe not. If he's having his first heart attack, he might find the pressure so unfamiliar that he thinks it's something else."

"Would he head for the men's room, like for water, or something?"

"Funny you should ask; that's what I was going to mention. There's so much pressure, and a sense of dread and denial that comes over them, that they misread what it is, and think that they have to move their bowels. He might think it's urgent and head for the john. It sounds like a bad joke, but we find lots of heart attack victims sitting on toilets with their pants down."

"So it wouldn't surprise you to find a guy having a heart attack running for the toilet and keeling over in the stall?"

"Is that what your lawyer is going to say?"

"Lawyer?"

"I read the papers."

"Debbie, I didn't kill anybody, and they think that he had a heart attack."

"So who stabbed him with your knife?"

"When this is all over, Debbie—"

"Yes?"

"You and your husband are going to have to come over for dinner, and I'll tell you about it. Bring the kids, maybe a picnic or something."

"I'll hold you to that, Paul. I'd love to see you again, and see that you got all fat and bald, and I wasted those nights pining for you."

"Debbie!"

"So, I'll go home with the man I love, instead. Still, it would be nice if you'd grown a wart, or something, you know? Kind of a friendly gesture?"

She giggled. "It would be nice to get together."

"Thanks for your help, Debbie. I think I have some ideas from what you told me. I appreciate it."

"Don't forget dinner. Take care."

"I won't forget. I'll see you soon."

I hung up softly and scribbled some notes on my legal pad. I made coffee, and started to arrange my notes. On my time line, I figured that the Congressman started feeling the effects of a heart attack and headed for the nearest men's room, the one in the bar. He got in while my attention was elsewhere. Sarah, the waitress, could have missed him. The customers might have seen him without noticing. A man headed for the men's room wouldn't draw any attention.

I checked my email. Nothing. No email from somebody telling me how to cause a heart attack. The CIA gentleman had seemed unlikely to forget, and I had no way to reach him. I had to wait, if he decided to keep me waiting. He had already admitted that there was a way. If that had to be all I got from him, I could live with it. Maybe he was a fraud, working for the Department of Labor, but I didn't think so.

When the phone rang, I was startled enough to leap for it. My heart rate was still up when I answered. "Hello?"

"Paul?" It was Dana, finally. "I'm sorry about the phone tag. It's been crazy. Not just the Congressman, but a couple of other cases, and I really wanted to talk to you, and to see you, but I've been running around, and it's—"

"I'm just really glad to hear your voice."

"Indeed?"

"Yeah. I'd like to see you," I said, with adolescent nerves.

"Good. I can't leave Boston, though. Can you meet me up here?"

"I'd meet you in Anchorage."

She named a Japanese restaurant on the South Shore, shortening my drive as much as she could. I told her I'd meet her there at eight and we hung up.

Then I sat down with the medical stuff and tried to decipher it. I saw the Myocardial Infarction, and even saw the probability that the knife wound was barely ante mortem, or probably postmortem. There was a whole lot about toxicology and mass spectrographic analysis.

I knew a doctor. I called Debbie's office and left a message. Ten minutes later, her receptionist called and asked me to fax the report to the office. I hadn't seen a fax machine in years. I didn't have one, so I saddled up and drove to a print shop, where they sent the fax for me, with a short note. I told her about the phone tap, so the notification wouldn't surprise her It cost me a buck a page, and I had to use my debit card. I didn't like the state of my finances, but I had unjustifiably great expectations. I was home in time to meet Marisol. We had the last of the blueberry muffins, and she ran to get her homework done, so we could get to the library to do the research for her special project.

I hustled up some frozen ground beef, and put it into the microwave to thaw, while I poured a cup of coffee for myself. I brought a glass of milk and a few cookies to 'Sol's room, feeling like a mom in a Norman Rockwell print. She looked up, said "Thanks," and went back to a word problem.

Later, we drove to the library. On our way home, I started to tease her about how many books she'd gotten, and how it would make Mr.

Emmet Davis so happy. She poked me in the ribs. She hit one of the sore ones, and I hissed.

"Sorry, Daddy, sorry. I'm so sorry," she said.

"Honey, it's okay, just an accident. It's my own fault for zigging when I should have zagged. 'Sol? It's okay, honey, really."

"I just want things to be the way they were. I want you to work so I can miss you, and come home, so I can be glad to see you. I want to make coffee that you pretend to like. I want Mrs. Pina not to look scared and mad. I want you to not be all bandaged. I want to fly our kite."

"Sweetie," I said, but stopped. I wanted a lot of that, too. I also liked feeling more alive and connected. I didn't like being hurt, but I enjoyed mixing it up. No way was I going to tell her that.

"Honey, I'll get back to work, soon. Things will be more normal. We just have to get through this. We've been through hard times before, right?"

She nodded.

"And we know how to get through them, right?"

She nodded again; her head was up and she was looking at me directly.

We lugged her books to her room, and stacked them on the floor next to her desk. She never used it to do her homework, but we both pretended she did. I marked the book return date on the calendar in the kitchen, and called Mrs. Pina. I took my time getting dressed, settling on a jacket, slacks and a tie. I planned to pick up my weapon, and the jacket would help to conceal it. I wanted to get used to wearing a gun again. It was best to have it and not need it, than to need it and not. It wasn't profound, but it was true.

Mrs. Pina and Marisol grinned, and nudged each other and whispered as I left. I mugged a scowl, and I stopped at the bus terminal and signed for my package, bringing it to the car unopened. I clipped the holster and weapon on, and put one of the extra magazines in the inside jacket pocket. I found the restaurant, fifteen minutes early.

So, I sat in my car, sipping cold coffee. A Boston cab pulled up, Dana got out and paid the fare through the window. Her hair was up in some kind of twisted arrangement at the back of her head, leaving her neck exposed. There was an erotic charge from the way her neck moved that was out of all proportion to what she revealed. She was wearing a suit of some dark material, with slacks. When she bent over to pay the cabbie, they drew snug across her rear.

She saw me, and her face brightened. The look was worth the long drive. Except for 'Sol, Mrs. Pina, and the occasional thirsty customer, no one had looked glad to see me in two years. She walked over, put her arms around my neck and drew herself to me. My arms went around her waist, and I had my face in her hair. I smelled her cinnamon perfume, and her shampoo, and drew back to look at her. I kept my arms around her waist, and she had her hands draped loosely behind my neck. "Hi," we both said at once.

"I missed you," I said. It was true, and it was what I felt. I had probably spent less than four hours with her, but it was true. She was looking at my face, and the bandage above my eye.

"How does the other guy look?"

We walked into the restaurant. The tiny Japanese hostess wore a formal kimono, and bowed as we came in. I nodded to her. We removed our shoes, and Dana took my hand, walking beside me.

"Well, that certainly explains a lot."

I spun towards the familiar voice, and Dana wheeled with me. I hadn't realized that I'd pulled her along. Detective Petersen was sitting or kneeling at one of the low tables with a pretty young woman. She looked familiar. On the floor, with a table in front of her, I couldn't place her. She wore a formal looking green dress, with her hair loose around her face. She looked embarrassed. "Seems like if the suspect fucks one of the investigators, another one gets fucked," he said, too loud. His date looked down.

I remembered. She owned the first pair of bare breasts I'd seen in more than two years. I gave her a five-dollar tip at the strip joint. I looked over at Petersen, and did a lot of guessing for a few seconds.

"Sure, you start seeing the Fed, and suddenly you're not a suspect, you're packing heat, and I'm off the case, because I know—"

"Petersen—"

"It's Detective, asshole!"

"Sorry, Detective Asshole." His date got up and headed for the ladies' room. I felt Dana's hand give mine a warning squeeze. I'd been looking forward to my time with Dana, and I'd been looking forward to this moment with Petersen. Anger won out.

His face got red, and he started to stand.

"Let me explain things to you, slowly so even you can understand." I was pleased with my level tone. "You're off the case because you lied about an investigative matter, and you got caught. It was a dumb, bad lie. You're off the case because you lied to hide how close your association is with that strip club," I nodded towards the ladies' room, "and its employees. You're off the case because people are starting to wonder how you afford your expensive, yet tacky wardrobe. Most of all, you're off the case because you failed to tell anyone about your relationship with the late Congressman, and half-ass pimping for him. Finally, you're off the case because you're an incompetent doofus who was in way the hell over you're pointy head." "Doofus," was one of Marisol's favorite insults, but I stole it without shame. I was watching him closely, as he tried to stand.

I looked around the room at what seemed like a cast of thousands staring at us. "Petersen, if you so much as hint at reaching for the two thousand dollar phallic symbol, I will break some bones. Then I'll take your cannon and use the barrel to turn you into a lollipop. You didn't have to lie, because nobody would have cared. They knew where I was going and why. If you didn't want to go in and be seen, you could have said that the place was too empty to follow me in. Nobody would have thought twice, and I might still be a suspect, Detective Asshole. Frankly, if I were you, I'd collect my date, and bug the hell out of here, after you pay your check and leave a generous tip. Then again, that would show a bit of class."

His hands were trembling, and his face was the color of old bricks. When the girl returned from the ladies' room, he took her hand, nearly dragging her past the frozen patrons, waitresses, hostess, bartender and bouncer. I was glad I didn't have to sit in the passenger seat of his car for a long ride back to Providence or wherever.

"Well," said Dana, softly, "I'm comfortable."

"Yes, that went well."

"Miss, could you show us to our table, now?" I said to the hostess. I was still holding Dana's hand, and we walked together to our table. I was proud of her poise, despite the scene. She folded to the floor, and was instantly in a comfortable and attractive position. I got down there and adjusted myself, without whimpering.
Dana ordered for both of us, starting with sake, and going on from there.
"Dana, I have some notes back in my car, and I really need some expert opinion about some of the things I ran into down in D.C. On the other hand, I don't want to ruin our evening with shop talk."
"Sake first, then food, then we'll decide what to talk about, okay?" She had one warm hand resting on my knee, and I wanted it to stay. My mouth was dry. I took a sip of ice water.
"Paul, about Petersen…" She stopped when the waitress showed up with a tiny ceramic carafe and little cups. She dropped them off with hot damp towels and a couple of empty bowls. We wiped our hands on the towels, and put them in the empty bowls. She poured the warm sake into our cups, and we gently toasted, without saying anything. The tiny contact felt intimate in the soft light. I noticed that all of the tables were sited so that each customer or couple owned a bubble of privacy. We could have been alone in the place.
"About Petersen, how much of what you said is provable fact?"
"Probably all of it. His clothes are expensive, although unsuitable."
"I got that part, but if he lives modestly in other ways, he could just spend most of his money on clothes."
"Uh-huh, and jewelry. The watch is worth about a grand and a half, retail. His weapon is two grand. That all adds up to a lot of skimping on meals, and living in a small apartment, and driving a car like mine.
"He lied. You remember that part, and he was avoiding anything to do with that strip club. His date is a dancer there."
"Does she look that good when she's, um, you know."
"She seems more like artwork than a human."
She murmured something about art to herself, but I let it go.
"And the bit about the Congressman?"
"He frequented strip joints and hooker bars, and places where he was likely to find Petersen. The congressman had ways to keep his fun

and games private. A pet cop seems helpful. Petersen knows his way around and, knowing Morley, there was a quid pro quo for whatever Petersen did for him. I could be wrong, but I don't think so. You saw his reaction when I tossed that one at him. He could have hit it out of the park if it wasn't true, and he didn't even swing."

She nodded.

"Talk to DaSilva. He's a good man, and he's straight. His good will couldn't do any harm."

She was looking hard at me. "You really have gotten back into the swing."

"Maybe, or maybe it's just the bartender coming out. Getting along with people is a big part of it."

"You could be doing lots of other things, so why do you do that work?"

"Trying to improve me?"

"Nope." Her hand on my knee slipped upwards a fraction. My eyes went wide, and she smiled. "I'm just curious."

"Uh-huh."

Her hand slipped a tiny bit higher, then lifted from my leg completely.

I shifted to ease the erection that was tenting my trousers, getting it to settle into a bearable position. The soup was gone, and the bowls were whisked away for a small plate of sushi.

Rather than answer her, I started to talk about the whole Morley bunch. It took concentration, because I could see her breasts rising and falling with each breath, smell her scent, and hear the whisper of fabric slipping over smooth skin. She listened silently. We finished each course as it came, ending with green tea ice cream and ginger sauce. Her focus was almost physical. I saw the agent who could conduct complicated investigations, and the woman who could have been a therapist.

"What kind of opinion are you looking for?" she said when I had wound down.

"I don't know. I mean the whole scene was disturbing, you know? I guess I was hoping to get some confirmation that I wasn't imagining the whole thing."

"The spook you referred to, what about him?"
"I'm pretty sure that he was, and is, having some sort of affair with Mrs. Morley. He seems like a senior guy, and has whatever it is that CIA guys have in their attitude. Probably that's why it's always so easy for the bad guys to catch our guys."
"You've known CIA officers?"
I nodded.
"I've never worked that kind of case, but I think I know what you mean. You can tell DEA from ATF and so forth, just by meeting the agent or operative."
"So, what do you think?" I asked.
"It's been awhile since I did anything clinical, but you're on the beam as far as I can tell. There's pathology there, or a whole set of them. The level of ongoing trauma and stress could have driven her into all kinds of illnesses or possibly a mixed set of disorders."
I thought about that. "So, she's pretty ill."
"I'm not going to try for a diagnosis, but for discussion's sake, she's in a lot of trouble. It's not impossible that she was sexually abused by her father, brother or both."
"I think she would have told me," I said.
"She probably would have, unless she repressed it so deeply that she honestly doesn't remember it. All she'd remember is tension, stress, fear, anger and a sense of betrayal. It may be hard to get at reality."
I nodded. I knew about denial, and the idea that it could become that extreme wasn't farfetched.
"The brother, Jason?"
I nodded.
" 'Psycopath' isn't a clinically accepted term, but there's really no better word for him. From what we found out—"
I raised my eyebrows.
She rolled her eyes and went on, "Okay, from what you found out, it's a case of 'like father, like son.' Adam, God knows. I could be wrong, but I'd suspect he'd go to prison rather than let one of them get punished. I'm still guessing, but I'd bet that Mrs. Morley's an alcoholic, emotionally retarded woman."
"A mess," I said.

"The good Congressman has a lot to answer for, wherever he is now."
"Hell."
"We can only hope."
I told her about the Morley house, and the beating that followed. I told her about Sandra, the TV person and how she'd helped. I told her that DaSilva had the file and my report, and she nodded as if she knew.
"I don't understand why they came to the motel and did that," she said when I was done.
I nodded to the waitress for our check, and we rose. She gracefully, like a gymnast finishing a routine. I didn't groan about it. I was proud of that, until she took my elbow and lifted gently as a hint to straighten. It hurt to take a deep breath. I reached into my pocket and took one of my painkillers dry. "Dana, did you ever hear the joke?"
"Which one?"
"Why does a dog lick his own balls?"
She grimaced, "I don't know, why?"
"Because he can. I think there's a lot of that in young Jason."
"That would fit, but he was taking a huge chance." We were at the door, looking out at a rainstorm.
"I hope it isn't an imposition," she said, "but I was counting on you for a ride."
My mouth was very dry, "No, it's no trouble at all."
"Maybe you could walk me to my door?"
"Sure," I answered, forcing the word over a sere tongue.
"And maybe you could come in with me?"
I nodded, and ran for my car.

Chapter 15

In the parking garage, I closed and locked her door, and we walked to the door of an apartment building. She took my right hand and dropped a set of keys into it. I fumbled and unlocked the door and held it open for her. She stepped inside, and turned and looked at me.
"Paul?"
"Yes?"
She started to grin, "Care to see my etchings? Maybe you want to slip out of those wet clothes?" I swallowed and managed a smile. At the door to her apartment, she drew me inside, by the hand.
We were in a short hallway, at a small table with a lamp on it. There was a light blinking on the answering machine. She kept walking, still holding my hand, so that our arms stretched out and I followed her into the living room.
She stopped, standing next to a table that ran the length of her couch, along its back, and reached inside her jacket. The gun, holster and extra magazines hit the table. I took mine off and placed it near hers. She turned, and we were holding hands, standing face to face.
"Do you think you're ready?"
Instead of answering, I stepped forward and drew her closer at the same time. Freeing one hand, then the other, I took her face in my hands, and bent closer. The universe stopped. An eternity passed, as I slowly brought my face closer to hers. Her eyes searched mine. She saw something, and her expression relaxed, just as her face went out of focus. My lips brushed hers, and we were apart, then together again.
Her lips parted and my tongue slipped easily past her teeth, before we began to invite each other's entrance and retreat. My hands slipped to her neck, and then down, until they reached the small of her back, just above the swell of her buttocks. I felt the fabric of her jacket, then blouse, some silky lingerie, and finally, the smooth skin beneath.

Her hands came up, one around my shoulder, the other reaching for my neck. I felt her nails pushing against the skin, causing something that might have been pain any other time. We were pressed together, from our mouths all the way down to our knees.

Pushing herself away, she pulled her blouse up and over her head, where it joined her jacket. She kicked her shoes away and tugged her pants down, stepping out of the pool of cloth at her feet.

I kicked my pants, shoes and socks loose, into a pile behind me. "What about a bed?" I asked, my breathing ragged.

"Too far," she said, whispering with long breaks between the words, "We'd never make it." The minutes that followed were consumed by blind, urgent needs answered, sweetly and finally, with a gentle sense of completeness.

***

Afterwards, we sagged to the floor, and she pulled herself away, causing an amazing tingle. We kissed slowly. "Do you have to go, Paul?"

"Maybe not right away," I answered, looking at my watch. It was just about midnight. On her couch, we dozed and cuddled and kissed and touched each other for a while with almost no sexual appetite.

"I have to work tomorrow, and I have to get some sleep. If you can stay, I want you to."

"Well, I don't want to keep you from your beauty sleep, even if you don't really need it "

"Maybe I can get by with just a tiny bit less," she smiled, with a wicked, playful edge.

"Maybe more than a 'tiny bit,'" I said, and felt myself grinning with her.

Chapter 16

It was after three-thirty by the time I got home. Mrs. Pina was asleep on the couch. I got undressed and put my clothes in the bag for laundry and dry cleaning. I wandered into the kitchen and saw that I was due back for work that night. After a quick check on 'Sol, I staggered to bed, wondering where the guilt and pain were.

I woke up four hours later, feeling refreshed. Marisol was still asleep, so I took a quick shower and dressed. Shaving could wait. I left a voicemail for Dana at her office.

Once my bed was made and the house was mine, I sat down at the computer and logged on to the Internet. My email file was huge, filled with junk mail, because of all of the sites I'd been visiting. None were from my government acquaintance or anybody from the CIA, as far as I could tell.

The last was a long letter from Dana. She didn't mention the murder, the case or anything to do with it. The line that stuck with me was the one telling me that, "sensitive and generous lovers are as rare as diamonds."

It took me three tries to tell her how happy I was. I let it all hang out, and hit the "send" button before I could change my mind.

I looked at my watch and headed for the bathroom to shave. I had some things to do, and I didn't want to frighten women and children. It wasn't even nine o'clock, and I felt virtuous. I knew I'd be in rough shape after work. A quick inventory of the kitchen showed a lot of things that weren't there. Cursing softly, I grabbed my keys and headed out.

It dawned on me on my way to the grocery store, that Debbie Fugazzi's office wasn't far, so I doubled back and walked into the lobby of a nice building. She probably was as good with money as she was with everything else. Her husband was also her partner in her practice.

"Mrs. Doctor Fugazzi is with a patient, but Mr. Doctor can see you right away."

"That's nice and I appreciate your help, but it's 'Mrs. Doctor' I need to see," I said. The receptionist asked for my name, and said that she'd try to squeeze me in. I read old magazine articles about the habits and hangouts of unfamiliar stars. I read brochures on heart disease, alcoholism and Sexually Transmitted Diseases. Eventually, I was summoned to "Mrs. Doctor's Office," in tones of awe.

Debbie's skin had cleared up. She still had a lantern jaw and immense hands. Her glasses had never reached all the way to her ears, so the earpieces stuck into the tops of her ears and her glasses appeared to be falling off. She still kept shoving them back up her remarkably small nose. Apparently, she had no interest in cosmetics or taking care of her hair. It was cut short, and was going gray. She had a wonderful smile, and stood when I came in. She hugged me and then retreated behind her desk. "Sign here," she said.

"What am I signing?"

"It makes you my patient, with any conversations being completely confidential."

"Will I have to turn my head and cough?"

"Please do, I don't want you coughing in my face, after all." She was smiling. "Seriously, it's a good idea, and keeps the whole thing private."

"Whole thing?"

"Sign first, then we can talk." I signed and dated and initialed and slid the paper across her desk.

"And now for your physical," she said, rising. I pressed back into my chair, trying to slide it away.

"Paul, you should have seen your face," she whooped, "Omigodomigod. Physicals get done in examining rooms, you idiot."

Once she was seated, and settled down, she pulled out the fax I'd sent her. "This was both interesting and routine. He had what appeared to be a routine heart attack that killed him. His liver was shot, and he had the beginnings of prostate cancer. He had his appendix removed, as well as his tonsils. He got himself snipped, pretty recently. You know, a vasectomy. He was otherwise a healthy man in late middle age."

"Routine so far?"

"So far. Now, he had no signs of any heart or pulmonary disease except for the M.I. that killed him. That's not too rare. The knife in his ear was inserted, probably several minutes post mortem, or possibly just moments before he died. At the absolute outside, he was in extremis, and the knife was a coup de grace, but given the histamine levels at the site, or rather their lack—"

"Slow down, Mrs. Doctor. I'm but a lowly bartender. Histamine? Keep it simple, okay?"

"And I'm the next Miss Universe. Okay. Let me try it this way. If you're alive when you're injured, histamines are rushed to the injury. If you're dead, they don't gather at the site of a wound, get it?"

I nodded.

"There were virtually no signs of life, or signs that he was alive at the time the knife went in. The M.E. is hedging, but if he had more nerve, he'd just say that it was a post-mortem wound. Minimal bleeding, mostly like a slow leak. Get it?"

"Got it. Still it would take somebody cool, but angry to do it."

"Your department. Anyway, his stomach contained a lot of pineapple juice, and some kind of fruit derivative, and a helluva lot of alcohol. He was at least four hundred percent over the limit to drive. No matter what his tolerance, he was drunk."

"Yup."

"He'd had a roast beef dinner, with gravy, and some kind of pastry, as well as some coffee, less than three hours before he croaked."

"Is 'croaked' a clinical term?"

"Did he croak?"

"He croaked."

"So, may I continue?"

I nodded.

"The reason I'm going over his stomach contents is that they also found some tiny fragments of metal. It was a copper alloy, with remnants of a coating used on pills. You know, the 'easy to swallow' things?"

I nodded. My painkiller had a shiny coating on it.

"On to toxicology. This is where it gets weird. See, he had a high blood alcohol content, had taken Viagra, and had traces of something else that didn't show on a normal tox screening. Being a congressman, he rated some extra attention, and they took sections of liver, kidney, heart and stomach as well as blood and urine, and sent it to the State Lab."

I was leaning forward. She was still a fine teacher, and her voice was drawing me in.

"Did I mention that he'd recently had sexual intercourse? I should have, I guess. They found foreign pubic hair, and they checked his level of seminal fluid."

"Debbie," I said.

"Hey, this is clinical and kind of standard for a death like this. Did you know that men of his age have literally screwed themselves to death? That Viagra is potentially fatal, not from direct side effects, but from what it makes men who have no business—"

"Debbie, please."

"Oh, right. Well, none of us are getting any younger."

"Debbie, I'm begging you."

"Okay. They did some heavy checks. Things that they usually don't bother with. They booked and conducted gas chromatography," She looked over her glasses, and started again. "There's one that they bombard samples with radiation, crack it into its components and compare the signature they get with known substances."

"Never mind, Debbie. What did it show?"

"Also they got enough with the foreign pubic hair to get good DNA for a match later on."

"Nice. The chemicals?"

She was grinning. "He took some kind of derivative of digitalis. It's synthetic, and immune to a normal tox screen. If they hadn't gotten curious, they never would have found it."

"Does it occur in any way that could be explained?"

“I said ‘synthetic’. And it isn’t medicinal, and he had no signs of existing heart disease. It resembled digitalis, but wasn’t exactly a match. Paul, the congressman was murdered, but he was poisoned, not knifed in the ear. The M.E. said so, and it isn’t exactly my field, but I’d agree. Any doctor would.”

“How long would it take from the time he got it to the time he had the heart attack?”

“A few minutes after the metallic capsule melted. It would have hit his bloodstream with a bang, flooded him with cardiac stimulation. He would have been sweating, hyperventilating and feeling his heart pounding. There would have been immense pressure coming on within no more than ten minutes from the time it hit his blood stream.”

“So he swallowed it?”

“That’s the way it had to be done.”

“And the copper in his stomach?”

“I did some research on that. In some countries, they use metallic capsules to time doses of medication for release into the system. In Russia, they treat alcoholism with a drug that reacts with alcohol, and makes the person violently ill if they drink. It’s administered in a thin walled metallic capsule, of specific thickness. If the person doesn’t consume alcohol, the capsule should make it out of the stomach, and into the intestines where it won’t dissolve. Alcohol will dissolve it. You can make a drug sit in the stomach without entering the blood stream for a predetermined period of time. Here’s the cool part. If the person lives, for say, fifteen minutes, the metal melts and just becomes part of the goop in the rest of the alimentary canal.”

“Goop?”

“Another clinical term. Trust me, you don’t want to know.”

“Do you have the stuff on the Russian usage on paper?”

“Attached to my report and summary. Oh, yes, and my bill.”

“I hate doctors.”

“We like bartenders.” We were smiling at each other. “I have to tell you, this is a lot more interesting than my next patient’s phlebitis.”

“Probably not to him.”

"His insurance pays well and promptly. Here's the file, with your fax and my report. And bill." I paged through it.

"No bill."

"Oops. Watch for it in the mail."

"I'd never have made it to the Academy without your help. I think I thanked you, but not as well as I should have. Thank you. For this," I gestured at the file, "thank you, again.".

"I'd never have made it through High School without you, so I think we're even." She came around the desk, hugged me and gave me a kiss on the cheek. "Be well. It's not good advice, but I hope you get the bastard."

The woman at the front desk looked impressed when I left. No bill, a file, and a half hour with "Mrs. Doctor."

The grocery store was filled with lots of elderly people, a scattering of women with small children and not enough clerks. I spent an hour there.

***

I ignored my answering machine until the food was put away. There was only one message that interested me. I called Dennis Pereira back, and asked him if he wanted a couple of free drinks.

"Is a duck's ass watertight?" he answered.

"Must be," I said,

"Or it would sink," we said together. We'd been telling each other the same bad joke for nearly forty years, but we still laughed.

"I have stuff to tell you, but in person."

"Nine o'clock?"

"Nine," I confirmed and gave him the address and name of the hotel. "Casual dress, so you fit in."

"Fit this. I drink scotch."

Marisol came through the door in a jumble of backpack and jeans and sneakers and long dark hair and an unbroken monologue. She left a note from Mr. Davis on the table for me to read. Her day was filled with friends and boys who were "so immature and gross." There was a birthday party coming up for Terri. She got serious and asked if we could talk.

"Daddy, you know Miss Kilroy?"

It took me a minute to shift gears, "Yes, I do, honey." I said it slowly and carefully.

"While you were away, she called to tell me she was sorry for being part of all the trouble. We talked for a long time because we both were so worried about you. Then she told me how much she liked you and asked if I was upset about that. Of coursc I was, but I told her no, and then she asked if she could come over. Then she talked to Mrs. Pina, and after a while, Mrs. Pina was smiling, then she laughed and said something in Portuguese."

"Then she came over and we played cards and chess and backgammon, and we talked and she ordered pizza. She likes linguica, and I thought it would be okay if she liked you. So I told her so. Anyhow, when you went out with her, I was really happy, and she's nice and I like her. I know it isn't like she's going to be 'Mom.'" The last was said with near defiance.

"Honey, easy. It's okay. Okay? I like her too, and I'm glad you got to know her."

"So it's okay that I knew all about it?"

"Muffin, it's okay, it makes it easier. I was wondering how to tell you so it wouldn't hurt you or scare you?"

"Scare me?" She seemed outraged. "I'm not a baby, Daddy!"

"I guess you're right, 'Sol. I sometimes think that you're littler than you are, and I'm sorry. I should have just talked to you about it like you did. I have a lot to learn from you."

Her eyes shone. She got up and put her arms around my neck. I smelled mint, and pineapple from her shampoo. The shower was filling up with her "stuff" and I was dreading the next few years, with all of the girl paraphernalia that I remembered from my time with Isabel.

"Daddy," she said, "you're walking and talking better, you know? The gun scares me, but Mamacita said that it was okay, before."

"Gun?"

"I saw it, but I remembered not to touch it from when I was little."

"Good job, sweetie. Another thing I should have just told you about."

"Yup, but you're still learning."

I smiled into her hair and held onto her.

I started supper just before Mrs. Pina came downstairs. I was dressed and out on time, with the gun in the car. I couldn't wear it at work, but I wanted it nearby. I had limits that I usually didn't. Things still hurt, and I was slower than usual. It was good that the hotel was going to provide security that night.

I thought about the conspiracy of women in my life, and how it wound up with Dana and me on her living room floor. That thought sent an erotic charge through me.

***

It was early, and most of my orders were coming from the dining room, with a few people in the bar waiting for tables. Diane had traded shifts, so Sarah arrived dressed for work, except for her battered running shoes with white socks. Mike was with her, and they walked straight up to the bar.

Mike stuck out his hand, and I automatically took it. "I'm sorry about the attitude after he, um, died," he said. "Sarah was in tough shape."

"Thanks. We're still okay?" I asked.

"Don't worry, Paul," came Sarah's soft voice, "Marisol will still get the talk from me, just like we agreed."

"That isn't what I meant."

They were both smiling.

"Oh, you were kidding."

Right on time, Dennis walked in, dressed in a nice pair of slacks and a golf shirt. The slacks were tailored to disguise the bowed legs.

Dennis was at the bar shaking my hand, "Paul, how they going?"

I poured a healthy-sized single malt into Dennis' chilled snifter, and dug into my tip jar to pay for it. I turned back, and mixed a couple more orders before I got back to him.

Dennis grinned. "I contacted some friends, and friends of friends."

I nodded.

"Anyhow, the congressman was a client of an escort service out of Providence. He had a preference for the exotic, the offbeat. He liked twins and couples. Sometimes he hired someone for his son or a friend, or his servant. He paid extra to watch or film them."

"The night he died," he went on, "one of the girls, Miranda, came here to meet him. The fee was five hundred dollars, a straight date."

I had to pause to take care of a large order for Sarah, who was staring over at us between waiting on tables. When I returned, Dennis continued, "Miranda called the service when she arrived, like a good little call girl, and when she left the man's room. Nobody's heard from her again. Her driver didn't see her come out, and called to tell the madam so. He came in to the hotel to find her, but couldn't. As far as he knew before he called, she was fine and on her way out to the car."

"What time was their date?" I asked.

"Ten o'clock."

"And she was on time?"

"According to both her and her driver, she arrived at ten minutes before ten."

"What time did she call in to tell the boss that she was done?"

"Eleven forty."

"And the driver's first call?"

"Midnight."

"Did the Congressman make the appointment himself?" I asked.

"No, an aide. Pre-paid for the appointment."

"Did they know the aide?"

"No, the Congressman usually makes his own arrangements."

"So for all you know, it could have been anyone making the date."

"True. Still, the person knew enough to be accepted at face value."

"May I restate what you just told me?"

Dennis nodded, and made a regal "go on," gesture with the hand holding his drink.

"Okay, somebody made a date for the Congressman, paid for it, and arranged for Miranda, the call girl to arrive at ten. She did so, whatever happened privately, happened. She called in that she was done and ready for any more work."

He nodded.

"At eleven forty. She's never heard from or seen again, as far as anyone can determine, right?"

Dennis nodded.

I broke away, mixed, strained, poured and drew a couple of drafts. I fixed Dennis another drink, jotted the cost down to pay later on, and took away his empty.

"What can you tell me about Miranda?"

"What do you need?"

"Let me try this. If she could do her work, and still make more, would she?"

"Dress it up as pretty as you like. She was a hooker. Would she try to make more if the opportunity came her way? Yes, any of them would."

"I don't know Miranda. She is some man's daughter, though. Perhaps we can find her. I can't promise a thing, but I will make her a part of this."

"Why?"

"I have a daughter. I had a wife. Somebody should care."

Dennis thought about it. "I'm in, too, if you need me."

The shift went quickly, and I was tired to the soles of my feet, slowly walking out to my car.

After Dana and rising early, and running around, and then working, I was draining my tank dry. The next day was Thursday, and I had the day free. I scribbled a note to call Dana, and DaSilva on the back of a deposit slip, when I stopped to deposit my tips in the bank's ATM.

I sent Mrs. Pina off to bed, and staggered to my own room, finally falling on top of the covers in my shorts. I pulled a sheet over for propriety's sake, and fell and fell and fell.

Chapter 17

When I woke, I smelled coffee and English muffins, and scrambled eggs and bacon. It was eight-thirty. I grabbed one of the hotel's robes and headed into the kitchen. Marisol was stirring scrambled eggs, and Dana was draining bacon drippings from a pan. I bolted for my room, just as they both turned to look at me. I heard laughter and knew I'd never live it down.

I hopped and stumbled into a pair of jeans and dragged a shirt over my head, stopped in the bathroom, for a quick tooth brushing and tried to get my hair in some sort of order. By the time I made it back to the kitchen, a huge breakfast was ready. I sat down, and said, "Good morning." Both of them broke up. "What's so funny?" That only got them going, and it was contagious.

"Daddy, Dana called while you were at work, and I invited her over for the day. I wanted to take a mental health day; is that okay?"

"Honey, you can always invite friends over. It would be nice if I knew about it before I scare someone in the morning, though." 'Sol smiled.

"Bet she wasn't scared, Daddy. She has a gun."

"All the more reason, honey. Suppose she'd opened fire, thinking I was a mutant or something?"

"We try not to use our guns, even on mutants."

"I feel better then," I paused. Marisol was looking benevolently from one to the other of us. "I'm going to just dig in, here," I said. "If you two want yours to get cold, it's up to you."

They talked about who made what and I nodded and told them how good it was.

'Sol walked to her room and I turned to Dana. "Glad you're here. My daughter has excellent taste in friends."

She handed me some of the dishes from the table. "Serious for a second?"

"I was serious."

"Okay, serious about something else," she was grinning. Her tilted blue eyes were dancing. She was a woman, with a healthy woman's artifice. "You aren't thinking serious thoughts," she said, wagging a finger at me.

"Oh, not true. My thoughts were serious."

"The tap is still on your phone. It seems to be harder to get it off than it was to get it in the first place."

I remembered bureaucracy well, and that made as much sense as a lot of the problems I'd run into.

"Dennis Pereira?" she asked.

"An old friend, from way back."

"Anything to add?"

"He knows people who know people."

"He's a felon, on parole," looking down as she said it.

"Eagle scouts don't know the kind of people I need."

"Find anything out?"

"I can't bring any of it to you or DaSilva, just yet. I made some promises, I was trusted."

"You're on a quest."

"A little grand, but it's kind of like that," I answered.

She smiled, and nodded.

"In a day or two, I expect to be muddying the water even more, but it's going to take some help from DaSilva."

"What about me?"

"You get to be involved, DaSilva has to be committed."

"What's the difference?"

I gestured at the dishes. "Think of bacon and eggs. The chicken was involved, but the pig? The pig was committed. That's tomorrow, though. I have to make a phone call, but that's it. Today, we have some fun. Tomorrow is tomorrow's problem." She had a hand on my face, looking at me.

I had a thought. "Dana?"

"Yes?"

"How much plotting and scheming went on behind my back to get me to the restaurant and then your place?"

“Mrs. Pina has the soul of Mata Hari. Let’s just say that we had it under control.”

“I’m out numbered.”

“And surrounded.”

Marisol came out, wearing jeans and a shirt over a bathing suit. I looked at Dana, and saw that her white tee shirt covered one, too. Out numbered. Surrounded. “I’ll go put on my suit.”

I was rummaging around in the garage, looking for beach chairs, muttering curses, when Marisol came out. “Daddy, we’re waiting in the car. It’s packed already.” Females were thinking rings around me. I started the car and dropped the roof.

Marisol and I had always liked the beaches in Middletown, so I had wangled a parking sticker. We pulled in to the rock and surfers’ end. That was the best part of the beach as far as we were concerned. I lugged chairs and a picnic basket and towels and a blanket, while ‘Sol and Dana walked onto the beach, looking beautiful.

Marisol grabbed her boogie board and fins and took off for the water. The surf was moderate, and she was a strong swimmer. Dana and I sat in the chairs and watched her. We said little and held hands. ‘Sol came out of the water, shining, with strands of hair hanging to her shoulders. Her suit was a one-piece and from the distance, it was hard to tell whether she was eleven or twenty years old.

***

When we got home, Mrs. Pina was waiting for us, with dinner made. I looked at ‘Sol, then Dana. Mrs. Pina had her back to me, but her whole posture suggested she was laughing “The soul of Mata Hari,” I said aloud.

After dinner, it started to rain. I went to my room to change into work clothes. “I’m not ready to call it a day, Paul.”

“I won’t be in until the wee hours.”

“I’ll catch a nap, and we can talk when you come back.”

“Talk?”

“Your daughter is two rooms away.”

“Talk is probably a good idea. “

“Tardiness made Rome fall,” I said. She kissed me on the cheek, and I went to the garage.

It was still raining, but I made it to the bar in time to watch Diane stride in. "Sorry, the boys made me late. I have to get my ass to work. I'm sorry if I started your night off the hard way."

"Diane, it's a fine ass, and watching it work makes my whole night."

"Men are pigs." She smiled and ignited her sex appeal for the night.

Fine with me. I flipped a gin bottle and started an orange blossom.

The rest of the shift went quietly. After our clean up, I walked Diane to her car.

Dana was dozing in my favorite chair when I walked in. I tiptoed past her, and went to my room to change. The tuxedo shirt was a palette of colored stains from drinks. I changed into a pair of jeans and casual shirt, and turned to go back to her. She was standing in the doorway.

"Hi, there," she said in a Mae West imitation.

"I was just coming to see you."

"I could save you the walk, but I'd guess you'd like to stay in the living room?"

"Sorry, I wouldn't want Marisol—" I answered.

She nodded. "Me either. She's an amazing girl, Paul. You've done wonders."

"Her mother, Mrs. Pina and lots of counselors, mostly."

"I've seen you two together enough to know better."

She carried on the Mae West thing, doing a huge hip swing from side to side as she walked. It was such a departure from her normal walk that I smiled, swinging my head to match her rhythm. She settled on the couch and patted the seat next to her. "'My Little Chickadee' was on when I fell asleep,"

"You do it well."

"High School drama clubs. I got the part of Ophelia, because I could do accents and voices."

"I worked the stage crew one year, because I had a crush on one of the girls in the play."

"How'd that work out for you?"

"She started dating the porky kid who could sing. I learned to run the light board."

"Ah, the arts."

I sat down next to her, and put an arm around her shoulders.

After some time passed, I stiffened because I heard noises from Marisol's room. She flinched and quickly drew her top up and skirt down. I felt an ache that I knew was going to turn into cramps. She seemed to read my mind, and gave me a small smile. "Adventures in Babysitting," she said.

I grinned and went in to check on 'Sol.

She had been stirring, and talking quietly in her sleep. There was a smile on her face, and she giggled, still asleep. I was smiling when I went back to the living room. Dana had fallen asleep on the couch. It was four in the morning, so I wasn't surprised. I picked her up, got her into my bed, and covered her up. I went back to the couch. I was restless, aroused and sore at the same time. I popped a painkiller, and drifted off to sleep.

***

The phone was ringing, and I was disoriented. I got up, stiff and aching, and finally found the handset. "'Lo?"

"DaSilva, here, what's up?"

It took me a minute. "Paul, you awake?"

"Yeah, I'm awake." I remembered why I'd called him. "Listen, you need to get a warrant. The Congressman's place, videos, photos and journals, personal documents, letters, and personal diaries."

"We were already there. Nothing."

"There's a secret closet. I know how to get in, and I have written permission from the daughter."

Larry paused for a moment, "So? You're an official P.I., licensed and all. Go ahead and look."

"Ever hear of 'fruit of the poisoned tree?"

"Nah, you'd need to be a lawyer or maybe a detective to know about that. I'm just—"

"Sorry, but I think a defense attorney could have a real party with evidence provided by a suspect."

"You aren't a suspect."

"I was, right?"

"So, I'll call my favorite judge. What about Agent Kilroy?"

"I'll make sure she meets us there.

"Whyn't you just bring her?"

"Ever hear about knowing too much?"

"Yup. Oh, and Petersen wants to press assault charges. Says you made a terroristic threat at a restaurant, in front of lots of witnesses. No battery, though. Braintree cops laughed at him. Told him he could have arrested you himself, but they have better things to do."

"Sweet."

"I'll get back to you in a half hour about the warrant. I have to dream up some stuff about a confidential informant. That'd be you."

I turned, and Dana was behind me. "DaSilva," I said. "He's getting himself committed. We'll know in a half hour or so if you get to be involved."

She nodded, and yawned, only covering her mouth with one hand when it was half way over. "How do you do it?"

"Do what?"

"Keep these hours."

"Oh, that. Coffee and frustration help." I went into the kitchen and started breakfast. She came in and put bread in the toaster, and Marisol walked in.

"Good morning!" she said, bright as sunshine. "Daddy's back must be sore from the couch." She did a little pantomime of an old man straightening slowly, and groaning, it was a perfect imitation of the way I'd gotten up. She gave me a hug, and gave Dana one that made me smile.

"I'm supposed to go over to Terri's after school today," she said. "Yes, her Mom and Dad will be home, and it'll just be us. We'll be going to the beach with her parents, and I'll be home for supper. Did I forget anything?"

"Nope."

"Oh, and there's that note from Mr. Davis in the bill basket."

"Okay, honey. Is it a trip or anything?"

"No, Daddy, and it isn't a bad note. Just something that's going to happen at school. Some guest or something. He won't be talking about sex or anything interesting."

Dana broke up.

I just looked at Marisol. "So, am I taking you to Terri's or is she picking you up?"

"Her mom will meet us at school."

"I'll miss you."

"Miss you, too," said into my midsection as she hugged me again.

I dug out some cash, and packed a beach bag with towels and sunscreen, while she changed for school. She actually missed the bus, a first. DaSilva called to tell me he had the warrant, and that we should meet him at the Congressman's house in an hour.

We all piled into the Saab. I took a look at the sky, the switch didn't work, so I used a piece of foil to jump the roof open. "That's why I still smoke, honey," I said.

She gave me a sour look and we started moving.

After I dropped 'Sol at school, I pulled out a road atlas and picked a route to Morley's house. I made one stop for coffee.

"You're getting a habit, aren't you?" Dana asked.

"Getting? You wondered how I kept the hours I do? This is my secret."

We pulled up and DaSilva got out of a marked police car. I handed him the card from Charlene Morley, and he held it with the warrant. We all went to the door together.

We didn't have to kick the door in since I had a key, and we only had to leave the warrant somewhere in the house, to cover DaSilva. He hung it on a corkboard in the kitchen.

I walked over to the entertainment center and opened a drawer, pulling out a remote control, marked "VCR."

"Cellar stairs over here," called Dana. The lights came on as soon as we opened the door.

It looked like a basement. No manacles or trapeze bars, just shelves and paint, and boxes. Water heater in the corner, furnace next to it. Off to one side was a metal shelving unit. Something that looked like a motion sensor for a burglar alarm faced us from above the shelves.

I pointed the remote at it and pressed "rewind." There was a click and the shelves shifted towards us on one side. DaSilva grabbed the shelves and pulled. A door opened in the wall, slightly uneven, matching the pattern of blocks that made up most of the wall. When the door opened, a light came on in the closet. DaSilva whistled softly. Imelda Marcos had a closet just like it for her shoes. This one was lined with shelves and a dehumidifier hummed softly.

One wall was filled with books, another with videos, DVD's and small cases for flash drives. The back wall facing the door was filled with accountant's journals. The titles on the cases were professionally printed. Some had artwork. They were alphabetically arranged. Some of the women's names had roman numerals afterwards, as if they were sequels.

"Nobody touches anything else. Back out, and remember what you touched," said DaSilva. There were missing videos. I guessed that they were the ones Charlene Morley had mentioned. There were four of Camille, his wife. Charlene had left them there.

DaSilva called in for help. Dana put in a similar call. I helped to set up a card table with some chairs in the basement. An FBI agent sat at one side with a Newport cop across from him, logging in each video, journal, book and magazine. Two red spots appeared high on the cop's cheekbones, as he looked at the magazine covers. I thought it said nice things about him. He could be embarrassed. Probably he even liked dogs and small children.

A technician wearing white cotton gloves opened one of the accounting journals. "It's a diary," he said. Each book had a year printed on the cover. They dated back fifteen years. "It has the names of women, dates, and places, times, and what they did." He closed it and put it into a paper bag, and sealed the bag.

It was the technician who collected evidence at the hotel when the congressman was killed. He'd complained the whole time. This time he was no different. "Sick motherfucker, twisted bastard, Christ on a crutch, it feels like I should take a shower. Sick motherfucker," he was saying under his breath, over and over. “Book lists what videos to look at, too. I’m not sure which is worse.”

“Let’s break,” said DaSilva. “Agent Kilroy, you can witness me closing the door, and sealing the last evidence out in bags, then we’ll all go and get some air.”

Chapter 18

It was hours later when we finished. Dana and I were quiet on the way back to the house. We were quiet after we got back to the house, while I made coffee.

I handed her a mug and sat next to her. "I should get back to Boston, and make out some reports and maybe catch some sleep," she finally said. "Besides, I need to return the car, and get some clean clothes."

"How about a quick shower to get the cellar off before you go?"

"A shower sounds good right now. I want to catch whoever killed Morley, but I don't, you know?"

"Yes you do. You're a cop. Murderers shouldn't be loose."

She nodded. "Join me? It's a shame to waste the hot water."

I found some liquid soap, and climbed into the shower. It was already running, and Dana was gleaming with water. I squirted some of the soap onto my hands and worked it up into a creamy lather. Her head was leaned backwards, her eyes were closed and I drew both hands together from her throat, down, between her breasts and straight down. I crouched to work the lather into her legs, sliding my palms upwards. She gasped and jerked her head down to look at me, as I looked up at her. From the low perspective, she was beautiful in a whole new way. It was like seeing her for the first time.

There was a time where we were distant from the world in steam, hot water, soap and flesh.

The moment ended and we drifted back. I dried her back, and she did mine. We kissed occasionally, and parted for me to go and get my clothes on.

She came out, wearing a towel, and sent me to her car for an overnight bag. My room served as a dressing room for her. "I wish you were staying," I said.

Finally, she made it to her car. "Paul, when are you off again?"

"Tuesday night."

"Dinner? My place? I can cook, you know."

"What time?"

"Eight-ish, okay? Bring a bottle of red?"

"Red wine, Tuesday, eight o'clock, your place."

"Take your vitamins. Don't forget your gun."

I watched her drive away, and then got into my car to pick up 'Sol. I hoped that Mrs. Pina was out with her grandson getting groceries when I thought about how loud we'd gotten.

There were messages on the house phone from reporters demanding that I call them back immediately, to discuss "your side of this important story." I deleted them, listened to one from one of Marisol's friends. I know that her friend was speaking English, because I recognized the words. I'd never heard them strung together quite that way. They might have been plotting the takeover of Canada for all I knew.

The night passed, dinner went fine, except for a discussion of why the benefits of fresh spinach offset the icky taste and texture. Ultimately, even though I won the battle, the war wasn't over. She ate the two forkfuls I insisted on. After dinner, she flounced off, to "do homework, and maybe throw up." More experienced parents told me to enjoy this age, because it wasn't going to get easier. I sighed. It was, I thought, a good thing that I loved her.

***

The next morning I woke up before Marisol, and I got out my legal pads. I reworked the timelines, thinking about the timing, using Miranda, the call girl's known activity with Congressman Morley.

I was starting to hate somebody. Morley served best by leaving the world, however it screwed up my life. I had been trying not to think that thought. I'd been inconvenienced, but if people were dying, I had to keep pushing. I wouldn't recognize Miranda if she stood next to me, but I knew that she was a reason. How well would you have to know an innocent woman to keep her alive? It was possible that she was alive and in hiding, but barely. The killer or killers were willing to murder, and willing to frame me. Why not just kill a hooker?

I was sitting in my kitchen chair, sipping coffee, and sneaking an indoor cigarette. Marisol came in and glared at me until I stubbed out the butt. I tried to change my thinking. I didn't want to be angry, so I concentrated on my recent shower. It put a grin on my face that 'Sol imitated. There was lots of chatter about the beach, some boy named "Chad," and Terri and her mom and dad. Dana came up, and we talked about how much fun she was and how pretty and nice.

There was a note from "Mr. Emmett Davis" sitting in the bill basket, along with some bills. I looked at the clock and groaned to my feet. Mrs. Pina came in while I was changing for work. She seemed to have trouble containing a smile. I heard some softly spoken Portuguese. I only recognized the language by the slip and slur of it. Not a single word was audible. She had to have heard Dana and me in the shower. I was grateful for her and her love for 'Sol, but her omniscience was annoying.

She went to 'Sol's room, carrying cleaning equipment, her step rolling, like a sailor long at sea. I got my car running, and headed for work. I hated day shifts, but it was part of the price I paid for my week off. I had to cover another guy's shift so he could get a root canal. After four hours where I served two drinks, I was ready to change places with him.

Chapter 19

DaSilva came into the bar, with a detective I didn't recognize. He introduced him as "Phil Lacombe." Except that he had more hair and brown eyes, he could have been DaSilva's brother. He had brown hair, going to gray, combed perfectly, and a steady look. He was lean, and had tattoos visible on the backs of his hands. I'd have guessed a .38 revolver in a shoulder holster, and he looked like he had forgotten more about being a cop than Petersen would ever learn.

"Getcha anything?"

"Got coffee?"

"I'll order some up. How do you take it, Detective Lacombe?"

"Black." His voice was deep, and he spoke slowly. It seemed as if each word had weight. I punched the order in for the kitchen, and the lift sent it up. I sipped mine and looked at DaSilva.

"Phil and I have talked a bit about you, and we think it's okay to be sort of open with you."

I nodded.

"We've been looking at tapes and books and stuff," said DaSilva.

"A whole lot of suspects. Family and all," Lacombe went on. "We'd be done by now, but we have to stop and take a bath sometimes."

I nodded again.

"We're also sure that you know some stuff that we don't," said DaSilva.

"I don't have a thing that you don't that could get into court, no matter if I'm an informant or not. If I give it to you, it will taint your real work, and could screw up your case."

"So you give it to us, and we get it confirmed by other means, and it gets the bad guys into the pokey."

"Pokey?"

Lacombe looked out at me from under his eyebrows. "You prefer 'hoosegow?'"

"I was a lawyer, and Detective Lacombe, if I give you what I have, and you get it confirmed, it's still fruit from the poisoned tree, and therefore—"

"Inadmissible," finished Lacombe and DaSilva together.

"Certainly, we're open to suggestion," said Lacombe.

"You guys continue with your investigation."

"Okay, Mr. Costa, and you break yours off?"

"I'm a PI and I have a client, and as long as I don't interfere and do what I can to legally get evidence to the proper authorities, I get to do what I want." I said it quickly, and probably with more heat than I intended.

DaSilva raised his eyebrows. "Client?"

"Yup."

"Mind telling me who?"

"Yup. I don't have to unless my client is a suspect. Meantime, Larry, how about the tapes and such?"

"Bad. I'm not squeamish about sex. Hell, I like it. This is different. It isn't the sex. This stuff's awful, you know? Nothing a man would ever want to see. You keep picturing it as your wife or daughter getting treated like that. It's like they aren't people to him, or his kid, they're just things to enjoy."

"Objects of pleasure?"

"Like a good cigar or comfortable shit," said Lacombe. "Makes it harder to keep the edge, you know? This time I'm tempted to shake the perp's hand. We still have twenty or thirty videos, and lots of people to identify with his journal. We're interested in some stripper named 'Lois' or 'Lolita.' Know anything about her? He took movies of himself and his wife, and her with some other guy through a pinhole." I stayed still when he mentioned Lois. I didn't want to burn her or Tim Foley, the bartender at the 'club' anymore than the phone tap already had.

To cover, I said, "He had DVD's of his daughter, too. She destroyed them herself. If it helps you keep your edge, remember that the bad guy tried to frame me. Besides, there may or may not be another victim. Put up a watch for a call girl named Miranda. List her as missing, and use me as the reporting party.'"

DaSilva's eyebrows were climbing. "Got a description?"

"Nope, but I'll get you one by tonight."

"So how'd the mother's tapes get left? Wouldn't the daughter—" DaSilva stopped. "Shit, the daughter took her videos and left Mom's?"

"Not to mention that she directed me to that closet. Lots of anger."

"Fucking diseased, if you ask me," said Lacombe, " 'Lois' meant something to you, care to talk about that? No? Okay, Who's Miranda? How do you know she's missing, and why don't you have a description? No answer? What about the son? How do we like him for this? Myself, I like him pretty good. I think he's one sick little prick, myself. You're shaking your head, Mr. Costa, why's that? "

The way he jumped around from subject to subject, but never really let go of things made him a formidable interrogator. He had a mind that could go around corners and never get lost. "I'll get your description as soon as I get home, I know what I know. I think the son is sick, but his father was the source of his pleasure, and cover. I think he's got his own self-interest at heart. How'd I do?"

"You forgot 'Lois.'"

"No, I didn't."

"Suppose this 'Miranda' turns up alive and well."

"You'll want to talk to her."

"And if we suddenly know what you know?"

"Hearsay."

"You, Mr. Costa, are a piece of work. You say a whole lot without saying much. Ever consider being a cop?"

"Yeah, but the hours suck."

"Bartending's better?" We all were smiling at the same time.

"He ain't Petersen, Paul," said DaSilva, seeming to read my mind.

"Nope, he's a cop."

"I'm right here, you two."

"Yeah," said DaSilva, "But we're talking nice about you."

"Oh, well then, that's okay. I'm thinking looking at the family might be a good place to start. The percentages still work, mostly." He looked my way, "Miranda's description, Paul?"

"ASAP, Detective Lacombe."

Percentages? Police hate mysteries. Love, hate, anger, jealousy, greed and all of the other nasty emotions resided inside of families. It was the first place the cops looked.

"Thanks for the coffee, Paul," said DaSilva.

"Welcome, Larry. Detective Lacombe."

"Hell, if it's 'Larry' and 'Paul,' it might as well be 'Phil.'"

"We'll be in touch, but if you have any more that you can't tell us, give us a call, and don't tell us, okay?" Lacombe seemed to be enjoying himself hugely.

The rest of the weekend passed, and I found myself relaxing at times. Marisol did her homework, and I picked at some household jobs I'd been putting off.

***

Monday afternoon, I was in time to pick up Marisol at school, so I cut through town and pulled into the parking lot. I walked in, feeling guilty, as if I had cut class. I hadn't been to a principal's office for a talking-to in thirty years, but the memory cut deeply. Mr. Emmett Davis was there, collecting his mail. "Mr. Costa!" He shouted, as if meeting me was the best part of a great day. He always bubbled with enthusiasm and barely contained excitement. "It's so good to see you, again. Marisol is doing wonderfully. Her project on the Federalist Papers was absolutely great. I had high school students who couldn't have done as well." I nodded my thanks and tried hard to look into his eyes, instead of the architecture of his comb over.

"And to think that he's a friend of yours," he was saying. "It was so nice of him to make such a fuss over Marisol, and how well he knew you." I must have drifted off to insulate myself from his excitement. "I'm sorry, Mr. Davis, what did you say?"

"The aide, and son, you know, Jason Morley and the congressman's aide, Adam? Such a tragedy about the congressman. It must be a relief to you to be cleared, finally. Young Mr. Morley was so generous with his time and spoke to the kids about Congress and how it all works. He talked about lobbyists, and just lots of detail. The kids were rapt. You know, so many adults underestimate kids, but he didn't talk down to them."

I felt a crawling tingle descending my buttocks and climbing up to my scrotum. I felt my breathing deepen and accelerate, and the muscles in my legs tensed, bringing me to the balls of my feet.

"He was here? With my daughter?"

"Well, yes, Marisol and my whole class. I sent that note home to tell you about it. Well, you and all of the parents, of course. I was so pleased to get him to speak to us, especially during the unit on the federal legislature."

"You invited him?"

"No, that's the wonderful coincidence. He called the school, and offered to do it. The timing was so good, and it was so good of him, especially under the circumstances; so close to the tragic loss of his father. He was wonderfully gracious, especially to Marisol. Kind of making it clear that you're innocent. Generous of him, don't you think?" I nodded as if I agreed. That note. The one I'd been too damned busy to bother with. The one I could have been reading instead of playing with Dana in the shower.

I had three days, or at least two and a half. Too busy enjoying a beautiful woman's company to take care of my daughter.

"Mr. Costa?"

"Sorry, what were you saying?"

"Just that he told the whole class that he knew you, and did it in exactly the right tone and way so the other kids would understand."

"Has he left? I ought to thank him." I said, my tone nearly robotic. Even the teacher, in his haze of enthusiasm noticed.

"Something wrong, Mr. Costa?"

"Not with you, Mr. Davis, you did your job well, as always." He looked down at his shoes, blushing. He'd done his job, letting me know that my daughter was about to meet Jason Morley and the family fixer.

I was the one. I let myself get so involved that I neglected important family business. I was furious with Dana, and myself, and Mrs. Pina. My rational brain ridiculed me, while the old lizard portion had me ready to kill. With nowhere to go, the rage I was feeling formed a cold, nasty ball in my stomach. The ball was giving off a taste that was coppery, like blood in the back of my throat. I swallowed hard, and shook Mr. Emmett Davis's hand, just as Marisol arrived at the office.

"Marisol, I was just telling your father about Mr. Morley and Adam."

"Oh, they were so cool, Daddy! I really had a lot of fun, and they told the whole class that you're innocent and that I'm pretty and smart, which makes me pretty smart. That sounds lame, now, but the rest of the kids laughed and it was nice. The kids have been pretty mean, some of them, you know?"

I managed a smile, thanked her teacher, and we left for home. I was quiet, but 'Sol was happy to fill in. She handed me a calling card from Adam, rather than Jason, but it had Jason's autograph on it. "See, Daddy, there it is."

I made some sounds that I hoped sounded like a pleased parent, and felt dead inside. They may have touched her. I failed her. I'd never failed her before. She didn't think she did, my little "almost a teenager," but she counted on me, and I let her down. It was like a refrain from a song you can't get out of your head. "She counts on me, I screwed up, she counts on me, I screwed up."

The whispering of my ancestors grew louder, telling me to end this threat to my child.

I thought I could just let it all go, give it to DaSilva, talk Dana into a short leave, and take off. There were other bars. Other towns, other states. Marisol loved Florida. Maybe I should have let it all go before. As soon as I was clear, just hand it all off and go back to what I had. Screw Lois, screw Miranda and screw Sandra. They were all big girls, not my fault. Marisol was my fault, and I could get her clear and protect her.

I got her home, and Mrs. Pina was there. There were another twelve messages on the voicemail, and I briefed them on screening the calls using it, because reporters were allowed to call us now. Then I played all twelve messages. Three I wanted, nine I erased. The public had a right to know, I supposed, but not from me.

As I thought that, my right forearm brushed over the butt of my Beretta. Dana had supplied a couple of quick extraction pouches for me, so I had them strapped over my belt at my left.

I called Dennis Pereira and left him a message, asking for a description and a photo of Miranda. I told him that I was going to put her in as a missing person, without involving him. I realized that the house felt confining, and the weather was beautiful. A drive, it seemed, was a good way to try to sort things out.

In my car, I unloaded my pistol, checked all three magazines, tested the action, reloaded, holstered it and put on a windbreaker for cover. I pulled out and away, trying to decide if I-195 was the best route for me to take. To hell with the seals, I figured, and pushed down on the accelerator, watching the turbo kick in and feeling the push at my back.

All the way to no place in particular, I thought about the original killing, the Congressman's world, and Jason and Adam. I thought about Dana and Marisol. I had slipped up. It was my fault, and Dana wasn't to blame. We had a date in a couple of nights, and it was going to be hard to keep it, but miserable to break it. I kept coming back to Jason Morley and Adam, nearby, knowing where to find my daughter. It was my fault. Once in the clear, I could have dropped the whole thing, but I felt sorry for a reporter in Washington. I had to take on a call girl and a stripper as my burdens. It put my little girl at risk.

I caught myself slamming the heel of my hand into the gearshift knob as I drove. Things had been going well. I had a job. It wasn't great, but it paid the bills, and I had time with my daughter. I had almost come to terms with losing my wife, and Marisol was coping. Then all of this, and I fell right into it. Instead of leaving it alone, I fought back. That part was okay, but after I won my fight, I kept going. I kept on with it because I liked it. I wanted to keep going, keep feeling as if I was doing something worthwhile. The first threat to my family was over, but a new one came up.

If they wanted to scare me off, or get even, then maybe it was over. So what if they had backed me down. Didn't matter. My daughter mattered. I was working at convincing myself, but I remembered my wife, long ago.

She had told me, when I mentioned leaving NCIS to go into private life, practicing law, "Paul, you are my love. Not perfect. You are stubborn. You have a temper. You are brave, but not fearless. I am proud of you."

I felt grateful for her understanding and unconditional love. I missed the intelligence and insight that she directed at me. I missed it, but not with the usual pain. I seemed to be past that at the moment.

What I couldn't do was back away. Isabel had loved someone who fought back. If Jason Morley wasn't evil, then no human was. "You have no secrets, " he was saying. "I know how to hurt you, and you know I can do it." He wasn't afraid of tapes or books, or cops. He knew my soft spots. He liked the way he was, and he was going to make sure that I didn't stop him.

He didn't know that for the cobra, there's a mongoose.

The mongoose relied on response. The cobra struck with a fall from above, and the mongoose danced clear, leapt and bit the vulnerable area behind the snake's hood. A mongoose never tried to strike the cobra until after the cobra did. The mongoose positioned himself so that the cobra could only strike from one direction. I knew all of this because of a report I'd helped my daughter to do after they read Kipling's "Rikki-Tikki-Tavi." Nothing like a fourth grade report to bet your life on.

When I got home, I wasn't fuming anymore. I had to work that night, and I had to pick up a bottle of red wine for my evening with Dana for dinner. I didn't think her invitation was made lightly, and I didn't want to take it that way.

Dinner was blade meat and kale soup, a favorite, and I ate it mechanically, not enjoying the cumin and other herbs that Mrs. Pina used. Tender blade meat was the product of hours of cooking, with pauses to cool and reheat. It was a lot of work, but I was eating it without pleasure. Mrs. Pina probed with her eyes, without asking any questions. Marisol was too absorbed in the excitement of the day to notice anything.

After we cleaned up, I took Mrs. Pina aside and told her about Jason and Adam. I told her what they looked like and told her to call DaSilva, Lacombe, Dana and me as soon as she spotted them. They'd sent a message, and I remembered the beating that continued after I was unconscious. I called and left a voicemail for DaSilva to brief him. I made sure to tell him how worrisome it was. Laying a foundation couldn't do any harm.

I managed a shower and shave, struggled into my work clothes and left, after collecting my goodbye hugs and kisses from Marisol. I felt a physical pull, the urgent need to be home. I knew I couldn't live with that, every night. I could guard my house, all day, every day, or I could run away. There had to be another option.

***

The hotel bar had slowed down, after the notoriety wore off from the Congressman's death, but Sarah was on the schedule to work with me.

Business was slow, and we had lots of leisure time. Time to look at the harbor through the windows, then back at the clock, polish glasses that were already clear and wipe the spotless bar. We had time to talk, hum and think.

If Jason and Adam didn't bother us again, no contact or messages, no further threat pointed at Marisol, then they could go home to Washington, and maybe the system would do something about them. I would help it along, if I could. Otherwise, I'd have to act. I felt relieved by having a decision made, even if it depended on somebody else's actions. I caught myself hoping that the two monsters would head south. Hope isn't a good reason to let your powder get wet, but it isn't a bad thing to have.

The shift lasted forever. I was partway home, trying not to doze, when I quit fighting it. I found a donut shop that had its lights on, and bribed the kid cleaning the place with a ten-dollar bill for a pot of coffee. He passed three cups through the window at the rear, making me promise never to tell a soul. It got me home to stumble to bed, after checking on Marisol and sending Mrs. Pina to bed. An old western flickered on the TV set. John Wayne flipped a short carbine in one hand to cock it, flourishing a pistol in the other with his horse's reins in his teeth. He had a patch on one eye, and appeared to be long past his best days. "You'd better fill your hands, you son of a bitch!" he shouted, just as I switched the set off.

Had there ever been a time that simple? It was a good question to fall asleep with, so I did.

Chapter 20

I woke up in time to see Marisol off to school. When I'd had some coffee and felt more human, I called Sandra, the TV lady. She said, "Unless a civil war has broken out in D.C., you'd better be Brad freaking Pitt. And you'd better be horny, and recently divorced from what's her name."

"Um, it's Paul. Paul Costa?"

"Yeah, I'm listening. Who needs sleep anyway?"

"About Jason and his pet monster?"

"Okay, I'm really listening, now."

"I need to know where they are, and I need to stay aware of it."

"That's easy. The little shit is going to run for his father's seat. He's up your way."

"You're joking." I started getting queasy.

"I wish. Nope, he figures he learned at his father's knee, et cetera, et cetera."

"So he's here for a good long while?"

"Yup. Probably moving into Daddy's old digs, to set up residency. He may never have lost it, who knows? The good news is that he's not down here for now."

I spent a few minutes telling her about his visit to the school and the attention he gave to Marisol.

"Mother. Fucker," she said, carefully pronouncing each syllable.

"I need him tracked, if you can make that happen."

She was silent for a moment. "Our affiliate up there has an old friend of mine producing for them."

"Is that good?"

"Producers are serious journalists. They're the reporters who get the information for people like me to spend a few seconds on air. This guy was a pit bull. The best. If the junior asshole from Rhode Island is going to run, he has to stay on good terms with the media. I think it'll work, Paul."

"Will he do it?"

"I think so," she said slowly.

"Sandra—"

"You're welcome. That's what friends are for. Besides, there is the exclusive. I haven't forgotten."

"Neither have I."

We hung up, and I felt a little better. DaSilva knew that Jason made an approach. He and Lacombe would read that as a threat. I had someone who could trail along with Jason, and Jason would want him around.

It was still early, and I went to my computer, logged on to the Internet, and checked my email. There was one from "DennisTMenis." I opened it, and it was from Dennis Pereira.

"How're things?" it began. "The attached is a photo and description of Miranda, courtesy of the escort service. In the meantime, there really has to be a good way to make money with all of this computer technology. If you come up with something, let me know, and I'll split the take with you. Kathy Sousa says to say hi, and why haven't you called her, you dog?"

I sent an answer to thank him. I passed on a hello to Kathy Sousa, and told him that the FBI had a whole group that did nothing but go after on line scams. I didn't bother to tell him why I didn't call our classmate. Dennis would know that if I hadn't, I wouldn't.

DaSilva's business card had an email address, so I copied the photo and description file and sent it directly, with no trace of Dennis in it. I signed off and picked up the phone to make an appointment at the range for some pistol practice.

They had a small "Hogan's Alley" combat practice range, with a mocked up city street. It sounded like fun, until they told me it cost a hundred bucks for a half hour. Nope. They had a pistol range for target and one for combat shooting. Each went for twenty-five bucks an hour, plus target costs. They could sell ammunition, and they insisted on having my Beretta looked at by their gunsmith. It sounded like a professional operation, and it was just over the border in Massachusetts. My license was okay for Rhode Island, so I asked the guy at the range about carrying it over the border.

As he suggested, I locked it in the trunk, and drove up into the countryside west of Taunton. I checked my weapon in, and waited for about twenty minutes. The gunsmith bore sighted it for me, and cleaned it, adjusting the tension of the recoil spring. He gave me a signed card to present to the range master.

The concentration was just the thing to help me try to think. The range master had been in the Marine Corps, and didn't like my choice of holster position and orientation.

"Okay, so you can draw when you're sitting at the table. Great. While that barrel is clearing the holster, it's pointed at your waist, right into your guts from the side, about the worst way to get hit that there is. I don't like drawing across body, either, so that leaves the high right with the butt to the rear. The FBI does it, and it works. The weapon is safe until you level it, quick, natural and brings the gun right on line. Shit, Navy, even the SEALS do it that way."

We argued for awhile, enjoying the debate, finally getting into a shooting contest. I had him, until we got to twenty yards. At that point, he could just about write his name with the .45 he insisted on using.

I paid him off.

"Remember what I said, Navy, unless you plan to get into a gunfight sitting on your ass."

My early start on the day was great, in some ways, but it got me home with time on my hands. I figured I'd do some housework. As I pulled up to the house, another car pulled away. It looked like it had been parked outside of my house. I had my gun in the trunk, so I pulled straight into my garage, opened the trunk, and locked and loaded. I holstered it after I had gone through the whole house.

There was careful, and there was fearful. I didn't mind careful, but I couldn't stand being afraid. It made me angry. I was still angry when I picked up the phone, hung it up without dialing, and paced around the house. Then I started a pot of coffee, and picked it up again.

I called the strip joint, and got lucky.

"Tim?"

"Yup, this is Tim Foley."

"Hi, Tim, Paul Costa."

"Hey! How they going?"

"Okay, but we should talk."

"Drop by, I have to tell you something, and I still don't trust your phone."

"Give me an hour?"

"See you, then."

Chapter 21

I checked all of the locks on the doors and windows, left a note for Marisol and Mrs. Pina, and left. I made some turns to see if I was being followed before I headed for the "Gentlemen's Club."

If anything, Tim Foley looked bigger, and tougher than I remembered except for his boyish grin. He poured me a coffee, got his filthy old mug out and sat at a table with me.

There were no customers, and a couple of the girls were sitting around, looking like tired secretaries. A little bored, sitting casually, with legs crossed sipping coffee and chatting, except secretaries didn't sit around in the mix of outfits that they did. One looked like an underdressed cowgirl, with chaps and a thong, a gun belt and a cowboy hat. There didn't seem to be anything under the vest she wore, which somehow stayed in place. She was talking to a woman wearing an evening gown with no back, and very little front, along with opera length gloves. It looked like a Fellini movie.

He looked around and saw what I was seeing. "Pisser, isn't it?" He pronounced it "Pissah."

"How do you deal with reality when you leave here, Tim?"

"It's a crutch for people who can't handle booze, drugs and fantasy. You just get used to making the jump, I guess."

"I guess so, What's up?"

"Lois is back."

"That's good, right?"

"Yeah."

"Did she tell you anything about Jason and Adam?"

"She mentioned them. She doesn't like to talk about it."

"She staying with you?"

"No."

I thought again about how wise she was. "Jason and Adam are up here too; that's why I called." I told him about the school visit, and how close he got to my daughter. His grin faded. "If they know that you and I are friendly, and they know about Lois—" I started.

"I should be worried, right?" He sounded grim.

"Can you get her under cover?"

"I can get her to be careful, I hope."

"She has my number, and the cops are aware of things, but unless she's in Newport, they can't do much."

"She ain't in a running away mood."

"Since I'm here to bring you bad news, do you know a Newport cop, named 'Petersen?'" I asked, after a moment.

"He used to come here. He dated one of the girls, but she hasn't seen him in a few days. He's real bad news. I think he's on a pad. I know he and Morley were asshole buddies."

"On a pad?"

"Yeah, he gets paid off to overlook some things. He has to unless he has a family fortune or something. He spends more in here than an honest cop could. If you're on his shit list, there's lots he can do."

Now it was my turn. "Pisser."

"I'll call Lois. She may want to talk to you. Shit, I just wanted to tell you that things were looking up and that she's back."

"I'm sorry. Maybe I've brought trouble your way."

"Not you, man. I'll break their fucking backs if they come near her. I can be at her place from here or my place in less than ten minutes, and she always seems glad to see me."

I liked his smile. Acne and battle scars notwithstanding, when he smiled and thought of her, he had the pure joy and abandonment of a kid who'd just gotten the puppy he wanted.

I was home a half hour later, checking my mirror frequently and coming into my neighborhood from a different side, watching for cars moving and any other hint that my house was under surveillance. It seemed clean, but I was still cautious. I pulled into my garage, and searched my car. Short of using a drug dog, it seemed clean. I entered my house with my hand near my gun. It took me a half hour to search my own house. Paranoia, but even paranoids have enemies. A cop with a grudge could "find" all sorts of things.

I remembered Dennis Pereira's email about scams, and checked my files on my computer. No cookies or activity that I couldn't account for. I felt silly, but Tim had gotten me thinking. I was chasing my tail. Enough was enough. I had a date with a beautiful woman in a few hours. I had to go and leave my daughter, or let men who belonged in jail keep me at home.

I tried to think of how my grandparents would handle it. It was tough, because I couldn't imagine them getting into my situation. Still, my quiet and retiring grandfather had taken on the whole system for me and won. My grandmother's steely determination intimidated more than one person who spoke better English, was better educated and had more visible power.

Marisol came home with her flurry of books and energy, followed by Mrs. Pina. "You have a meeting with the FBI lady, tonight?" she asked.

"Yes, but I'm thinking about canceling. Those men I worry about, and the reporters. I think I should be here."

"I think different," she answered, with her chin pushing forward. "I think that this night is fine, and that I can protect our girl. I think that you worry about things that I can handle."

"Mrs. Pina—"

"Paul, you think I would not want you to stay if I was worried? You think I do not care about Marisol?" She was getting a little louder than I wanted, so I led her outside onto our front porch.

"Mrs. Pina, these men— I know you can take care of 'Sol. Maybe better than me, but they just like to hurt people."

Her purse was huge and could have qualified as luggage. Lifting it was an effort for me, but she lugged it all over the place. She reached in, and produced an honest-to-God Luger. Carrying seven rounds of nine millimeter, with the famous jointed action, it was one of the best designs for comfort and accuracy.

"Where in the world—" I started to say, and stopped myself.

"No one hurts our girl, no one gets in; no one bothers us. No one changes our lives."

"Have you ever fired that thing?"

"Manny's father brought it home from the war, and I keep it clean and I have fired it." Manny was her husband, dead for the past ten years.

"Not your job, Mrs. Pina, it's mine."

"I will be here, Paul, whether you go or not. I think you should go. I think you should spend time with her. It might be good for you. Bring her here, if it would make you feel better, but these men should not change things. You can't live afraid, you know that."

There it was. Our blood called to us. I was angry because she was right. Another man might have thought she was wrong, but she knew me well. I went over her gun, checking the tension in the magazine spring, as well as the action and trigger pull.

"Where did you learn to take care of a gun?"

"My father, in Angola, taught me." She was grimly determined. I hoped that no repair people showed up in my absence. I gave in to her, because I trusted her. It seemed irrational, but it felt like the right thing to do. I was hoping my libido wasn't doing my thinking for me. I gave her Dana's number and showered and dressed.

It was an occasion, so I hauled out my best suit and ironed a shirt. Marisol thought somebody was getting married or died or something, and couldn't stop giggling.

"Mrs. Pina won't stop looking out of the windows, Daddy. What's she looking for?"

"She wants to make sure the house is safe, that's all, honey." I doubted that she believed me, but she let it go.

After I left, I detoured to a liquor store that specialized in wines and bought a nice Australian red that I'd heard good things about, then headed up to Route 24 and the drive to Boston.

***

She was wearing a floor length black dress, and had her hair in a twist with some loose tendrils. I smelled cinnamon and coffee and a meal cooking. It blended into a net of different kinds of deliciousness. She looked beautiful, and when I slipped my arms around her, I felt the weight of fabric slipping over silk and skin. She finally broke the kiss, "I have to turn the fish, and if we keep that up, we'll never get to dinner." She asked me to open what I brought.

The table was set carefully. Her corkscrew was a good one, and I poured us each a glass. For the first time, I had time and inclination to look around at her home. I was standing in her living room. Some furniture was missing or had been moved. She had rearranged it to accommodate a dining room set from her kitchen.

There were four bookcases of different sizes and shapes scattered around, with titles that I was familiar with, along with some in French. Lots of Hemingway, Saroyan and Steinbeck were mixed with some textbooks, including investigation and forensic tomes. I found a small CD player and picked out a couple of soft jazz disks. I loaded it, and started it up on a random mix.

"Thank you," she said, "I meant to turn some music on." Her back was to me as she stood at the stove. I put one arm around her waist from behind, and passed a glass of wine over her shoulder. She took it after she stopped stirring something that smelled like lemon and garlic. She sipped and leaned back against me. "I missed you," she said.

"You too."

She rubbed the back of her head against my chest and chin.

"Everything looks nice and smells amazing. You weren't kidding about being a good cook."

"Thanks." She seemed to be considering something, and asked, "Do men look in medicine cabinets?"

"Nope, we like to preserve our illusions."

"That means I cleaned mine out for nothing."

"Men look at bookcases."

"And?"

"Yes, we're compatible, from a literary point of view.

"And others?"

"How's the wine?"

"Good, and I don't care about the rules, I like red, and I like it with fish."

"Then I think we're about perfect."

By unspoken consent, we stopped and sipped our wine. "Go sit down, I'll be right out with dinner," she said. The room was warm and welcoming. It looked like a comfortable place to sit and read, or listen to music. It was a great carpet to make love on.

Dinner was as good as it had smelled. Scrod, in a garlic and lemon sauce, some kind of Indian rice and steamed vegetables. Wine to stroke it down, and make the conversation flow.

When the last of the wine was gone, she took my hand, and led me into her bedroom. More modern prints on the walls, and a couple of lamps with simple shades. Over her bed, a good reading light was switched off. She was a reader. I had a similar lamp, and fought my loneliness with books. For her, and if I was honest, for me, the loneliness was a choice.

She turned, and her dress whispered to the floor. Underneath she wore a skimpy push up bra, and a pair of silk and lace panties that held up lacy garters with stockings. She left the heels on. Her look searched my face for my reaction. I don't know what it showed, but what I felt was raw lust. There was the desire to take charge in her manner. She pushed my jacket off of my shoulders, and undressed me.

She had trouble with my belt and trousers, but I let her fiddle until they came loose. When my clothes were in a pile next to hers, she put one hand in the middle of my chest and pushed me gently onto her bed. In moments I was engulfed, drowning in her.

Afterwards, I was trying to catch my breath when she turned to lie in the crook of my arm. She faced me directly and said, "You're welcome."

"There's no thanking you for that," I answered.

We cuddled, talked, sat up and talked, and made out, with no urgency, until it became urgent.

"You have to go home tonight, don't you?" I thought about telling her all about Jason and Adam, and held it back. It had nothing to do with her and the dodging I had done early on. That was part of getting myself clear of a murder charge. This omission was a different kind of deception, and made me feel soiled.

"Yes, I have to go, not right now, but I will have to be home by three or so."

"Paul?"

"Yeah?" I think that men fear two things: the snap of a rubber glove in a doctor's office, and that tone of voice from a woman. The one that means she wants to talk, and that she wants to talk seriously.

"Never mind, I guess."

I thought for a moment and spoke, hoping I was guessing well, "I'm a bartender, Dana. You're an FBI agent. You overachieve, and maybe I've given in or even given up. We need to keep that in mind. The other thing is that I was a suspect, and you're what you are."

"You're a really good father, and a gentle, tender man. I like being your friend as well as I like making love with you. I think nobody will ever know much about things you want to keep to yourself. You're a good friend and a fine lover. For now, that's enough for me."

I nodded.

"I should probably head for home. I want to be there when Marisol wakes up."

"If you gotta go, you gotta go, but before you go," she said, with a grin.

"Before I go," She rolled over, pulling me to her. I didn't resist at all.

***

I got home and noticed the message light on the machine blinking. I thought about playing it, but couldn't manage it. I collapsed into bed, still dressed.

I woke up before six o'clock. I felt as if I would roll to one side and find Dana next to me. I got my feet to the floor, feeling as if there was sand in the gears. A half hour later, I had a coffee in my hand, and heard Marisol stirring around. I hit the "Play" button on the voicemail.

"This is a message for Paul Costa. My name is Bill Latronica. Sandra, from DC asked me to call you with some updates on Jason Morley's activities. I've been with him, off and on for a day or so, all routine stuff. Last night and early this morning, he and his aide drove up to Newport, and went into a neighborhood. Kind of blue collar, but nice. Anyhow, they parked and seemed to be looking at a Dutch colonial." He read off the address. "It needs to have the lawn mowed. It's got cedar shakes and white trim that could use some paint."

I'd been meaning to put a coat of paint on it, and Mrs. Pina's grandson was due to mow.

"I have them on video, watching the house. I suspect that this is important to you, and you can reach me on my cell phone." He gave the number. I checked the time of the call, which came in about five minutes before I'd gotten home. I had to call him, but it appeared that they'd come to my neighborhood and spent some time watching my house. My daughter was in there, with a little old lady to protect her. A tough little old lady with a German Luger, but still a little old lady. The young girl had a perfectly good father, but he was out having dinner and sex, instead of protecting her. I wrote the phone number down and deleted the message. I was a little rough on the phone.

If Sandra's friend had been out tailing a political candidate until all hours, he probably needed some sleep, and I needed to think. I couldn't use the police. They had to worry about their superiors, and internal leaks. At least DaSilva did. If Petersen had worked for the father, it was likely that he'd whore for the son, too. All DaSilva or Lacombe had to do was say something in front of a cop who was friendly with Petersen.

I made a light breakfast, with the fruit that was still fresh. I cut away some bad spots and sliced fresh peaches and mixed it all up, gently. I used a dollop of whipped cream and made some toast. I was pouring juice when Marisol came out.

"Was it nice last night, Daddy?"

"Yes, honey. She's a good cook, and a nice person. She loves to read, like you."

"I like it that we're having company, sometimes. I think I'd like it if my friends could stay over, too."

"Would you like to have sleepovers?"

She looked down at the table. "Sometimes."

"If you ever want to have a sleepover party, we can do that, you know."

"I guess."

"Did I do anything to make you afraid to ask?"

"No, I just thought you want us to keep things the same." My heart was breaking. I felt like nine kinds of fool. She went with my isolation, because, "Daddy must know best."

"I was wrong. I'm sorry."

"It's okay, Daddy. I love you, and I sort of wanted to just be home and have you close."

"Is it different, now?"

"Yeah, I think so."

"Good, I'm feeling different about things, too. We'll work on it together?" She started to smile.

"Okay." She looked at the kitchen clock, and got up, heaving her backpack onto her shoulder. "Love you!" A quick kiss on the cheek and a one armed hug and she was through the door, as the bus pulled to a stop. I was already missing her. I watched for cars or pedestrians. I didn't see anything I didn't usually see.

I called DaSilva to check on his progress.

"If we can keep those tapes and their contents quiet, I'd be grateful," he said. "The family's lawyer is keeping it as quiet as he can, to protect the Congressman's image. The wife hasn't been told." Other than that, he was stalled. No luck with Miranda..

"Listen, Larry, there was a flashdrive called 'Lois,' wasn't there?"

"Funny you should mention that one, Paul, it was recorded over. Our technician said that it had an old recording, and that the other one was duplicated on top of it. The tech weenie couldn't pull up any of the old image. He could only tell us that there had been one. He said that was the only one that showed an old recording. The bastard used new tapes, then DVD's, then flashdrives for all of his other home movies."

"Shit."

"Why?"

"There's proof of a crime in that old recording."

"You're sure? And how do you know?"

"Before I try to tap dance around that, are you interviewing the women on those tapes?"

"No, I'm the Newport village idiot."

"I'm sorry. But how's that going?" I asked.

"They either deny knowing anything, admit to a past relationship, or cry and beg us not to let it out, ever."

"Blame them?"

"Hell, no. But you do have to wonder how they got into such a mess." That one could take all day to answer, and we could still be guessing wrong for most of them.

"Larry, can your technician copy one of those flashdrives, any one at random, and hide the woman's identity?"

"I'm gonna assume he can. Why would he?"

"So you can give it to me."

"Why would I?"

"Cause I'm charming and mix a great gimlet?"

"And because you know that a wiped out video had proof of a crime on it?"

"Will you do it?"

"Sure. Anything for a great mixologist."

"Will you pick one that has Jason and maybe Adam in action?"

"Since I'm at your service, why the hell not?" He was getting a little testy.

"Larry, I made some promises. I have a client, and this will move your investigation, I think." Just because my client hadn't hired me, didn't mean I couldn't use the excuse to keep things private. Just because my client was eleven and my daughter, didn't change things at all. "So, will you do it? And it would be just great if you didn't let anyone else know, especially a certain cop named Petersen."

"Petersen is on his way to suspension, I think. He's got an awful lot of explaining to do."

"Has he got friends?"

"Does a bear shit in the woods? Of course he does. Others like him, mostly, but some political weight, too. The heavy cover will go away as soon as things go formal though. Why?"

"Just checking my tail, Larry. You know how hard cops can make somebody's life if they want to."

"I'll talk to Phil Lacombe, he has an ear to the ground. If anybody would know you're on the shit list, he will. In the meantime, I'll drop your recording off at the bar, tonight."

I left a quick voice mail for Dana. "Just hi, and call me back, please." I looked at my watch and decided to wait to make another call. I headed upstairs to knock on Mrs. Pina's door.

"Paul, good morning." She was surprised, since we usually met downstairs.

"Mrs. Pina, I'm sorry to intrude on your morning."

"If it wasn't important, you wouldn't be here."

"True. There will be a time, pretty soon, where I'll need you and Marisol to be someplace else."

She didn't even blink. "I have a sister-in-law I trust."

"I'll let you know."

"We'll be ready."

"Thank you, Mrs. Pina."

"Meo pracer," she answered. She hardly ever spoke in Portuguese to me, unless she had a point to make. It reminded me of my ancestry, and my grandparents. Maybe that was all that she wanted.

Downstairs, I picked up the phone, and dialed a number that I'd written down earlier that morning. It took awhile, but finally, the TV news producer was on the line. "Paul Costa," I introduced myself.

"Hello, Mr. Costa, I've been expecting your call."

"It's Paul," I said

"In that case, I'm Bill. Sandra speaks pretty highly of you."

"You too."

"You got my message?"

"Yes, and you know that he was watching my house."

"I figured as much."

"Sandra tell you about this guy?"

"Enough to get me interested. I don't think he has much of a chance."

"Neither did Nixon."

"Now you're scaring me."

"Jason has a dark side. I know of at least one case, where he didn't even tell the victim to put ice on it."

"Proof?" He asked, starting to sound excited.

"Oodles of proof."

"And what do you want in return?"

"You have to trust me."

"I don't know you, but Sandra says you have an agreement to do an exclusive with her."

"True, but you'll get to produce it."

"Deal."

"Are you going to air the tape of Jason Morley and his thug watching my house?"

"For what? They could always say they were checking on the safety of neighborhoods in his district or some bullshit like that."

"Good. You say it for them. Something like this: 'A resident of Newport, well known to Jason Morley caught him on video, researching the safety of neighborhoods in his district. That same resident has an extensive collection of recordings of Jason and old family friend, Adam,' whatever the hell his last name is."

"Birch," he said. "Adam's last name is Birch."

"Anyhow, if you could mention that the station expects to be coming into possession of those additional tapes when arrangements can be made, that should do it."

"This is a set up and you're trying to roll me." He was nearly whining.

"Set up, yes, roll you, no. Whatever tapes I have, I will provide to the station, as promised. That's a fact." I was only going to have the one that Larry DaSilva was having made for me, but I figured that was information to keep to myself for the moment.

"Arrangements?"

"To be discussed later."

"What are you up to?" he asked.

"I plan to give Jason an opportunity. If he takes me up on it, I promise it will be newsworthy. If he doesn't, you still get evidence that will blow things apart."

"I don't like the sound of this."

"But will you do it?"

"I have to give this some thought. I'm supposed to report news, not be used, and certainly not create news. On the other hand—" He stopped. "Watch tonight's news at six o'clock."

"This would be a lot easier if I knew."

"It would, but I don't know myself," he replied.

"Okay, I'll watch the news, tonight. Either way, thanks for helping keep to tabs on him for me."

"Forget it. I owed Sandra one."

"At least stop by for a free drink sometime," I said, and told him where I worked with a couple of nights that I could be found there. I cleaned up the kitchen and made my bed. Marisol had made hers, but left some laundry for me to pick up. There were still favored stuffed animals on her bed, and dolls sitting on her bookcase. I could see the little girl in her room. Then I looked around and saw posters of boy bands, teenaged movie actors and pictures of her, with me, with her mom, with both of us, and one of our wedding pictures. The budding young woman filled me with mingled pride and worry.

With thoughts of parental inadequacy following me around, I dug out my legal pads and began to write some notes. The situation with Jason and Adam might or might not fit into the murder of Richard Morley. I thought that they were just wild cards.

Somebody killed the Congressman in a very professional way. Jason had the houseboy. Adam wouldn't have taken a leak without someone pointing out which urinal to use. His haven was threatened by Morley's death.

Adam seemed to rely on the authority and direction from his employer to act. He had been tentative at the Morley house in DC, allowing me to react. He had vague orders, subject to interpretation to "show me out." At my motel, he'd taken immediate control. I'd have bet that he had specific orders to do so, and carried them out once he knew what was expected of him.

I had to wait for the six o'clock news. My grandfather used to say that things would be ready, "Bye and bye." He usually found something productive to do while he waited for them to gel. I took my work clothes to the cleaner we were supposed to use, and grabbed some groceries. Paid my phone bill and my electric bill and looked at my account balance. Not pretty, but I made a deposit of tips and my paycheck.

That killed the morning. I was emptying the dishwasher when the phone rang. "Paul, it's Larry DaSilva." He sounded depressed, and while businesslike as a rule, he was rarely down. I hadn't heard it in the time I'd known him, anyway. "Miranda turned up."

I knew what he was going to say.

"She washed up near Tiverton. They used dental records to identify her. Coroner and M.E. are working on her, but it's going to be tough to say much of anything. She's missing her lower legs, and there isn't much left."

"Shit," I said. I didn't mean it to be profane, but I had no real words to use. "Any family?"

"I just made the notification, myself. Her uncle's going to claim the remains. You don't seem surprised. Pissed off, I think, but not surprised."

"I'm not. Not really."

"Better tell me about it. The whole thing. Right now. I want to keep you out of the shitpile, but I need your help to do it."

I started with the night that the congressman died. "Somebody made an appointment, requesting Miranda," I began. When I told him about Miranda's vanishing act, and brought him up to the point of the body's discovery, there was a long silence. "I don't get the knife, Paul. If it hadn't been for the knife, he'd just be a dead guy."

"How about his life insurance? Anything if he's found to be murdered?"

"You mean double indemnity, like the movie?"

"Well. Yes, I guess I do, Larry."

"The policy pays five million regardless of cause of death, except for suicide. The money goes to a trust, with an attorney as a trustee, and all of his family as beneficiaries. Evenly divided, basically."

"Anyone in the family in financial trouble?"

"You been hanging around with Phil Lacombe? He spent two days on all of that. The bad part is that I didn't do it sooner. The good part is that it didn't make any difference. No reason on the money side to kill him."

"Smart cop."

"And he's dying."

"What?"

"Liver cancer. He has maybe six months. He used to be this big burly guy, but now he's leaning out. He can only work for another few weeks."

"Family?" I asked.

"Nah, his wife died three years ago, no kids, no fucking nothing, except the job."

I was silent for a time, thinking, before I spoke. "Nothing to say. It sucks. I'm sorry."

"I'd like to make sure he shows up on the arrest."

"If I can help, I will."

There was a pause, while he thought. "Want to hear about Petersen?"

"My favorite guy, sure."

He brightened for a moment, "Well, Pus Pockets Petersen is going to be arraigned, on Monday. The State guys found all kinds of money he can't account for. His wardrobe is supplied by some clothing store that he works for. He keeps building inspectors and so forth away from them. There may be enough to show that he did some side work for Morley. Should make it an interesting trial, if it gets that far. I think he'll make a deal. Even that atomic cannon he likes to carry was a bribe, and the ammo is way the hell outside of guidelines. He's suspended and his assets are locked up. It'll be in the papers by Monday night or Tuesday morning."

"I needed some good news. I know it isn't really good news, but you know what I mean. I hate to ask but do I have to keep looking over my shoulder for traffic stops?"

"I'd be careful for a bit. He made a lot of noise about you and how he's gonna get cleared and how you framed him, and like that."

"You watching your back?" I asked.

"Yup, and Phil is, too. Phil's sort of old fashioned. And doing a politician's dirty work? Phil hates politicians."

"Sorry I opened the can of worms."

"It would have happened anyway. Petersen's too stupid to last much longer," he said quietly.

"Still, it can't be good."

"Yeah. Now they'll look at the whole department, and it'll show up in the news for a while. Plus he could have been a good cop. The only good thing is that we tipped off the State guys ourselves. We don't have an internal investigation group. Never needed one before this. Makes us look a little better, anyway. I know he's dirty and all, but he was still a cop, you know?"

"I guess I do. In a way, I'm sorry I was right. Look, try to keep your head up. You got a couple of kicks in the balls, but it's not like there haven't been others."

"And won't be more, I know."

"Take care of yourself," I said, as if it meant anything at all.

Marisol came in a few minutes after we hung up. She caught me staring into space, sitting on the couch.

"Daddy?"

"Hi, honey. How was your day?"

"Great! I got my grade for the special project and I got an A, and they cancelled gym. If it's okay, Terri's coming over tonight," I agreed, remembering the call I'd made to her mom.

"That's slamming, Daddy. Mad good." I was pretty sure that meant she was happy. Then I stopped dead. If the news guy did what I wanted, then another little girl would be here, so I couldn't send Marisol and Mrs. Pina for their "visit" to keep them clear.

"Daddy?"

"What, 'Sol?"

"You just kind of stopped, like you remembered something."

"You don't miss much, do you?"

She went to her room to do some homework.

While she was doing that, I called Bill the TV guy. "No, I tried, but I couldn't get it into tonight's budget."

"Budget?"

"Yeah, we get twenty minutes, total, that's our budget and there was a huge fire down in Westerly. The local politician thing wasn't enough to make it in. I have a commitment for Monday, if nothing major breaks, though."

"That works out better, Bill. By the way, anyone hurt or anything in the fire?"

"Two firemen and a lady firefighter treated for smoke inhalation. How they inhale smoke wearing those masks is one of the mysteries of the business. Monday is better? Better for who? Sorry, whom."

"Just plain better."

"Okay, then, don't forget that I produce Sandra's exclusive, and you owe me some video."

"I owe you a free drink or two, too."

"Love a guy with a good memory. I'll be keeping an eye on our sleazy young politico."

I was making my interpretation of a fast food burger meal, when Mrs. Pina came to the door. Terri and her mom were behind her with an overnight bag. They were both grinning about something. "Thanks." I took her bag and walked with her to Marisol's room. Mrs. Pina began to set the table.

"Hey, there, muffin. Look who's here."

"Terri!"

"Hi, Marisol!" They were hugging and I liked how it looked. Marisol walked Terri to her room. I smiled, and waved to the two of them and went back into the kitchen. This would be good practice, for a full blown sleepover, I hoped.

I was an audience for supper. Mrs. Pina, Terri and Marisol chattered and laughed and teased me. It was a wonderful time. My graying hair came in for some humor, as did some of my speech. 'Sol got some mileage out of the way I said "Fall River, New Bedford and Warwick." I went to my room to dress for work.

I came out and they were sitting around the living room. The stereo was playing one of my jazz CDs. "You were born to wear black and white," said Mrs. Pina.

"That's because I have no color sense."

'Sol giggled.

"You ladies have a fun evening. Call me if you need anything." I couldn't help thinking that they couldn't wait for me to leave.

The Saab started on the first try.

***

Diane and Teddy were both working, and the hotel had hired a dance band, and had some specials on drinks. Of course, nobody changed the prices on the computer, so I was adjusting as I went.

It was busy, and the tips were good. Larry DaSilva stopped over and dropped the flashdrive. He stayed long enough for a beer and left for a weekend with his family. The crowd was friendly, older than usual because of the band, and was ordering drinks I hadn't mixed in a long time. It was fun, and my tricks earned some applause and a few big tips. When the shift ended, we were tired, but smiling.

I got into my car for the trip home. There was a set of headlights behind me. They were brighter than usual, and bluish. They followed me until I turned into my street, slowed after I turned, then sped off. He was almost quick enough to hide the plate. The car was a silver Infiniti sport sedan, just the kind of thing that Detective Asshole Petersen would drive. I wrote the number on the back of an envelope and carried it into the house with me.

It was ten or so when I woke up, and smelled coffee. We sat around for an hour, sipping coffee, eating muffins and trying to make plans for the day. Finally, I herded them into my car and headed north, then east for Cape Cod. I parked at one of the huge lots in Woods Hole, and we caught the ferry to Martha's Vineyard on time.

The day trip was a big hit with them. What was left of the weekend was spent playing board games, cooking, eating and dozing through the day. Very early on Monday morning, Marisol was in the bathroom when the phone rang. "A little shop talk?" Dana asked.

"Sure," I answered.

"Petersen."

"According to DaSilva, he gets arraigned this morning."

"That's for state and local stuff. We haven't taken our shot at him, yet. His involvement with the Congressman and the overall law enforcement overview thing is ours to use, as well."

"Has he got anything to trade?" Which reminded me. "I have to remember to tell DaSilva about the car that followed me."

Dana sounded tense, "You were tailed from the bar?"

"Might be paranoia."

"And they watched your house?"

"Might be somebody else."

"Did you think that maybe I should know about all of that? Being the FBI agent in charge of the case?"

"Dana, I should have, and I'm sorry. I guess I forgot about that, with what we have, it's like you work for the FBI, and I work for the hotel, but that isn't what's important."

"I'm a Special Agent." Her voice was cool and different.

"I did say I'm sorry. I think about you, not your job. That isn't trying to ignore it."

Her voice softened. "I think I understand, because I haven't been chasing you for answers, either. Could you maybe try, say, once a day, to ask yourself if there's anything you should tell Agent Kilroy? Then maybe you could think about how wonderful I am."

"Sounds reasonable."

"And if you forget, I'll shoot you in a place that will only hurt for a month or so."

"Can we get back to Petersen?"

"Sure. The US Attorney is looking. It looks like Petersen had a couple of friends in Newport, one or two in Warwick, and so forth. He was a busy boy, and probably worked into Massachusetts, Connecticut, too. That makes it Federal, and we should be able to make it. He can only trade his colleagues and the operations of the people who paid them off. Depends on what he can offer."

"So?"

"Somebody would have noticed something pretty soon, but, yes, we do owe you one."

"I'll take it out of your hide."

"Promises, promises," she said, just before we got off the phone.

Terri's mom showed up to drive the girls to school, and I was left alone.

***

It was the day for Petersen's arraignment, so I went to the courthouse. There were quite a few TV vans, with their phallic antennae extended towards the sky, with cameras and earnest-looking people speaking into microphones. As I threaded my way through the crowd, waving my brand new badge, I was stopped by a guy in jeans and a golf shirt. "Paul Costa?"

"Yes," I said warily.

"Bill Latronica." The TV guy that had followed Jason and Adam.

"Hi, it's good to meet you," I extended my hand.

"You, too. Listen, we're on for six o'clock tonight."

"Outstanding!"

"About the tape and the exclusive?"

"After the hearing, I'm parked over there. If you can bring a blank tape, can you dupe it in your van?"

"Yup. So, I'll meet you out here after the hearing? So what's your interest in this guy Petersen?"

"He was involved in the initial investigation into the Congressman's death."

"And?"

"And he wasn't, after awhile."

"Will I get anymore when you talk to Sandra?"

"Whatever you want," I said it over my shoulder, headed into the courthouse. At the door, I had to check my pistol into a lockbox, and empty my pockets and walk through a metal detector, twice. I was scanned by an electronic wand, and showed my permit three times. Finally, I made it in, and bullied myself into the courtroom.

DaSilva was there, with Phil Lacombe. They saw me at the same time, and Larry made a face. We squeezed in, three middle aged male butts packed into a space that could have handled one and a half. We rose when the judge entered, sat when she told us to, and waited for her to adjust her glasses and shuffle some papers. A clerk stood and whispered to her.

The clerk announced "Case this" and "Docket that" and "State of Rhode Island versus David Laramie Petersen." He was led in through a side door, handcuffed and dressed in a set of red surgeon's scrubs, with RICI stenciled over the pocket, on his butt and back. Both Phil and Larry looked down, Larry shaking his head.

Bail was set, and a Police Union Representative stepped forward to make bail on the bond. It all took less than fifteen minutes. The stripper girlfriend, dressed in a conservative pantsuit, handed

Petersen's lawyer a suit on a drycleaner hanger and a pair of shoes. I noticed that the shoes were two-toned and hideous. The judge rose, we rose, the judge left, and we shuffled out of the courtroom.

We hadn't exchanged a word, but I shook hands with them. I asked DaSilva if he would be around later, and he nodded. "By the way, that plate number, the one from the car that followed you? It came back as belonging to a rental company. I'll let you know who rented it." They left the courthouse together, but each seemed isolated. Cameras crowded around them, and they "no comment-ed" their way through and got into a marked police car. They had to use the lights to get the crowd to part.

There was a rush towards the front doors as Petersen appeared, with his girlfriend and lawyer. They finally pushed their way down the stairs to the lawyer's SUV. The District Attorney came out, made a speech and turned to walk back into the courthouse.

Bill Latronica walked up to me, looking gleeful. "I think this one is going to go national."

"And that's a good thing?"

"I'd rather work for a network than an affiliate."

He had thinning sandy hair, blue eyes and pale skin. Except for a plastic digital watch, he wore no jewelry, and his waist had fallen to make a rain gutter for sloping shoulders.

We walked over to my car, and I handed him the tape. "I need a copy," I said.

"I remember." At his van with its garish sides, he handed it to a technician who made a copy.

"I'll watch this on the way back to the studio," said Latronica. "Watch the news tonight, Paul. I wrote the narration almost word for word as you gave it to me. You might consider coming to work for us."

"No, thanks, too much excitement for me," I said with a grin. I could have added, "And I prefer honest work."

When I got home, I did some housework, and pulled together a clean outfit for work. There was a brownie mix in the cabinet, so I made that up, and had it cooling on a rack when my daughter got home from school. She was subdued, but didn't seem sad or upset, so I gave her a brownie and a glass of milk, poured myself a coffee and sat down with her. We chewed and sipped and looked at each other once in awhile. She gathered up her backpack and headed into her room to do her homework. "Anything you think you might need help with, muffin?"

"No, thanks, Daddy. It's all easy stuff."

I sauntered to her door. "Everything okay, honey?"

"Yeah, I guess I was hoping Dana would be here."

"You know that her job's way up in Boston, right?"

"Uh-huh. And it takes a long time to get there. We went to Boston to see the Red Sox."

"That's right. She'll come again, or maybe you and I can go up and visit her sometime soon."

"That would be cool!"

"I don't know when or how soon, but we'll see, okay, honey?"

"I know, Daddy, and I have to get all this dumb stuff done."

"And I have to go to work, tonight." She ran over and gave me a quick hug and kiss on the cheek. It felt sweet. I held on too tight, and maybe a bit too long, but she stayed with me.

"Love you, Daddy!"

"Love you, my sweet Marisol." She craned her head up to look at me.

"Do you miss Dana too?" It was tough to get anything past her, even if she was guessing wrong.

"You only hug me that tight when something's wrong, Daddy."

"Everything's okay, honey." I left her as Mrs. Pina came down the stairs.

She walked in, carrying her huge satchel. She patted it, and nodded.

"Tomorrow, Mrs. Pina, can you pick up 'Sol at school and take her to your sister-in-law's for the night?" I asked.

"Yes."

"From tonight, onwards, I will need you to be on guard. Tomorrow, you and Marisol have to be away, probably until Wednesday."

"Will it be over then?"

"One way, or the other."

"It shall be your way, Paul. You will do what you must."
"It won't come to that."
"Sometimes, I know about things, a little before they happen. Be hard, my son."

I felt my eyes sting, but managed to hold it in. "VooVoo, please take good care of my child for me."

Her eyes filled and spilled over. "She'll be safe, and so will you."
I got to work early, and watched the six o'clock news. Just before the weather, a short clip of Jason and Adam, parked two houses away from mine appeared. Then the magic words. "This video showing congressional candidate, Jason Morley, surveying one of the district's neighborhoods will soon be followed by others, as soon as suitable arrangements can be made. We look forward to obtaining more on this candidate's work with the voters."

Perfect. I had to move quickly, but for now, I had a bar, and a quiet night to look forward to. It was one that seemed to last forever.

After we closed, Mike met Sarah at the door, and Detective Sergeant Larry DaSilva met me, with his friend and partner Phil Lacombe. They all nodded at one another. Mike looked at me.

"It's okay, they just need to talk to me about something," I said.

He smiled and left, holding his beautiful wife's hand. They glanced back at us once, in unison.

"I suppose you have an explanation for tonight's news?" Phil Lacombe said.

"Sure do."

"I suppose you'd rather not share it with me?"
"Wrong. You and Larry and I need to talk, follow me home?"

Larry nodded, and we walked out to the parking lot.

***

"I don't like it," said Larry, when I finished.

"I'm not going to hang around, waiting for him to have his shot at my daughter." We were sitting in my kitchen, drinking coffee and eating brownies, and speaking softly. Phil was only picking at his.
"Could be entrapment," he said.

"Nope. We're not trying to get him to do anything criminal. I'm trying to give him something, and get him to stop harassing me. I just want to talk to him. I'll sign an affidavit to that effect."

"Just setting up a meeting?"

"Right."

"And we'll be there just to provide any protection that might be required," said Phil. "Does it matter that I really like them for the Congressman's murder?"

"No, it doesn't. They're suspects, because they stand to gain, I guess. I don't think they did it, but if you do, I trust your instincts."

"So why the news guy?" asked Larry.

"So that little prick doesn't make it to Congress. You saw those tapes."

"Smells like a set up to me," said Larry.

"And that's a problem? I fill out a report about the harassment; I set up the meeting with Jason and request police protection. The media happens to be there. "

"And then what happens?"

"I can't predict it. I can only provide the situation, and let it play out."

"Still smells, Paul."

"So you won't do it?"

He leaned over and whispered to Lacombe. It went back and forth a couple of times. "We'll do it. If nothing else, we get leverage."

I drafted the affidavit, laying out the plan, the need for police protection and read it before I typed it out, printing it from my computer. We all signed it, me as the party, and them as witnesses. There were three copies, all signed as originals, and they each slipped one into their pockets. "By the way, Larry, who rented the car that was following me?"

"Oh, yeah, I knew I forgot something."

"So, who was it?"

"The Morley's go-fer, Adam Birch."

"Still think I should let it go?"

"Yup."

"Would you?"

He ignored the question. Phil handed me a cell phone. "It's programmed to page both Larry and me. Set the meeting as we agreed, and page us with the time. If it has to change, call and let us know where and when. It'll get either of us or both anytime."

"See you around, Phil."

They left, driving their crappy looking Ford. It was late, so I decided not to bother with trying for some sleep until after Marisol left for school. I didn't want to miss her leaving. I sat down in front of the TV and pushed an old video in. When Marisol was three, her mother and I had taken her to Disney World. I'd rented a huge video camera, and Isabel had laughed at me dragging it around with us.

My wife's face and voice poured off the screen and my little girl smiled out at me. She stared in wonder at the characters and the rides. The tape ended with Marisol asleep on my chest while I snored, to Isabel's soft narration. The screen went blue and I turned it off.

I went to the kitchen table, and got out my cleaning kit. I cleaned and tested my Beretta, all of the magazines and checked each cartridge. I polished the loading ramp, to make sure it had no nicks to catch and jam. I took it all to my room and changed into a pair of jeans, deck shoes without socks and a tee shirt. I pulled a windbreaker from the closet, to cover the gun.

When Marisol got up, I told her about her visit to Mrs. Pina's sister-in-law. I'd expected lots of questions and arguments. She didn't disappoint me, but gave in. I packed her an overnight bag, and gave her a note, excusing her from school until Thursday. Mrs. Pina would pick up the bag right after 'Sol left for school. Our hugs and kisses were longer than usual, and she didn't complain. When her bus left, I followed it to school, dropping back, and pulling up close at times.

Chapter 22

The message light was blinking. One message. It started with a phone number, and the two-word message, “Call back.” It was Jason Morley’s voice. I hoped that my phone was still tapped.

“Okay, smart guy, I guess you didn’t get the message.”

“Hello, there Jason, nice to talk to you again.”

“I figured you’d back the fuck off.”

“Thank you for your concern, but I assume that there’s something you want?”

“I want all of the tapes and any other recordings you have. I want you to shut the fuck up. I want you to leave me and my family the fuck alone.”

“It’s good to hear your lyrical wit, I can understand why politics is your calling. If you want the tapes, you’re going to have to give me some sort of guarantee that you’ll be out of my life, my family’s life, and the lives of anyone I care about. It has to be a guarantee that I’ll believe, and it has to be one that will screw you up if you break it.”

“I know where your daughter is.”

Oh, no you don’t, asshole.

“Here’s what I know, Jason. I know you had Adam tail me from work; he really needs to work on his skills. I know that you need the tapes back. I know that you want to follow in Daddy’s footsteps, and you have to have all of your little piles of shit cleaned up before Petersen pukes up everything he knows. I want peace of mind; you want peace of mind. I don’t give a shit if you run for Congress. I don’t give a shit if you win. I just want you off of my radar screen and you want me off of yours. See that, Jason? We have a commonality of interest here. A confluence of needs, if you will.”

“So how do we make the deal?”

“We meet. I give you a video, and you give me your guarantee. Think hard about that guarantee, Jason. If I believe it, I’ll send you the originals of the recordings from Daddy's little treasure trove. One for each month I'm left alone. At some point, you and I will have developed a level of trust. I'll send you proof that all of crap has been destroyed, or I will send them to you for destruction. Unless you didn't learn a lesson from the old man."

"No fucking way."

"Then I send the tape I have to a certain TV personality, and you get to answer some hard questions. Then you get to answer even harder ones. After that, it'll get worse. I take my chances with you and your little organ grinder's monkey, or whomever you hired to do your daddy in."

"Fuck you! I didn't kill my father, asshole. You're all fucked up. You come after me for that and your head will be so far up your ass, you'll never see daylight. I'm thinking that if you want to play rough though, your little girl is sweet and might be fun, if you know what I mean."

"Then all bets are off." I was straining to keep my voice level. "You have a perfectly reasonable offer on the table. If you didn't kill your father, fine. Whoever did will either get caught or won't. Personally, that isn't important to me, since the cops know I didn't do it."

"What about that bitch down in DC, the TV slut?"

"Can't solve that one for you. You need to fix your problems one at a time."

"She gave you some information."

"Right now, I'm your problem."

"Where and when?"

"You, alone, at Quonset Point. Park at the Seabee movie theater at nine o'clock, tonight. Wait for me there."

"I don't like what that does for my security."

"It won't be full dark, and I really don't give much of a rat's ass what you like, since we're being so frank."

"Bring the flashdrive, asshole."

"Bring your guarantee, Jason."

He won the race to hang up first. I pulled the cell phone from my pocket and hit the keys to page Lacombe and DaSilva.

I made a call to Bill Latronica. He agreed to show up with a camera, some night vision equipment and a nondescript vehicle instead of the usual van. I told him where to set up, and how far away it would be.

"This had better be good, Paul."

"I can't tell you what's going to happen, for sure, but I think there'll be something interesting, and if you bring the mike that you use for football games, you should hear a few things. Be there by seven, and make sure you're well undercover. I'd suggest a truck that looks like a freight delivery. The loading dock faces the theater and should give a pretty good view."

"See you, there, Paul." I hung up and the phone rang almost immediately. I hadn't taken more than a step when I turned and picked it up.

"Paul? Larry. We'll be there early, just Phil and me. No one else knows, no leaks, it's set."

"Thanks."

"Don't look for us, okay?"

"I'm not the Newport village idiot, either."

"No, but it's been awhile for you."

"It's like riding a bike, they say."

"Yeah. Listen, just like we talked about, okay? Don't push him, just let it flow as if it's a real deal."

"Larry, if it looks like he really wants to deal, I go through with it. You'll be on your own for any criminal stuff that you want to make stick to him."

"All kinds of stuff I can do there, but it would be nice to catch him trying to tamper with evidence and show that 'Consciousness of guilt' you shysters love to throw around at the end of a trial. It gets him into a cell, and off the ballot, too. Sure you want to do it?"

"I'm sure I don't. I have to, though."

"Phil has a saying when we have to go through a door. He says, 'Let's just fuck 'em where they breathe.'"

"He's a poet."

"Just keep your head and do what we talked about, and we'll fuck 'em where they breathe."

"I'm on my way," I said, as if I was eager.

"So are we."

We hung up and I got into my car. I paused to look back at my house. The lawn did need to be mowed, and the trim needed paint. I wanted nothing more than to get to work on it. Instead, I pulled out and headed north, then east.

***

In its day, Quonset Point had been a sizable base, with Seabees and a naval air contingent. They could dock an aircraft carrier. It had been converted to civilian occupations. The airfield was part public and part Air Guard. Most of the existing buildings housed small to medium businesses except for a submarine builder, a company that built oil barges and a few others.

I parked at a daycare center, looking out at a sculpture of a huge Seabee, the tommy-gun-toting bumblebee with tools held in the other four legs and a sailor's hat on a ferocious but cute head. I opened a thermos of coffee, and looked at my watch. It was eight o'clock and my car was in deep shadow. The cell phone played a merry little tune I couldn't name, and I fumbled for the right little button to push so I could talk. "Yes?"

"Lacombe. We're in position. Where are you?"

I told him.

"Okay, we got it. You okay on the play?"

"It's fine. I got nice hot coffee, a comfy seat and a videocassette on the passenger seat. I have a nice view of the road."

"Betcha got a gun, too," said Phil.

"Did I forget to mention that?"

He chuckled.

"We're gonna fuck 'em where they breathe, Paul." He hung up. Or clicked off, or whatever you do with a cell phone.

I was scribbling on my legal pad, when I saw a car go by, moving slowly. I pushed the buttons on my cell phone and Larry answered, "Yeah?"

"Light blue or maybe gray, medium sized sedan, Rhode Island plates, I think."

“Wait one.” There was silence for an eternity, probably less than three minutes in the real world.

“Yup, got ‘em. He pulled into the theater lot, facing out. Lights are on, but it looks like two heads in the car.”

“Adam?”

“I’m guessing that it is.”

“I’m moving, now, Larry.”

“Hang up, we’ll be watching you. We’re close by.” I could feel my pulse coming up, and my toes bunching inside of my shoes. I had to force myself to click the cell phone off, and loosen my grip on it. I unsnapped the spare magazine pouches, and the thumb break strap on my holster, and made sure my jacket covered it.

I pulled onto the road, bore left and headed for the theater. I passed signs for construction and demolition companies, electronics and other businesses. I looked at the speedometer and realized that I was barely moving. I got it up to a reasonable speed, until I reached the theater with the car parked next to it.

I pulled up, facing them, leaving my lights on. Their doors were both opening.

“I said ‘alone,’ Jason.”

“I didn’t trust you, but it’s cool.”

“I want you both out of the car, with your hands in plain sight.”

They got out, holding their hands out to the side. “Turn in a complete circle and stay right where you are.”

“Look, Costa, this is stupid. Let’s get the deal done.”

“My guarantee?”

“I’m running for fucking congress, for chrissake. You think I can afford to be going after a fucking bartender? Or his stupid kid? I need to be clean, and I need those tapes.”

I thought about that. Who gives a shit if one more sociopath makes it into congress? “You are more dangerous to me, than I am to you,” he said.

“And your father’s murderer?”

“Look, go get him. I hope you catch him, or the cops do. I want that tape, and the promise that you’ll hold up your end of the deal.”

I had the tape in my left hand, and started towards them. My right arm swung back as I walked and the Velcro on the sleeve caught the side pocket flap. It pulled my jacket open, and my gun was visible. I saw Adam reaching to the small of his back. I dropped the tape, reaching up and back, lunging to one side at the same time. I drew my gun and brought it up two handed, chest high, centering my body mass directly at Adam's.

"Freeze, freeze, freeze!" It was Phil Lacombe, coming from behind a dumpster, into the open. He had a gun up in a two handed grip, right in front of his face.

"Phil, Shit!" and Larry was up and moving, with his gun out.

"You lying prick!" yelled Jason Morley, reaching under his left arm. Adam spun towards Lacombe and DaSilva, swinging his gun up one handed. There were explosions from him, and from the dumpster, and I saw Jason bring his gun up, awkwardly gripping it two handed. There was fire from the dumpster towards me, and I stepped to my right. Phil and Larry were firing in my general direction from over there, so I kept sliding right. Things slowed down and got silent. It was familiar to me. When I boxed, I never heard a sound, and everything seemed to happen in some kind of dreamy slow motion.

Without thought, my feet were planted shoulder width apart, left foot slightly ahead, both pointed at Jason. My gun was still at chest level, and I was pointing it at him, not aiming. I yelled at him to drop his gun. I couldn't hear myself, and there was a perfectly round blossom of orange and blue and yellow. I was on one knee, and my left shoulder was hot. I brought my gun up to eye level, dropping the barrel's line and sight onto Jason's midsection, I saw him struggling to bring his pistol under control, and level it at me. I had no cover, and I started squeezing the trigger. Twice quickly, then again. Grouped pairs of double taps. I continued doing it until the slide locked open on an empty magazine. I never heard my gun, but I felt the recoil. I couldn't get the magazine out of the pouch with my left hand. I ejected the empty and was fumbling right handed for a full one, when Larry walked up with his gun dangling at his side. "He's gone, Paul." My ears were ringing, and I could feel a burning and wetness at my left shoulder. I felt dizzy and nauseated.

"Jason?"

"Yeah, and Adam, and Phil."

"Phil?"

"Yeah. Adam got him twice, once in his hip, and one in the chest. Phil got him on his way down. I might have hit Adam once, but I don't think so. Phil's dying and he's still a better shot than me. Him and that stupid little fucking thirty-eight." DaSilva's voice was lifeless, but calm. "How bad, Paul?"

"What?" I asked, absently.

"You're hit, upper left arm, how bad?"

"Don't know." I was sleepy, and felt stupid. "Morley?"

"At least five hits, three in the upper chest, probably all fatal, and a couple more that he might have survived. He's dead."

I turned my head and vomited. There was just enough warning to turn away, but not enough to stop it. One second I was talking, the next I was throwing up.

"Jesus Christ on a crutch!" It was Bill Latronica. "I called an ambulance and the North Kingstown cops are on their way. State Cops, too. I don't think I forgot anyone. This is gonna be huge. I'm sorry about your partner, and we'll make sure we don't exploit it," he couldn't seem to stop talking. Not an abnormal reaction to what he'd seen, but I was tired and felt empty. I couldn't form sentences, or find the strength to make him shut up.

We set our guns on the hood of my car, and Larry got his badge out to wait. I was holding my left arm with my right. The pain felt good. I deserved to hurt.

Chapter 23

I'd been grazed just below my shoulder. The heat from the bullet had cauterized it, so the bleeding was minor. The EMT bandaged it, and they checked it out at the emergency room. A local and a couple of stitches after the doctor debrided it took care of it. "You'll get some amazing bruising soon, but there are no fragments. Some muscle trauma, but no nerve damage. You'll have an interesting scar." He looked at me as if I was supposed to say something.

"Thank you, Doctor." I wasn't feeling witty.

DaSilva waited for me, and we rode to the barracks in East Greenwich, in separate State Police cars. I was relieved to be alone. I had nothing to say to a man who'd lost his friend. The sling on my left arm made it hard to balance, and getting out of the car was a trial. The young trooper steadied me gently and led me into a conference room.

There was a TV with a VCR and DVD player on a rolling stand at one end. Bill Latronica was there, and he pushed a tape into the machine. "Thank you, Mr. Latronica, but we will require privacy from here on out." Her voice was familiar, yet strange. Dana Kilroy was standing next to a State Police Lieutenant, and she looked beautiful, remote, and cool. There wasn't a hint of warmth or welcome on her face or in her eyes.

"All present? Good. Let's review. A United States Congressman is murdered, and Commander Paul Costa is present to find the body. Time goes on, and Detective Sergeant DaSilva and Detective Lacombe, with the assistance of Commander Costa, set up a sting operation, involving Jason Morley. We have an affidavit to show why it was done. Good work on that one, Commander. Even the assistant U.S. attorney was impressed by your draftsmanship." Her every word was lashing at me.

"One way or another," the sarcasm was almost physical, "a camera crew was on hand to film the whole thing. The recording that was to be traded showed Jason Morley having sex with an unidentifiable, unconscious woman. In the meantime, you bush league hot dogs managed to turn a simple little sting into the shoot out at the O.K. Corral. The result is that a congressional candidate is dead, shot by the good Commander there, eight times no less, the candidate's aide is dead, shot by the late Detective Lacombe, three times. Commander Costa is wounded by the aforementioned candidate and the first time the North Kingstown police, the Rhode Island State Police," she gazed at me, "and the FBI find out is after the smoke clears. Did I leave anything out? Let's all take a nice look at the home movies, now. Perhaps I should order some pizza or popcorn?"

The sound was excellent, and the images were clear. My conversation with Jason was there, and I saw myself walking towards them. Then Adam reached for his gun, and I pulled mine, Phil stepped completely out of cover, yelling and the tape ended with Larry kneeling at his friend's side. I heard myself yelling and I saw myself hit and dropping to my knee, the burst of fourteen shots, and fumbling for a new magazine, before Larry got to me.

"So, what happened?" said the Lieutenant, speaking for the first time. His voice was higher than I expected. He rewound the tape and played it again, in slow motion. "It looks fine, and then the gofer goes to his gun, and all hell breaks loose."

Dana was looking at me. It was a look filled with anger. "Anything to add, Commander? Did you wish you had more bullets or anything?"

"No, Agent Kilroy. I think the video speaks for itself."

A man in civilian clothes at the back of the room spoke up. I hadn't noticed him before. His suit looked too big in places, as if he'd taken it off and put it back on. My watch showed two-fifteen when I glanced down at it. He'd probably been dragged out of bed to this meeting. "I agree, in this case. I'm the Assistant US Attorney that Agent Kilroy referred to. We'll be conducting more rigorous investigations, but I see nothing criminal, yet." He walked out without a further word.

"While it appears that Agent Kilroy's characterization of you three as bush league hot dogs fits, and there are some jurisdictional issues to work out, I agree with the AUSA, there. In the meantime, I'll be in touch with your chief, Sergeant DaSilva," said the State Police Lieutenant. "I expect you'll be in for some heat on your end. Off the record?"

"Yes, Lieutenant," answered DaSilva, looking him straight in the eyes.

"May I express my condolences on the loss of your partner. He seemed to me to be exceptionally brave and clear-headed under the circumstances, and may well have saved Mr. Costa's life."

"Thank you, Lieutenant."

Dana smiled, but there was a bitter curl to her lip that I hadn't seen before. I looked back at her, and she nodded as I left.

DaSilva drove me home, arranging to have my car brought home for me. "Tough to drive your car with just one hand," he said.

"Larry?"

"I think maybe you and I should hold off until tomorrow," he said. "I lost the best friend I ever had tonight. He was dying anyway, and maybe he was hoping to get shot, instead of flickering out with the doctors, but I wasn't ready."

"Can I say that I'm sorry?"

"Yeah, but leave it there, okay?"

He needed to get used to the idea. He had to be hurt and angry for a while. Maybe he needed to have his wife hold him and to hug his kid. I needed to hug my kid.

He steadied me as I got out of the car, and watched to make sure I made it to the door. I spent an hour or so on my knees in front of the toilet, finally walking to my room in a kind of daze.

By eight o'clock, I staggered out of bed. I removed the sling and tossed it into the trash. It felt about like I thought it would. It hurt. I made some coffee, and an English muffin, then called Mrs. Pina.

"I know, Paul, it's all on the television. I have Marisol locked away from it, but she saw enough to know what happened."

"Damn."

"She is okay, Paul. She understands, I think." I wanted to ask her what she'd said, but she had more wisdom and judgment in her little finger than I had anywhere.

"Thank you, Mrs. Pina. I have no way to repay you."

"There is nothing I would want. Is there trouble with the law?"

"Probably not. They want this over with."

"I think you are right. They said on the news that they believe that the son had his father murdered."

"They are wrong."

"Yes? Well, what does it matter, now? 'Sol is safe, and things can go back to the way they should be."

Except that a good man was dead, the woman I cared for was furious with me, and my daughter watched a film of me gunning a man down in a close quarters gunfight.

Still, Lois, Sandra and probably lots of other women could breathe again, knowing he was gone, along with Adam. I spent the day on the couch, waiting for Marisol and Mrs. Pina to come back. I turned down the phone, and let the answering machine handle all of the calls. I dozed once in awhile. When the ache in my arm woke me, I popped a couple of leftover pain pills and went back to sleep.

I finally woke up and flipped on the television. It didn't take long. The tape was edited, but they showed Adam reaching for his gun, and Phil stepping out. They cut it there, and showed me shooting Jason. They blanked out the jerking puppet-with-strings-cut movements as my bullets slammed into his body. I saw myself wounded again. There was a greenish tint to the images, because of the light enhancement, and my blood was a splash of chartreuse arcing over my head as I slipped to my knee.

The District Attorney came on for a brief interview. No charges to be filed. Detective Lacombe died doing his duty in the finest traditions of law enforcement. Mr. Costa was cooperating with the investigation as a licensed private investigator, licensed to carry a firearm.

He hinted, without saying so, that this would clear the death of Congressman Richard Morley. Detective Sergeant DaSilva would deliver the eulogy at Philip Lacombe's funeral the next day and the city of Newport could be proud of their police department, despite recent disclosures about one bad apple. I turned it off.

I had managed a shower and a shave, and was dressed before Mrs. Pina and 'Sol arrived. They were both quiet, and Marisol seemed distracted. She hugged me, hard, and went to her room to unpack. We had the rest of the day off. I wrote Mrs. Pina a receipt for two month's rent, and handed it to her.

"What is this, Paul?"

"I can't charge family the same as I would somebody else."

"You don't owe me this much."

"I can't pay you what I owe you, VooVoo."

She smiled. "Okay, if you say so, my son."

Marisol came out of her room, and was wiping her eyes. "Daddy?"

"Yes, muffin?" She shook her head.

"I'm too old to be 'muffin' anymore, Daddy."

"I slipped, honey."

"Daddy, what happened?" Mrs. Pina was looking hard at me, so I figured it was time to give her as much of the truth as I could.

"'Sol, let's go sit in the kitchen and I'll tell you about it."

She almost brightened. "I'll make coffee."

The version I gave her didn't leave a lot out. I shied from rape and drugs and pure evil. I felt like it was a lot more than any eleven year old should know, but she deserved the truth. She'd watched her father, who never spanked her, shoot a man.

"Sergeant DaSilva's friend is dead?"

"Yes, honey."

She stared down at the kitchen table.

"Honey, do you think we should go see Doctor Don?" He was a great counselor and helped us both with our own grief and mourning.

"Maybe."

That meant "Yes," so I jotted down a note to make an appointment.

"Daddy, what's it like, to kill a man, I mean?"

"It isn't good, honey. You feel sick and empty all at once. It's like you did something too big. The only thing that makes it a little okay is that he was trying to kill me."

"I'm glad he's dead, Daddy. I mean I'm not glad he's dead, but I'm glad you aren't. Would he have hurt me, Daddy? I remember him at the school, and he seemed nice, but some of the girls said he was creepy."

"I wouldn't have let him, muffin."

She nodded. I decided to let her think about it, and see if she wanted to talk later on. After our brunch, I played the messages from the machine. Almost all were from reporters, one from Sandra, two from Bill Latronica and one from DaSilva. Nothing at all from Dana. My stomach shrank or fell or something. It definitely felt lousy.

"Sergeant DaSilva."

"Paul Costa, returning your call, Larry."

"Hi." There was a pause. "Is your daughter okay?"

"I think so. I think she will be."

"Good." He still sounded half asleep. "Paul, I think if you can manage it, it would help if you could come to Phil's funeral."

"I was hoping it would be okay with you if I did."

"Yeah, that would help," He'd already said that. It wasn't like him to be vague.

"How are things at work?"

"Oh, the chief thinks I'm an asshole. He thinks I should consider my retirement benefits."

"He's got his head up his ass."

"Nah, no room. He's got the States and he's got the FBI up there, reaming him out already. You know, shit flows downhill."

After a pause, he continued. "Both Phil and I wanted the Congressman's killer."

"According to the DA we got him," I answered softly.

"You don't believe that anymore than I do."

"Doesn't matter."

"Bullshit. I think you have the answer, whether you want to admit it or not."

"I don't know it. I have a couple of guesses,"

"You're a good guesser."

"I'll see you at the funeral."

"See you there." He hung up without saying any more.

My next call was to Latronica. "Sandra's been calling me all day. She wants to know about scheduling that interview," he said.

"I have a message from her, too. I'll be talking to her, and I haven't forgotten our deal. I want to get through the funeral."

"Funeral? Oh, yeah, the cop who was killed."

This was getting to be a hard guy to like. "Yes, the cop who was killed. I'll be in touch with Sandra and once we get something going, I'll make sure you're in on it." I hung up without saying anything else. I dialed Sandra's number.

"So, hello. Long time no nothing."

"Nothing to say until now, Sandra."

"No? Bill Latronica has you as Wyatt fucking Earp, on tape no less, and you didn't think I might want in on a story like that?"

"I promised you an exclusive interview, Sandra."

"It'll be old news by then."

"Really?"

"Yes, Paul, really. I know it sucks for people in the real world, but your fight and the loss of that detective will be page three tomorrow and back section by Friday. Won't even make the local broadcast after his funeral."

"Even if the Congressman's killer is still on the loose?"

A breath hissed into my ear. "Is he?"

"Or she, Sandra, don't be sexist."

"Screw you, Costa. Seriously, is there still a story, here?"

"You tell me. The whole ménage, Morley, the son, Adam, the killer of the congressman. Sex, lies and videotape. This could put you as a permanent on one of the cable channels as a criminal conspiracy insider. You could get funny horn rimmed glasses and bad neck ties, and—"

She interrupted. "If you are screwing me, here, I swear I'll come up there and tell the world that you're gay or something." She got me to smile.

"On a more serious note, Paul, are you okay?"

"If I said it's fine would you believe me?"

"Probably not, but you'll say it anyway, right, tough guy?"

"No point in talking about it, Sandra. It's pretty awful. If it wasn't for me, a good cop'd be alive, and so would Morley and Adam."

"I knew Morley and Adam. They're no loss, and I saw the whole tape, you all tried to keep them alive. You can kick the shit out of yourself if you want to, Paul. I'm no shrink, but I know about hurting. I think you did your best, tried to do it right, and those two goons made it go sour. What's the other cop saying?"

"DaSilva. Larry DaSilva. He isn't much of a talker."

"You think he blames you?"

"No, I think he blames himself."

"Christ, Paul, you've found yourself a soul mate. Look, solve the mystery, call me and I'll make you the most famous bartender in Rhode Island. People will be falling all over themselves to tip you. Beautiful women will throw themselves at you. Oh, wait; we already do that, don't we? Skip that one." She paused.

"Seriously, call me if you need to talk. I think you did the right thing, and I think the cops did the right thing. It isn't your fault."

"Everything is somebody's fault, Sandra."

"Sure. I have to run." She hung up.

Marisol had been standing in the living room's archway until I was off of the phone. "Daddy, I need something dark to wear to the funeral, and I don't have an outfit that fits. I want to look right."

"The funeral is at ten tomorrow morning, so let's go pick something up now. I don't have to work tonight. Mrs. Pina, would you like to come?"

"No, thank you. I should go to the funeral, but I have plenty of funeral clothes. You make sure of that at my age."

We headed for the nearest mall. She picked out a pair of loafers, dark tights and a navy blue dress, with a hat. I was pleasantly surprised to find it all on sale.

I checked and found that I had a dark suit, still in the dry cleaner's bag, with a white shirt and gray tie. We avoided broadcast TV, and I played rented videos until it was time for her to go to bed. She was reading a book to me, when she stopped and looked up. "Will Dana be at the funeral?"

"I don't know, honey."

"Can you call her?"

"How about if I call her and let you talk to her?"

I was a coward. Still, I had to find a way to talk to Marisol about Dana and how maybe things had changed.

"She'd like to talk to you, Daddy," she said, handing me the receiver.

"I was kind of hard on you, at the State Police Barracks."

"Yes, you were."

"You screwed up, you know."

"I got that."

"And we need to talk."

"I'll be at the funeral." We sounded like strangers, arranging a first time meeting. "I'll meet you right afterwards."

"I know an ice cream bar that Marisol might enjoy."

"Okay, that sounds fine."

I thought about the passionate and lusty woman. I thought about that, for a long time that night. I thought about it until dawn. I finally felt sleepy, and it was time to get moving.

***

Larry DaSilva was in full uniform, including gloves and medals. Some of them I didn't recognize, but I saw a Silver Star along with two Purple Hearts. I assumed the others had to do with his police work. There was a black mourning ribbon around his badge, but he looked erect and well rested.

His eulogy was plain spoken and low key. Police from all over the Northeast were there, and they applauded. Cameras followed us to the cemetery and filmed the volleys and Larry, standing at rigid attention, his hand up in a salute that would have made a Marine DI proud.

He walked right over to Marisol, Mrs. Pina and me. He bent from the waist, took my daughter's hand, and shook it gently. "Thank you for coming, Miss Costa," he said, formally. She took one look into his devastated face and threw her arms around his neck.

"I wish you hadn't lost your friend, Sergeant." I heard cameras clicking all over the place, and began to regret coming, until I looked at DaSilva and saw how much that hug had meant.

Mrs. Pina smiled sadly at him. "I hope you will accept my condolences." She had struck the correct note. Still, she probably got more practice than I had.

DaSilva's wife was a pleasant woman, with short blonde hair cut in some kind of bob, wearing a simple black dress. She had short, clean nails and I got the feeling that whatever she did would be low maintenance. She looked like someone who had to be ready for something on short notice, so she kept things simple. He introduced us and she shook my hand and Marisol's, then Mrs. Pina's.

"Larry speaks well of all of you, Mr. Costa. He seems to consider you a friend, though he'll never admit it. Your daughter is wonderful."

"She gets me by in lots of places, ma'am."

"I hope your troubles are behind you, Mr. Costa. I really liked Phil and in a way, I think this was the best thing that could have happened. That sounds awful, but he didn't deserve to suffer that way. I like to hope. I'm a policeman's wife, and we're good at hoping." She and Mrs. Pina nodded to one another, like members of a secret club. She walked away for a short distance to give Larry and me a moment, looking like a woman who'd once been a cheerleader, or maybe a softball player.

"I have to go," said Larry, shaking my hand, "and this is too public to talk. I'll stop by the bar tonight."

"I'll see you there."

"Thanks for coming. All of you." He walked off, looking self-conscious, with all of the cameras. When we walked to my car, Dana was waiting. She was standing next to it, with her arms folded. She was wearing a charcoal gray suit, with her hair up very tightly. She looked stunning in a severe way.

Marisol walked quickly to her and put her arms around her waist. Dana hugged her back and looked over 'Sol's hat at me. The expression was neutral, except for the hurt around her eyes. Despite her careful makeup, I could see the effect of a long night. She looked tired, and I wanted to hold her. When she released Marisol and stood, Mrs. Pina and I were standing in front of her.

Marisol and Mrs. Pina looked from one to the other of us, and stepped back. It was slow, but we came together, and my arms slipped around her waist, she took my shoulders, but it was like holding a statue. She was careful of my arm, but that wasn't the problem. While I held her, I could feel that she wanted it to stop. I gave in and released her.

"Paul, we do need to talk."

"You told me everything you need to just now."

Mrs. Pina made an odd noise, a kind of click from the back of her throat. We all turned and looked at her.

"Marisol, please get into the car." She did and closed the door.

She stood for a moment, looking at Dana, then she turned towards me. "Stop talking. Stop trying so hard. You think it's a decision to make. It isn't; you either have something together, or you don't."

She stepped into the car like a queen and softly closed the door.

"Paul?" asked Dana quietly.

"Yes?"

"Are you sorry you killed him?"

"I'm sorry that Detective Lacombe is dead."

"That isn't what I asked."

"I know. No, I guess I'm not. He drew a gun, shot me, and I shot back, and he's dead. He had a better chance than I had. He ruined a lot of lives, or helped to ruin them. He threatened my daughter to control me, and he tried to kill me. I don't think I'm sorry. I'm sick, my head hurts, my arm is giving me fits and I'm having trouble sleeping. But I'll never be sorry for killing him."

"You kept me in the dark. You kept me away from it. I thought I made you understand how important that was. You emerged victorious and unscathed—"

"You can try to make me into the bad guy, but no matter what, they tried to kill two cops and me. To you, I'm wrong because I didn't tell you about it; or maybe even because I won. Tough shit."

I managed to get the “shit” out before she turned and walked away, with a stride that I admired. There was the hell of it. I wasn’t what she wanted.
When I got into the car, I was careful to close the door gently and drove out of the cemetery slowly. Neither ‘Sol nor Mrs. Pina spoke, but reproach was clear to see on their faces in the mirror.

Chapter 24

Larry DaSilva walked into the bar shortly after nine o'clock. It was a slow night. My left arm was throbbing, and my feet were killing me. Even my ribs felt a little tender. "Evening, Paul."

"Evening, Larry," I answered, sliding a coaster in front of him, and mixing him a whiskey sour without being asked. I added a glass of ice water and poured myself a coke from the gun.

He picked up his glass, and held it up. "Absent friends."

I returned the toast with my coke and we sipped quietly for a moment.

"Agent Kilroy?" he asked. I shrugged.

"Beats me, Larry. I don't know anything about women."

He looked at Diane, standing near the wall, leaning hip shot and looking sensual without effort. "Makes two of us I guess." He held up his glass again. "To women, life's second greatest mystery."

I clicked my glass against his and we drank them both down. "What's first?" I asked.

"Hell if I know, but I'll be damned if I'll give women first place."

I had to go down the bar to a customer. I took his cash and rang it up before I went back to Larry.

"I'm not ready to talk, I guess," he said, "can I come by your house tomorrow?"

"Sure. Another?"

"No, I have to get home." He walked out, right past Dennis Pereira walking in.

Dennis was alone, and came to the bar. He extended his hand to me, and sat down in one of the stools. He picked the one that wobbled a bit. He got up and glared at it, moved down one stool and ordered a Perfect Manhattan.

He said, after taking one sip, "This is really good. I never had one before. I think it's my new drink."

"Good."

"I guess I came to make sure that you're okay. I know I'm barking up the wrong tree and all." He'd driven for an hour instead of making a phone call. I took his hand, and gripped it hard. It was painful, but I raised my left hand to hold his elbow with it. Words wouldn't come. We told each other old stories, the ones that we already knew. There were people we talked about, some girls and old friends and enemies. He told me how pretty my daughter looked on TV and said I didn't look as old in person as I did on camera. The shift passed and he left before closing. All he did was drive down and have a drink. All he did was talk to me like an old friend.

"So, who was your cute little friend?" Diane was leaning slightly over the bar.

"An old friend, that's all."

"I'd wrap him up in a handkerchief and take him home. Maybe put him on a shelf or something."

"I'll let him know."

"Paul, you don't sound so hot, are you okay?"

"Sure."

"Uh-huh. Well, I'm not going to push, but you'll figure out a way that it's your fault. You shouldn't have that much gray hair, for God's sake."

My ride home gave me some time to think, but I wasted it. I thought aimlessly, circling around how I was feeling. I'd had lots of practice at loss, but somehow I had never gotten to be good at it.

I was surprised in a way, that when I went to bed, I slept. My jaws and teeth were sore when I woke, so I knew I'd been grinding them.

Chapter 25

When I woke up, Marisol had already left for the day, and I was alone. Her note said she had to stay after school and asked me to pick her up there. I made a pot of coffee, and sat down with my legal pads. I listed the people who might have killed the congressman. I made a list of what it would take to do it. It wasn't a long list; it had "money," access to information and motive."

The killing was personal, the knife in the ear said so. Never listened? Didn't hear? The equivalent of a stake through the heart? The message could be any or all of them, or none of them at all. The knife was impromptu, with an evil serendipity surrounding it.

Who's left? Whoever had the money and the access to information; who had the motive and the trust of a pro.

When the phone rang, I started, but picked it up. "Hello?"

"Paul? This is Larry. Larry DaSilva."

"Hi, Larry. I was just thinking about you."

"That's nice, Paul, but I won't play dress up."

"Feeling more like yourself?"

"It'll be awhile. The good news is that I think I will someday. Yesterday, I had my doubts."

"Yeah."

"How about you and Dana Kilroy?"

I was silent.

"Want to talk about it?" he asked.

"I already told you that you're a piss poor cupid."

He almost laughed. "Do you still need one?"

"Screw you, Larry."

"On another subject?" he said after a moment, "The Gentleman from Rhode Island?"

"My phone still tapped?"

"Hell if I know. I haven't heard a tape in awhile, but it's possible."

"Was the house ever bugged other than the phone?"

"Nope."
"Want some coffee?"
"Did you make it or did Marisol?"
"Larry, what are you trying to say?"
He chuckled. "Nothing, nothing. Give me a half hour."
"Half an hour." I put a pot of coffee on while I waited. I was drinking some of it when there was a knock on the door. I made sure my gun was at my waist, at least. Larry DaSilva was at the door, with a box of donuts.
Leave it to a cop, I thought, noticing that it was from the best place in town. He dropped the box on the kitchen table, grabbed one and ran back out to his car, returning with a file folder, some colored pens, a clipboard and three videocassettes. "I'm on leave, Paul, so this file that I'm holding doesn't exist. Naturally, I wouldn't have a file I'm not supposed to."
"You sound pissed off."
"Damned District Attorney. He's going to officially close the case by next Friday, unless 'something else crops up on his radar screen.'"
"You'd think a lawyer wouldn't mix his metaphors."
"You'd think he'd want to solve the fucking case, too."
"Let's take a look at that file," I said.
"Then?"
"Then we fuck 'em where they breathe."
He smiled.
Most of the file I'd seen. It had some investigative notes about me, about the murder itself, the M.E's report and Coroner's conclusions, references to multiple evidence numbers, and most recently, the DNA evidence showing that Miranda, the call girl had deposited three pubic hairs to mix with the Congressman's. That cinched that part of it, anyway. There were lots of pages of interviews with the ladies on the tapes from Morley's cellar. I flipped through them, and then checked the conclusion of each. All of them said, "N.R.A." at the end. I pointed to one of them, with my eyebrows up.
"No reportable action," he said.
I took out my notes and gave him the qualification list I had come up with. He nodded.

"Makes sense."
"Any of these women fit? Do their families?"
"We have to check. I have some tapes. I thought you'd like to take a look, so I brought copies."
I grabbed a calorie bomb from the donut box and brought the box and the coffees into the living room. I was eating the donut while he sorted them, I was grateful for Marisol. If it hadn't been for her, the VCR still would be blinking "12:00 Sunday."
"I'm going to do this in a particular order, okay?" he said.
"Works for me."
The TV screen went blue, then the little "Play 0:00:00" came up. The sound came up before the picture. It was Camille Morley's voice. "Dick, I know that you're in the mood, but you've been drinking and you know I don't like that."
A male voice came from right next to the camera. "Look, Camille, it's been a long time, and I really want you."
"Maybe if you could wait until morning?" Her voice sounded frightened. It was nothing like the mistress of her home voice that I had heard not long before.
The Congressman, demanding as he was when I met him, came back. "I don't ask you that often and I always manage to rise to the occasion during those ever so rare times when you seem to be interested. I'm sorry about your frigidity, but I do have my own needs." I felt itchy, but couldn't put my finger on the reason. It was somewhere between embarrassment and shame.
He came into view wearing boxer shorts and a tank style sleeveless undershirt. I'd overheard Diane calling them "Beater shirts," because all of the wife beaters on TV seemed to wear them.
Morley flipped the sheets and blankets off of his wife, who was wearing pajamas of some shiny fabric. He reached to her waist and pulled them down. She lifted her hips, and he threw them to the foot of the bed. She was looking directly at the camera. I'd seen the expression she wore in a photograph somewhere, but I couldn't place it.
She was lying on her back, with her knees up, pressed together. I was looking at a woman, nude from the waist down, but didn't want to

see more. I wanted to close my eyes and block my ears. There was nothing about this that I wanted to know. He knelt so that he was above her, looking down. "Camille, you still look wonderful," he said, as he reached with both hands to pry her knees apart. Then he mounted her. There was no better way to describe it. It was like watching a stud mounting a dam. I thought of lovemaking, and realized that he behaved like a guy standing at a urinal. There was pressure, and convenient relief.

She continued to look at the camera with that same lifeless expression. Her hands stayed at her sides. Once he reached and grabbed her hair, pulling her face around to kiss her. As soon as he released her, she turned her head back to stare, seemingly straight at me.

I felt sweat starting at my hairline and reached for the remote. Larry put his hand out. "No. It doesn't last much longer."

Sure enough, a minute or two later, Morley started bucking with no particular rhythm, "Fuck me back, you frigid bitch, what's the matter with you?" He started grunting, and she gave a slight lift with her hips. That seemed to be enough for him, and he groaned, and sagged onto her. As he rolled off, he pulled up his shorts.

"How was it?" he asked.

"Just fine. Thanks for being so patient with me." Her voice was lifeless. The picture froze, and I was left looking into her eyes.

Then I remembered. It hadn't been a woman in the picture at all. It was an American Marine, standing guard over a row of body bags. Had he not been standing, holding his M-16, he would have looked as dead as his comrades on the ground before him.

"Is that it, Larry?" My throat was dry, and it came out as a scraping sound. I cleared my throat.

"Yeah, the rest of the tape is just like that. Him sleeping and her staring right at us, until it runs out."

"The others that bad?"

"One is."

The third was different. Morley wasn't in it, and his wife was a joyful participant. The man's hair struck a chord, but I couldn't quite reach a point of recognition.

Just as they reached for each other, Larry clicked the remote and switched the tape off. I looked at him, a little surprised.
"This one's different, Paul. It's a couple making love. I saw it, and I'm embarrassed about it. If I just said that you never see the man's face, would you be willing to let it go?"
I nodded slowly.
Larry was staring off into the middle distance, and I felt as if I could almost touch his concentration, like a physical manifestation. His fists were clenched, knuckles white, and his brow furrowed, all the way back to his clean, shining scalp.
I ran my hands over my face. "I shouldn't even say it out loud, but that is one son of a bitch who needed to die."
"Yeah. Now, what else?"
Larry and I were still sitting in front of the television. The tapes were out of the machine and next to him on the couch. We had emptied the box of donuts. I was pretty proud of myself for switching the coffee maker off. In the past two and a half years, I'd burned out three of them. I had two pages of notes, and he had diagrams in multiple colors. So we knew what we knew. I closed my eyes and tried to remember the bar during that night.
I never saw anyone who stuck out. There was the guy with his hands all over the woman, and there were the three middle aged couples at the table. One couple was holding hands, under the table. They all looked wealthy and well dressed. There were a few other customers, but that was it. Someone had seen me slicing limes and lemons. Someone saw where the knife went.
There was a table with three couples. One of the couples was holding hands under the table. From behind, they looked like typical tourists, nothing remarkable. They never let me see their faces. I had been tending bar for quite awhile, and I always tried to see my customers' faces. They never let me see their faces. They were slim and fit and carried themselves as if they were attractive.
They never let me see their faces. They held hands. "Larry?" Something in my voice got his attention.
"Yeah?"

"You and Petersen interviewed everyone who'd been at the bar, right?"
"Sure, of course. Nobody saw—" he stopped dead. "Somebody did more than see. Aw, shit!"

Chapter 26

"Paul?"

"No question about it."

DaSilva was rubbing his eyes as he spoke, "From behind will never hold up in court."

"I bet that your interview will ring a bell with them. They gave you names and addresses and phone numbers, right?"

"Of course," he said.

"Ever try to contact anyone for a follow up?"

"Not me, I left that and the witness interviews to—oh fuck me." It came out as a groan.

"Petersen, right?"

He was biting his lip. "Yes, that's drudge work and it always goes to the junior guy."

"Petersen might have seen an opportunity."

"Oh yeah, that bastard has a nose for nasty shit. He would have switched bosses, right on the spot. Now I have to check all of the interviews. Phone numbers, names and addresses. Get alibis. Break those alibis. If they have an alibi, we know that it's bullshit. Maybe they came in and out, one day. Minimum exposure. So why would they even be there?"

"If you hated somebody that much, wouldn't you want to be sure he was dead?"

"Using the knife to make some sort of point, I guess. Hell of a risk."

"On the other hand, they still might get away with it."

"Nope."

"Nope?"

"They aren't going to get away with it." His expression was neutral.

"Larry, we are a long way from anything you can bring to the DA."

"I know. But you know what, Paul?" He didn't wait for my answer.

"I've been a cop for a long time. My best friend on the job is dead because of them, and if that isn't enough, they have seriously messed

up your life. They killed a call girl, like throwing away a gun or a knife. They play with people, as if we're tokens in some board game," he pointed with his chin to the Monopoly set.
"What about your job, Larry?"
"I got six weeks of vacation and sick time coming to me. The department is understanding, since I lost my partner." He said the last part with some bitterness. "I'll check the interviews, make copies of it all, and put in for some time off."
"And you're on leave for this," I said. "Could cause you career problems."
"Tough toenails."
"Toenails?"
" My wife doesn't like me to say 'shit.'"
"How does she feel about you risking your pension?"
"She'd probably rather I said 'shit.' She's known me since I was a brand new Marine. I can't surprise her, anyway. I'll stay in touch; we'll talk tonight, okay?"
"I'll be working, but you know where I'll be."
"I'll drop by as soon as I can."
He left carrying the videotapes and file. While Larry had been there, I'd turned down the phone, leaving the answering machine to deal with any incoming calls.
There was only one. I picked up the phone and dialed her number. If I remembered her schedule, she'd be home. She was.
"Hello?"
"Hello, Sandra. Paul Costa, returning your call."
"Uncommonly decent of you, Paul."
"Am I in some sort of trouble?"
"Bet your ass you are."
"Why's that?"
"I want that interview. My boss wants that interview. His boss wants it."
"When I do it, it won't be for them."
She was silent. "Thank you, " she said. "I think that was pretty nice."
"Sandra, there's stuff I know and can prove, and there's stuff I know but can't prove."

"And this is important to me because?"
"Because I'll give you the first word on the arrest or arrests, if any. Because after that, I'll tell you how it happened, on camera, with that dweeb Bill producing, because I promised him that. And most of all, because we're friends and I need elbow room. Probably only for a little while longer."
She breathed quietly for a moment. "You silver-tongued bastard, you."
"Thank you. I try to use this power wisely. For good and not for evil."
***
I was early picking Marisol up, so I went to the office to meet her. The hurley-burley had calmed down to tired teachers and secretaries closing out their day.

Chapter 27

“Daddy?” We were buckling our seat belts in the school’s parking lot.

“Yes, honey?”

“I have a permission slip for a field trip, and are you a murderer?”

I almost missed the last part. “Honey?”

“If you kill somebody, that’s murder, and you killed that Mr. Morley who came to the school, so you must be a murderer. That’s what a couple of the boys said.”

I took a deep breath. “Well, I shot that man, and he’s dead because of it, right?”

She nodded. I drove in silence until I was out onto the main street. The lawyer in me warred with her daddy. I’d fired at least one counselor for talking down to her. I wanted to pick my words so that she understood, but not commit the sin.

“Daddy?”

“I’m thinking, honey. I want to make sure I make sense.”

“Because I’m only a little girl?” She said it with some heat.

“It isn’t you, honey, it’s your dad the dope that needs to slow down, okay?”

“You’re not a dope.”

“You’re not a little girl, unfortunately.”

“Almost a teenager.”

I thought teasing was a good sign. “Don’t remind me. Okay, if I screw up or start acting like you’re a little girl, you stop me and I’ll start again, right?”

She nodded and turned in her seat to look at me.

“Marisol,” There, a good start. I didn’t call her a baby name. “Jason Morley was the son of the Congressman who was murdered at the hotel bar. I found out that they did terrible things to people. There are quite a few women who have a lot of bad times because of them.

Is that enough explanation?" I said it as if I was ready to answer any questions she had. I was praying that she wouldn't.
She nodded solemnly. "Jason, I mean Mr. Morley seemed nice, when he was at the school. He didn't look like a bad man."
"Bad guys don't wear black hats. The only way to tell is by what they do, not what they look like or act like. Remember about strangers?"
She rolled her eyes. "I remember, 'even people who act nice,' blah blah blah."
"Blah, blah, blah?"
"I didn't think you'd want to hear it all.
"Is that why I was visiting with Mrs. Pina and her sister?"
"That's right."
"Was Dana there?"
"Nope."
"Is that why she's mad?" She had her mother's mind and a child's openness.
I was determined to be honest. "Yes, but she's still your friend and she isn't mad at you."
"Uh-huh."
"You saw some of the news, right?"
Marisol nodded.
"So you remember that Adam and Jason started shooting and we all shot back?"
More nods.
I didn't mention getting grazed. I said it fast at the end, and realized that I was breathing hard, and couldn't seem to get enough air.
"Daddy?" She was looking at me with a worried expression. Good, if you're going to have a panic attack, do it in front of your child. I got control of my breathing and loosened my grip on the steering wheel and gearshift.
"It's okay, honey. I'm okay. It's just hard to talk about."
"We don't have to."
"Yes, Marisol, we do. It isn't fair to keep things from you, almost a teenager and all," I managed a smile. "You deserve to know. So I did kill Jason Morley. If I hadn't, he would have killed me. A small lie of omission. I didn't mention that he damned near had. "They call

that self-defense. The law says that you can defend yourself. If you do, it isn't murder. Murderers go to jail, I'm a free man."

"Does it make you feel bad?"

She never ceased to amaze me.

I nodded. "Sometimes, when I think about it, I feel awful."

She did it in a singsong, "Would you do it again?" The test that I told her to use to check herself. Perhaps I told her a bit too often.

"Nobody likes a smart mouth,"

"You do. You have one, too. Mamacita always said I got it from you."

"Mamacita always said anything she didn't like was because of me," I answered. "But can I tell you a secret? She got a kick out of my smart mouth, and she'd tell me all about yours and laugh."

"It used to make me sad to talk about Mamacita, but now it makes me happy, is that wrong?"

"Maybe we still miss her, but we're happy for the time we had with her. Ever hear of the Quakers?"

She glared at me. "Mr. Davis did a whole chapter on them."

"Well, one of the things the Quakers do when somebody dies is have a celebration. They celebrate his life, or hers."

"Can we do that sometime?"

"I think we should have done it sooner. Let's plan it for the last weekend this month. We'll invite lots of people and show some videos and put pictures of her out for people to look at."

"Daddy, what do people do at a sleepover party?"

"You mean besides sleep over? Looks like some research may be called for, if you're planning to host one."

"I want to try."

"I'll find an expert and pick her brain."

When we got home, I called Sarah, the waitress, and left a message that I needed some advice.

Supper was one of 'Sol's favorites. I made a huge country breakfast, and we sat down to drown our problems in cholesterol. I read about the field trip to an art museum in Providence. They were going to be showing primitive art and crafts from late colonial and early Federalist period. Mr. Davis' note said that it would integrate the way life was "in a day-to-day sense, to round out the children's classroom-based understanding of the broader scope of conventional history." I guessed that he liked art and wanted an excuse to go. Still, it was educational, and would only cost eleven bucks and some cash for a lunch.

They were looking for chaperones. Marisol looked at me. "I'll die if you do, Daddy."

"Well, I certainly wouldn't want that, honey. Am I that embarrassing?"

"No, it isn't that." She made some vague gestures, and I thought about some of the things that she'd heard at school.

"I understand, muffin. It's okay. Maybe the next trip?"

"Maybe."

I wondered if she meant if I could avoid finding murder victims, shooting people and getting the snot beat out of me. It seemed little enough to ask.

I signed it and put it back in the envelope, slipping it into 'Sol's Social Studies book, where she was sure to see it. Only Mr. Emmett Davis would take the time to stuff envelopes. The other teachers folded their notes and stapled them. Not him. He addressed each envelope and closed it with a nice gold seal. I was going to miss him the next year. I'd had a couple of teachers like him. Their students got excited, and worked their tails off. I knew 'Sol would remember him. I made a note on the calendar. She'd want to give him a gift, and I thought he deserved something special. Maybe I was getting the hang of it.

'Sol still had to do her homework, even though she'd done some after school. She called me in once to help out with a word problem. She did it out, and I checked her answer on the calculator. "Muffin, we're geniuses."

"We?"

"Okay, I'm a genius, honey."

"Hey, Daddy the genius?"

"Yes?"

"Aren't you going to be late for work?" And right on cue, Mrs. Pina walked in.

"You are smiling as if you both discovered teeth," she said, and smiled with us. "It's good to see."

I managed a shower and shave, but my bow tie wasn't fastened when I got to the hotel. Diane was there, and fixed me up. I looked at Diane's outfit, relieved that I didn't have to wear high heels.

"Good to know you're still looking," she said.

I got through the shift. I didn't remember much of it, and a couple of drinks came back to be re-mixed. I hated that. It was just a drink, it was easily fixed, but it was the job I had. Not a great job, but my grandfather had instilled it in me at an early age. Take the job, do the job. So I was irritated with myself.

Chapter 28

DaSilva showed up an hour before closing, carrying a file folder and a notebook and a pen. He seemed edgy and excited. "The men's room is over there," I said. "I can have a drink waiting for you."

"Yeah, maybe later, just a beer, okay?" He was up there, sky-high. I remembered the feeling. It was like watching the bobbin on a fishing line. You saw the first little jump, and waited for the fish to turn and come to really bite. Your pulse got faster, and your breathing shallower. Movement was a need instead of a way to get from place to place.

"You have something?" I asked.

"Oh, yeah."

"I made the calls, and two names didn't check out. They weren't guests at this hotel, and no such people exist. They didn't 'borrow' names, they made them up."

"Shit."

"No, now wait. Doesn't matter, Paul. That's courtroom evidence, we still know, and here's the good news. They're in town, and we can hit them tomorrow."

"Okay, so I have an idea."

"So, what are you proposing?"

"Tomorrow, Larry, I need you to go with what I come up with. I promise you, you won't be compromised."

"It would help if I knew what you were planning."

How nice it would be to have a plan. "It'll look better if it's spontaneous on your side."

"They're ready, and smart."

"Doesn't matter. I won't be applying technique. I'm going to use his weakness and I'm not going to show any fucking mercy."

"I can't let you hurt him," said Larry, suddenly a cop again.

"It isn't going to leave a mark. He won't be able to say a damned thing about it, if it gets to trial. His lawyer won't. Too damned bad for all of them. I've had it. Someone stupid enough to turn his throat up, fine, I'll be the alpha damned dog this time."

"Easy, take it down a bit." I looked around, to see customers and Diane looking at me. I'd let my voice rise. My early training, both as a Portuguese-American kid and then a naval officer had brought the volume of my voice to one that polite people said "carried." Isabel referred to it as shattering. I waved at the customers and put out a round on the house. Nothing like free booze to smooth ruffled feathers.

"I'll pick you up at eight tomorrow morning," said DaSilva.

"I'll have coffee made."

After work, Diane asked for a glass of white wine and I sipped an Old Fashioned. We didn't talk much, but I noticed she had a different manner. Her appearance and body English still oozed sex, but there was restraint to her. "That little outburst with you and your cop buddy."

"How do you know he's a cop?"

"Well, let's see. He looks like a cop, he talks like a cop and he moves like a cop. Nice try changing the subject, but I'm not that easy."

"So what was the question?"

"Paul, tell me to mind my own business if that's what you want. Okay?"

"Diane, I'm sorry. It's been a rough few weeks, and I finally have a chance to put it all behind me. I got kind of vocal."

"You may not realize it, but you have a little bit of the hard ass that only shows once in awhile. It gives you an attractive edge and all of that."

"Me?"

"Yeah, you. When you go for a customer who's out of hand—I've seen guys a hell of a lot bigger and meaner than you back away when you're coming to walk them out. It wasn't that you were loud. Even the cop was leaning away from you."

She looked down into her wine glass. "I'm sorry, I had no right."

"I don't think of myself as a violent man."

She snorted.

"What?"

"Think about it. You could be doing lots of other jobs. I know you like being friendly without making friends, even though that's starting to change. The other bartenders don't try to handle what you do. They call hotel security. You have the situation already over by the time they even show up in their nice blue blazers. Usually, you give the guy a shot at you."

"It does seem to come my way."

"Paul, don't get me wrong. I can get away with flirting and 'look-I-have-nice-boobies' when you're on."

Considering what I was up against, if I had done things differently, would I be in this mess? I could second-guess myself forever.

I looked up, and Diane was looking thoughtfully at me. "Welcome back," she said.

"Good to be back." I smiled back at her.

"You do go away like that sometimes, but a few seconds before you return to earth there's usually a change of expression. This time, you were smiling."

"See, Diane, I'm a nice guy."

"It wasn't a nice guy smile. Goodnight, honey, I need to get some sleep, I'm supposed to work tomorrow morning at the restaurant."

"I'll walk you to your car."

"No, you relax, wouldn't want people to talk."

"Bullshit, Diane."

"You had your chance, never mind the sweet talk." She was still chuckling as she left. I let her have the last line. I rode the elevator down, nodded to the night clerk and security man and headed for the back door and the parking lot.

Chapter 29

The next morning, Mrs. Pina came downstairs early as I'd asked the night before. We were quiet together, and she sighed, got up and poured us each another cup of coffee. She scrambled some eggs, and Marisol started to stir. I went to my room and pulled on jeans and a shirt and grabbed a windbreaker. I put on some deck shoes, laced them more tightly than usual, and slipped my gun, holster and extra magazines onto my belt.

'Sol chattered the whole time until the bus came, carrying a conversation that never would have happened without her. She would be in Providence for the day, and would need to be picked up at four. I kissed her on the forehead, meaning to keep it light, but suddenly my arms were around her, holding too tight. She noticed, but didn't say anything.

"How close?" asked Mrs. Pina, once we were alone.

"Close. I have to end this."

"You will. They have tried to destroy you and threatened our girl. Soon, either you will end it, or I will be taking care of Marisol alone. You cannot let that happen, so you will not."

"Mrs. Pina, I'm curious, is there anything that escapes you?" She smiled with that shy old world smile. Her teeth were white, straight and her own.

She went to the door to let DaSilva in. I was sure I heard Portuguese, because DaSilva answered her in that language.

I handed him a cup of coffee He took a sip and glared at me. "Plan to tell me anything about it?"

I shook my head.

He shrugged, sipping his coffee. "No harm in trying."

"Ready to go?" he asked.

"Fine, you drive."

"We need to talk about what we're going to do."

"Have you got a wire?"

“Yeah, I can set it up and a tape will be running. But it won’t matter without a court order.”

“Don’t you have a warrant to electronically monitor me?”

He stopped and considered. “Telephone, cell phone, or other occasions as investigative circumstances dictate and permit,” he said. There’s a helluva lot of leeway in that one.”

“So you’re monitoring me. And happen to get a conversation. Two of us in the room? A good prosecutor can demonstrate that they had no reasonable expectation of privacy.”

“You’re assuming a prosecution.”

“There will be a reckoning. I’m not going to hurt anyone,” I said, intercepting the look he gave me. “I’m not going to sit back and wait, anymore, either.”

“I remember. You said that at the bar, too.”

“Probably getting old, and forgetful.”

“Probably,” he agreed.

“Probably what?” I asked.

Chapter 30

He drove over the causeway to Goat Island, and pulled into the hotel parking lot. A valet approached and was greeted with a badge.

"Sonny, if my car moves an inch, if the keys are not in the ignition when I come down, or if there's as much as a scratch, then you will never move in this town without a cop demanding ID. Are we clear on that?"

The kid looked at him, goggle-eyed.

"I'd be surprised if a police officer had ever even spoken to him before," I whispered when we got into the elevator.

"Well, now he knows that we're here to serve and protect."

"Room number?"

He gave it to me.

"What if they're not there?"

"Would you for chrissake relax? I'm not an amateur. He used the same fake name to check in. What are the odds? They have adjoining rooms. She used her real name. Room service delivered a champagne breakfast for two to her room, less than," he looked at his watch, "fifteen minutes ago. I arranged to have them stall until then, so we'll be getting here just as they finished up."

"What if they slept in?"

"Their flight leaves from Green at eleven-thirty. They can't sleep much after nine, regardless. Worst case, we get them out of bed. Yesterday, they hung around the city, shopped, hit the galleries and played a round of golf. He bought a small sculpture at one of the galleries for four grand."

"What'd they shoot?" I asked, just for something to say.

"Eighty-two and a seventy-nine, playing from the blues."

I looked at him.

He grimaced, "I have no damned idea. I know they played golf, okay? Jeeze."

He knocked on the door, and said "Room Service," in a cheerful voice.

I heard a man speak, "We already have our order."

DaSilva knocked again, "Maybe there's a mistake, but the first order was incomplete, sir." He was perfect.

I heard movement and stepped to the latch side of the door. Out of sight, I drew my Beretta, and held it to my side. The door opened, and Rob of the CIA, wearing a blue blazer and gray slacks was looking at me.

He started to speak, and to push the door closed, when he looked down and saw my pistol, cocked and pointed at his midsection. "May we come in?" I asked.

"We were eating, and we have a flight to catch, but please do, as long as you can keep it brief."

I raised the pistol, and that was the first DaSilva noticed it. He didn't blink, drawing his and holding it at his side as he entered, moving to the opposite side of the door. "Sergeant," I said, "I wonder if you would make sure of our privacy?"

He quickly checked the closets, the bathroom, and locked the door to the adjoining room.

"Clear, Mr. Costa," he said, and holstered his weapon. I nodded toward Rob, and he quickly patted him down.

"Let's all sit down. Mind?" I said, pouring myself a cup of coffee.

"No, help yourself, Mr. Costa," the widow Morley said.

"Sergeant?"

"No thank you, I'm fine."

"Everyone comfortable, then?" I said. "Well, Bob, it's good to see you again. I had a long night, and it's been awhile since we spoke, but it's a genuine pleasure."

"It's Rob, Mr. Costa,"

"Okay, Bob, but for now, I'd like to keep things moving along. You do have your obligations, don't you?"

He nodded, and Mrs. Morley nodded. She seemed puzzled, but willing to let her lover take care of matters. His face showed some annoyance over the name. I liked that. DaSilva stood with his arms folded, looking like a cop.

"So, Bob let me tell you what I've been up to, and how your life is about to take a serious turn for the worse. Would you like to hear all of that?"

"First of all, Mr. Costa, there's nothing legal about what you're doing here, and I promise you can't do a thing to my life. It's fine as it is. I assure you that I will use whatever means I have to alter yours. This is unconscionable."

I smiled at him, and for the first time, Mrs. Morley spoke, "Rob, what is this all about? Is he here to kill me, too? Mr. Costa, is that it? Will you finally kill every last member of my family? Rob, why is he here?"

Rob stood, "Mrs. Morley is quite correct, it's time for you both to leave."

"Sit down, sir," said DaSilva, in a quiet voice. I looked over at him and saw the kind of anger that should make people afraid. Rob recognized it and dropped back into his seat. "I spoke to an old friend from my time in in Recon, about his time in Viet Nam and in the 'company,' and found out all about you, Mr. Singer. Your grandfather, the anti-Hitler Prussian officer and you, the second generation 'Company Man,' and all of the games in Nam. Before your grandfather came to the States, your family's name was 'Von Singler und Ettlinger,' right? Wonder if that's where your sense of entitlement comes from."

"Sergeant, word of your inquiries reached me," of course. Your acquaintance was a fine and loyal officer. He spoke quite well of you, too. This behavior is a surprise."

DaSilva said, "My friend and I lost close friends, we did horrifying things, and we were lucky to come out of those hell holes you sent us into with minds and souls intact. Do you understand that? We thought we were serving, but it turns out we were game pieces for overeducated, elitist assholes, like you. Someone treating you like the felon you are is long overdue, in my opinion. To me, you're a traitor, a war criminal, and at this moment, you could be charged with homicide and conspiracy. My behavior is just fine, thank you." His face was tight and it matched his voice. "If I were you, I'd give Mr. Costa a listen, and stop making idle threats."

DaSilva's eyes were narrow, and he was leaning forward as he spoke. "You and your kind got at least one war going, thinking you knew best. You were there. What you did resulted in an explosion in the 'law of unintended consequences.'"

Singer's eyebrows went up.

"That's right, I can read and write. Just like in Viet Nam, and some other shitholes, you set off a chain of events here in Newport, and the genie got out of the bottle. Just like Viet Nam, you've been trying to stuff it back in. The result is Mrs. Morley's sick son is dead. Again, the law of unintended consequences." Camille Morley was staring at Singer, with dawning awareness. I could almost see connections forming.

I didn't expect that.

DaSilva said, "You'd think after you got fifty thousand American kids killed that you might have learned a little something. Guess not. Paul, you'd better take over, before I forget what I am." His fists were so tight that the knuckles were smooth and white.

Rob spoke for the first time in awhile. "Camille, why don't you go to your room and finish packing?"

"Camille, these are things you need to hear," I said.

"You mind your station and your own business," Singer snapped.

"Let me think about that, Bobby. No." I lifted my pistol a scant inch and saw his eyes go to it. "So, where to begin? Well, I'll start with what I know, then I'll review what needs to happen next, Okay? Sergeant, how does that sound?"

DaSilva nodded.

Mrs. Morley started to rise. "I think I'd like an eye opener."

I held my hand out to her. "I'll get it for you." I went to the bar near the television set and began to break seals. There was a bucket of ice, and a carafe of orange juice. I mixed her a weak Orange Blossom, and handed it to her.

"There. Everyone set? Good. Bob-bo, it seems that your first mistake was in enhancing the work of your professional. The Congressman would have been a natural causes death, and you could have gone on with your life. Was Camille the woman in the bar whose hand you were holding?"

He shook his head. “You are speculating.”

“Nope, the hotel security system videos show you and your female companion in the hotel at the time of the murder. The waitress that night saw both of your faces. She’s currently under police protection by the way, so don’t run for the phone.”

DaSilva never batted an eye. There was no video, and Sarah didn’t remember anyone at that table.

“Female companion, Rob?” said Mrs. Morley. “Do go on, Mr. Costa.” She took a sip of her drink.

“You hired a call girl, who got a pretty unusual drug into the Congressman. You or someone you hired eliminated the young lady to hide any traces, and dumped her body into Narragansett Bay. She was just a loose end to you. Her uncle claimed her body, what was left of it. He had to see that. Guess she wasn’t real to you or your employee? Still, you’d be in the clear if you’d left it at that.”

Camille Morley was looking at him, now. Her look was one of bitter amusement. Her voice had a cold, ironic tone to it. “Dick was a manipulator, but I’m beginning to see your mastery of the art.”

Rob looked back at her. There was passion, desire, longing and the knowledge that he would never see it returned again. He slumped in his seat. “This is nonsense, you have no way to prove anything, because I did no such thing.”

“Must have been a shock to you and your lady friend when Morley stumbled into the men’s room. But you’re an operator. You remembered the knife and probably saw me toss it into the dishpan. The timing was right, and you picked it out, and went back to your seat, I’d guess. I didn’t see this part, but at one point you rose and went into the men’s room. You found Morley, probably dead. If not, he was dying. Here’s where it gets kind of shaky.

“Mrs. Morley, you know that Friedrich/Rob/Bob, Singer or whatever, is in love with you. It’s hopeless, depthless and without any limits. You’re both lucky and cursed. It’s fortunate to find someone who is even capable of that kind of love. He thought of the abuse you’d suffered. He thought of all of the small scale evil the Congressman did, and his love for you was overcome by his hate for what your husband had done.

"Anyway, Bobby, you looked the knife over, and held it by the blade, lining it up as you were taught to do, and pushed it into Morley's ear with the palm of your hand. You simply had to act against him, or what remained of him. I can't say I blame you, there. But it was a lapse. Internet is a great thing. You know that technique has been taught all the way back to World War Two and the OSS? Women were taught to use hat pins."

"I'm not going to listen to this nonsense."

"Oh, yes, Bob, you are. See, it continues to get better. Your method of demonstrating your hate dropped me into the shit. That probably wouldn't have bothered you or stopped you. Even now, I'm easy to rid yourself of, in your mind. I thought, until a minute ago, that the woman in the bar was Mrs. Morley. Sorry, Camille, I misjudged you a bit. Turns out you're more than I thought you were. Still, I don't think anyone would blame you."

She nodded, and her eyes were filling.

"We'll come back to the woman. Earlier that evening, I met one of the men from that table when he came up to the bar, and assumed that I knew all about the people sitting there. Singer, I saw you holding the woman's hand, and it bothered me. I still missed my wife, and I was jealous. So I remembered."

Singer simply stared ahead. "Camille, we can have a good life, what's left to us. I love you, you can come to love me again," he stuttered to a stop. His composure and reserve shattered like spun glass on the stones of her new strength. No one should ever witness what had just happened to those two. If it had been different, I would have been embarrassed.

He wasn't denying any more.

"So, you returned to DC, comforted the widow, and probably her daughter in an appropriately avuncular way, and waited for the bartender to get charged, arraigned, tried and convicted. Long before then, you would have your bride and a fine life. Even with the knife, it could have worked. The FBI was under immense pressure to get me into custody over that. I don't suppose you'd care to talk about the source of that pressure, would you? No."

"May I get up, please," he said, "I really need to stand." He was asking for permission. I was pleased by his demolition.

"Sure, but you will stand right there, until you sit. You will keep your hands in plain sight, and you will make no sudden moves. Is that clear?"

"Clear," he said in a lifeless voice. He rose.

"Back to events. When it was thought that the congressman died of a heart attack, I was free to visit the surviving Morleys down in the capitol. That must have turned your classy poop watery, Bob. Then Mrs. Morley referred me to you and set up the meeting. You had to do it. I wondered about that, until just now when I realized that Mrs. Morley didn't know about your actions. You attended the meeting, gave me a lot of non-information and promised to send more to me. But you never did anything, did you? The last thing you wanted was to help me. That was your second mistake, Bob," I said.

"Please, I hate that name, call me Rob, or at least Friedrich."

I threw him the bone. "Okay, Rob. No problem. Now, it gets even more interesting. You bought Detective Petersen, maybe that night, or maybe a little later. Doesn't matter much. Whatever influence you had with Petersen, you didn't know how corrupt he was. His aggression towards me, along with his actions got him investigated, and he's going to prison. He will deal to get that sentence down. You could be part of that deal. He will offer you to the Feds, if it gets that far, and let the locals have the ones they'd be interested in. We'll see. Still, if I were you, I'd be worried about ex-detective Petersen."

He started to speak.

"No, Rob, I still have the floor. See all of this opened a huge can of worms related to the unlamented congressman's personal life. He left too many tracks. One of his numerous victims set up a Dead Man's Switch to protect herself."

He looked up, sharply.

DaSilva was looking from one to the other of us. "Rob, care to explain the 'Dead Man's Switch' to Sergeant DaSilva, here? See, he does honest work and wouldn't know about your slimy business."

He shook his head. So I explained it quickly.

"Mrs. Morley, I thought at the time that the Switch that the young lady set up was overkill. After I met Jason and Adam, I hoped that it would be enough."

"You did kill my son, Mr. Costa, I haven't forgotten that."

"I never will, either, Mrs. Morley. I hope knowing that he and Adam were trying to kill me will help us."

"So, Rob, that got Adam and Jason involved. That got me a severe beating from one or the both of them. Adam probably for fun and revenge. I'd put him down at the Morley manse. You found out about it, maybe from Jason himself, or maybe from Adam. You may have already owned a piece of that psycho, by then."

"How about that, Friedrich? Was he your boy when he beat the snot out of me? I know you had some ownership and mutual trust within a week, because that's when he accepted the contract on me, isn't it?"

Mrs. Morley gaped at Friedrich. "What are you?" she asked.

He hung his head and said nothing.

"I wished Dick dead more times than I could ever count," said the widow.

He looked up, and a glimmer of hope showed in his eyes.

"When you killed my husband, and never told me, and when you hired a killer to kill Mr. Costa, and never told me, and kept trying to control and manage, did you once think what it would do to us when I found out? Was your respect for me so limited? Did you truly think I'd never find out? Was all of this," she gestured vaguely, "all of this, to keep it from me? Was it, Rob?"

He nodded. "It's all been for you, Camille. From the moment I met you, whatever I was able to do, I did. What I was unable to do, I arranged. I love you, Camille. What I had, I put at your service; I laid at your feet. I saw your suffering, and I had to end it. Do you understand? Your son was probably beyond help, but I wanted to help Charlene, too."

"Charlene?" she almost shouted. "What have you done?"

"Mrs. Morley?" I said.

"Yes, what is it?" lots of impatience showing. She had a lot to say now.

"Let's stay with what we were doing. I think we need to get through it all, okay? You and I can talk about Charlene, if you really want to, after that."

"If I really want to?"

I continued as if she hadn't spoken. Rob looked older than he had twenty minutes before. He had the "thousand-yard-stare" of recent combat. If I thought about him too much, I'd pity him. I had to remember that he'd handed me the weapon, but never believed I'd be able to use it against him.

"So, you offered Adam some money to kill me. Probably not a lot, but I think he'd have done it for free, as long as there was someone to ask or tell him to do it. You didn't know about the tapes, though, did you? You would never have held on to evidence like that. Morley needed those tapes on some level, and his son enjoyed them, too. I had come into arm's reach, and even a dope like me would eventually realize that you'd stonewalled me. You had only one reason to do so. You're good, but you had to hope I'd slow down before Adam killed me."

The best he could do was shake his head from side to side.

"Want to deny any of this, Rob? Should I go on?"

He looked up at me, his face showing no sign of anything but misery.

"So, Jason decides to run for Daddy's seat, and starts testing the waters. Unfortunately, he and Adam knew I was digging around, and the TV message about the tapes got his attention. Before that, he went to my daughter's school and trailed her a time or two, for my benefit, to warn me.

"Camille would understand. I'm told you're childless, Friedrich, so you can't understand as she does.

"I set the sting up to catch Jason on film, taking the tape, and saying more incriminating things than the tap on my phone had already caught. Sergeant DaSilva and Detective Lacombe came to help protect me, and the TV crew was there, as arranged.

"Adam lost his head, and thought about solving Jason's problem and collecting his money, all at once."

DaSilva didn't flicker. He kept his basilisk stare on Singer, his arms folded.

"As Sergeant DaSilva pointed out, 'the law of unintended consequences' took on its own life, somewhere along the way and one good man and two evil ones died." I glanced over at Camille, and saw that she was crying, holding her drink in one hand as the ice melted.

"Mrs. Morley, I'm sorry, but Jason was poisoned from an early age."

"I should have left that man and exposed him. I'm a coward, I guess. I kept trying to hold it together. I'm sorry, sorry, sorry." She wasn't apologizing to anyone in the room, I knew. "Law of unintended consequences," she said, bitterly. "Take it back a few more years, Mr. Costa. If I really want to think about it, this whole thing is my fault."

"No, Camille. That's my routine. You do the best you can, and keep hoping it will get better. 'Maybe this,' and 'I should have that' is different from setting up a murder." I gave her a half beat, but she remained silent, her careful makeup smeared by tears.

"Back to recent events. Adam had failed and brought matters to the surface. I was a serious problem. Rob, I do hope for your sake that you contracted for this from your own funds. If you took Company money to do your personal work, I doubt that you'll get much help from them."

Rob wasn't biting.

Camille was staring over at him. "His child would have been an orphan. Why? For me? You did that for me? Did you know me at all? I'd have continued as we were, for as long as you wanted. I would have divorced him for you, and blown his career apart for you. I'd have changed my life to be with you. You knew that. Do you remember? I was yours for the asking. You never asked. Just asked. You wanted to maneuver and control and you wound up killing. Of all you killed, you killed us, too."

The affect of her cold voice on him was hard to watch. Each word sank into him like a blade. Each one stole more life from him. If I'd briefed and trained her, it couldn't have been worse. The room was so silent, that we could hear the curtains stir in the air conditioning. His breathing was audible. DaSilva moved slightly and I heard a joint crack.

"How are we doing on time? Don't want to miss your flight, do you?" I said.

"I'll call and cancel," said DaSilva. Nobody protested as he went to the phone. "All set, your reservations for today are cancelled, but your tickets are useable." He said it as if he'd provided a vital service. What he'd done removed any doubt that we were in complete control. They were going nowhere without our permission. Their lack of resistance spoke volumes. Mrs. Morley noticed that she was in a nightgown and robe.

"I'd like to get dressed."

"Not just yet, ma'am, but your dignity is fine." She settled back into her chair. DaSilva had struck the perfect note. He was polite, professional, and in absolute control.

"So, Rob, back to business?" I spoke with an artificial lightness, trying to get his anger to focus on me. He didn't take me up on it.

"Lawyer," he said, at last.

"Oh, I think that may be premature, Singer. I think you want to hear me out."

"Heard enough." His old-fashioned speech was gone.

"Want to hear your way out? Does that interest you?"

He looked up, a suddenly elderly man.

"Cancel any contract that you're considering, now, immediately. Irrevocably. I have a Dead Man's Switch set up, but I want that community to know that I'm a sacred cow. That's first. Second, resign from your position. You are too dangerous there, and you certainly don't need your salary. If you do those two things, I'm out of your hair, out of your life."

"Why resign?"

"Sergeant DaSilva here thinks you screw up, and when you do people die. Soldiers, kids, mostly. See, you get mixed up in things like that, and the best young men leap into the breach you created. Then they die, or get wounded, crippled, emotionally, physically, whatever. You've done enough for the country, I guess; or maybe you've done enough to it. Regardless, if you fail to resign, I'll drop all of this right into the FBI, and your own Counter Intelligence folks. There'll be audits, and you will be seriously screwed."

"How will you know if I comply?"

I didn't answer. I could have been speaking to a machine.

"One more thing, Singer," said DaSilva, "I want a statement from you, signed, that will never see the light of day unless some unpleasantness arises."

"No."

"Then all bets are off. Paul has his needs; I have mine. I want satisfaction. I want to know."

"Why is that so important to you, DaSilva?"

"'Sergeant,' Singer. It's 'Sergeant.' I worked hard for it, and I earned it. I will have it. Say it."

"Why is it so important to you, Sergeant?"

"It's the last duty to an old friend."

"I have a question about my daughter, Mr. Costa," Camille said.

"That will be a condition for you, Mrs. Morley. She needs to be hospitalized, and immediately. You will have seventy-two hours to get that done, or I will."

"I know she's fragile, but she gets treatment."

"I guess I'm going to have to back up for a minute, while Sergeant DaSilva gets his statement."

Seated at a table on the far side of the room, their voices murmured as DaSilva wrote, edited and rewrote to the point where Singer nodded. Then they went on. DaSilva's assumption of authority over Singer was timed perfectly. To the CIA executive, I was the enemy, so Larry could be his mentor. He was starting the rebuilding process to get the help from his subject to a degree that an outsider would never understand. We had just broken a trained intelligence operative. It would have been harder, but we had the help of the woman he loved.

"Well, Mr. Costa?" asked Camille Morley.

"Once I realize how badly I'd misjudged you, I had to concentrate on Singer alone."

"Do you have any idea how cruel that was?" she whispered, glancing towards him.

"I'll be sick later, Camille."

"That night, I saw a middle aged guy come up to the bar, and I saw his wife, and two other couples. The two women I saw appeared to be around the same age. I saw them as 'types' rather than individuals, see what I mean?"

"I'm sure you have a point, Mr. Costa."

"Getting there, but it's important that you kind of see what I saw. I saw one of the women nearly full face, and one in profile. They fit the type, so I filled in the blanks on the one I couldn't see. I'm sorry Camille, but I put your face on her."

"You think it was Charlene?"

"I'm sure of it. What do you know about Charlene?"

"She's depressed, social anxiety. Earlier, we had to work on anorexia, but that's over." Her expression was the same as every worried parent I'd ever seen including mine, for that matter.

"Camille, you know about your late husband's secret closet?"

"Of course. When he was feeling particularly controlling, he'd send me down to get tapes for him, before he came to bed." She was blushing.

"So tapes of Charlene and her first love wouldn't surprise you too much?"

She shook her head.

"I know this is awful, but I need you to hold up, okay?" I said softly.

She nodded.

I went on, "She broke into the closet and took her tapes. I think there were tapes of your husband having sex with Charlene."

Her mouth formed the "O" from the "no" but no sound came from her.

"While she was in that closet, not far from her tapes were yours, Mrs. Morley. All of them. You understand, right?"

"Yes. It was awful." She bowed her head. "A woman with any self respect would have left him."

"My point was that she took all of the tapes that directly affected her, and told me about the closet. She knew it would point us at Jason, and hoped it would point me at you, too. She could have tried to save you. She chose not to."

"She left mine and took hers?" Her voice was like a small child's on the final, magic Christmas.

"I'm sorry. Her anger at you must rival how she feels about her father. She was the woman with Rob at the bar. I think she got wind of his plans somehow and she forced her way into it. I believe she wanted to see her father dead."

"Why would he indulge her? Rob, I mean. Why would he?"

"He might answer that."

I stopped to listen to DaSilva and Singer. They seemed to be reviewing the contract with Adam.

"I think he believed, honestly, that it would help her. His slip that let her into his planning might even have been deliberate. Maybe something in his past lead him to believe that it would make her better."

"Why hospitalize her, though?"

"I think you're next on her list, Camille."

"Me?"

"You're her mother. Her father was having sex with her. She denies it, but I'm sure of it. I don't know when it started, but you could probably remember when she started to act troubled. Anorexia, trying to be unattractive to her father, might have been a response."

She looked exhausted, like something had just drained out of her. For the first time, she appeared old. "Thirteen. She was thirteen."

"Her brother may have—been encouraged by your husband. I'm not so sure of that, but he may have been her target, by sending me to that closet.

"It's likely that her emotions never got much past those of a thirteen year old girl. In many ways, still a little girl, a child. In others, hormones raging, and the beginning of sexuality. She could still play with dolls, talk to imaginary friends, while showing interest in boys."

She was almost smiling. "Yes."

“A girl that age would expect protection and sheltering from good parents, wouldn’t she?”

“And I failed her.”

“What we think isn’t important. She may have decided you weren’t up to being his wife. She may have been told you were frigid, so her father was entitled to her. Charlene has a stack of stored up resentments, stewing for a decade. Some could be valid, and some, the perceptions of a thirteen-year-old girl,” I said.

Camille was sitting with her knees apart, and her forearms resting on her thighs. Her head hung forward with her hair hiding her face.

“It fits. It makes so much sense. My God, my God, my poor little girl.” There was a primal woman’s moan, “You bastard, my little girl!”

“Seventy two hours from five o’clock this evening Mrs. Morley. Seventy-two hours and one minute, and I contact my friends in the media, the ones who hound me every day. I’ve promised an exclusive to one of them. Are we clear?”

“I don’t know how.”

“Call your lawyer, he’ll have a tame doctor on retainer. That’ll get her in there. After that, she could start to get better. I hope so.”

DaSilva and Singer were sitting silently. I picked up the phone and handed it to him. “You still have conditions one and two to meet, Singer. Better get at it.”

DaSilva rose and walked over to Mrs. Morley to have her witness the signatures. I saw signatures and the date at the bottom of each page, and initials all the way around. Perfect. I read page after page of beautifully clear handwriting.

Singer made one phone call, and told the answering party that the game was a rainout.

“You can resign upon your return, Rob. You have seventy-two hours. Not a minute more. That’s it. If I don’t see your resignation within seventy-two hours from five o’clock this evening, I will consider all of our agreements null and void, and I’ll blow it up, publicly. I won’t care who gets hurt, or how badly. Nothing will be private. Nothing. Do you understand me?”

“You are making a terrible mistake, if you do that,” he answered.

"You're a fine one to talk," said DaSilva.

"Still, there are things you don't know."

"About Charlene, you mean?" I answered.

His chin sank to his chest and he was silent.

"Seventy-two hours. There's a flight in an hour."

"You got painfully close, Mr. Costa. Almost right." It was a woman's voice coming from the doorway. A young voice.

"Hello, Charlene," I said.

She had a pocketbook slung over her shoulder, with a hand inside of it.

The door closed softly behind her, slowed by a closer and air brake.

"You missed a couple of things. You guessed about my father. I guess you really do have a knack. Bartenders are supposed to be insightful and great listeners. All kinds of wisdom, right?" The sarcasm was heavy, but the gun inside of that purse was too obvious to let me push her.

"And mother, he even figured out what a waste of skin you were. Too polite to say so, though." I saw the same heat coming from her as I'd seen at the health club. A primitive anticipation. Her forehead was shiny with feverish perspiration. She licked her lips, over and over again.

I glanced over to see her mother sag even further. "It's true, Charlene. I failed you. I failed your brother, too."

"Jason? Jason? My second lover? Oh, mother, he was very successful. Not to worry, he was just what he was supposed to be." Her speech was so fast that it was difficult to understand. Her tone was getting higher, and I felt my neck prickling.

"It's all taken care of," Rob interrupted. "They know everything, how I let you into the plan, everything."

"Oh, you let me? How fucking generous, Rob. You really are the gallant, aren't you?"

I saw that DaSilva had moved, so slowly as to appear still. He was moving to her side, so she'd have to turn to see him. Charlene saw him at the same moment and turned to face him. She seized the straps of the pocketbook with her free hand. She began to pull her other hand from the bag, and I caught a glimpse of the gun she was holding.

"No! Charlene, stop!" It was Rob's voice and he took a quick stride in her direction. She wheeled on him as the gun came clear. I brought mine up, and saw DaSilva do the same. Both guns were leveled at her, but the only threat she saw was Rob, who was too close to her for either of us to take a shot. He was too close for her to miss.

***

He seized the gun as she fired and dragged her to the floor with him. He let out a long, soft groan after the shot. As far as I know, he never made another sound. Nothing in Charlene seemed human. She was uttering a stream of grunts and whispered shrieks, hammering at his fist with one hand, and pulling the gun with the other. A death grip is hard to break. As small as she was, it took both DaSilva and me to restrain her. The shy, pretty young lady may never have existed. When the police came, she was finally in handcuffs, sitting on a chair, while her mother cradled her.

Camille Morley was crying, continuously and silently, while she was allowed to dress. At the door, with a female officer, she paused. "It was her, wasn't it? She controlled it all. She manipulated Rob, she fooled me, her brother—all of us. Was she sleeping with him, too?"

I shook my head. "No, that wouldn't have been the button to push, He truly loved you, the best way he knew how. I'd be guessing, but I think she made sure he knew how badly you were being mistreated. Probably cried a lot and made him believe she was grieving for you."

She nodded, with tears still spilling over. "My fault. Your daughter, Mr. Costa, is she all right?"

"She's fine, Mrs. Morley."

"See that you keep her that way. I'll find a way to live through this, if I know something came out right."

I understood, somehow, what she was trying to say. "She'll have the best life I can help her find."

Her head sagged as she turned and left. I remembered the elegant and assured woman I thought I met in Washington. It was hard to believe that I was looking at the same person.

We didn't seem to have the strength to leave the room. "What do you think, Larry?"

"His statement, your story? The tape, with Charlene's little surprise? We have enough. I'll get his statement on record with the DA, along with the tape from the wire and a transcript. The call to the killers won't do any harm, and Mrs. Morley's reaction."

"You were fantastic, by the way," I said.

"Yeah, next I'm gonna go out and beat the shit out of some little girl with a rubber hose."

"I know."

"I see what you were saying about using his weakness."

"Yup, I'm a fucking prince aren't I? Not to mention that I thought the daughter was just along for the ride."

"I'd kind of like to have let them have their lives. I mean in a way," said Larry.

"In a way. Maybe if I could have been sure that he'd let me live, too."

"There is that."

I was home before one o'clock. I had three hours to kill before I went to Marisol's school to pick her up.

Chapter 31

DaSilva had promised to contact Dana to update her. He could argue jurisdiction and bring her into the investigation. The FBI getting one over on the CIA would gain her a lot. She'd probably wind up thanking DaSilva.

I called Dennis.

"Good news?" he asked.

I told him most of the story. "Christ, Paul, you wound up playing in the bigs. Shit. Are you sure it's over?"

"Some details and loose ends. You had a lot to do with saving my ass."

"So, maybe I can get a free drink out of that?" He laughed and hung up, promising to let the right people know. I hoped it was enough.

The next morning, DaSilva and I went to the cemetery. I waited in the driveway, while he stood in front of Phil Lacombe's grave. It was mounded with raw earth, covered with an artificial grass carpet. He patted the stone like a friend's shoulder, and turned away.

We were walking out together, and he stopped. "It's likely finished, one way or the other," he said. "See you around, I guess."

"I'm not hard to find, stop by anytime."

"Yeah, but not to hurt your feelings? You or Mrs. Pina make the coffee, okay?"

I smiled before he turned away.

At home, I sat at the kitchen table, trying to think about anything other than my recent life. I hadn't moved, when the phone rang. I looked at my watch. I'd been sitting looking into my cup long enough for it to go cold. "Hello?"

"Paul, Detective Petersen is dead," it was Dana's voice.

"Dead?"

"In his car, one shot behind the right ear. He was behind the wheel. His car was found at the National Seashore on Cape Cod. No fingerprints anywhere. The whole car was wiped. A professional job."

I considered a lot of things to say. Then I rejected them all. "Thanks for calling. Did you want to talk about anything else?"

"Thought you might want to talk about what I said. Like maybe who you suspect?"

"Did you talk with DaSilva?"

"Yes, he told me about that, and how you two solved the case and all. It was really nice getting all of that second hand like that."

I ignored the icy sarcasm. "So, Rob cleared up a loose end, I guess."

"That's it? Have you ever bitten into foil stuck in a piece of gum? That's what you're like for me."

"Petersen isn't my problem. Or my fault. Did you read a threat? If you had, you'd have had him in a safe place, right?" There was a silence. "I have enough to carry around without him."

"And now we never will get a thing from him."

I waited for her to speak. When she didn't I asked, "Is that it, Dana?"

"That and to tell you I've accepted a transfer."

I knew it was over, but the reality of it struck like a slap. "Where?"

"Washington. I'm going to be the agent in charge, heading up the investigation of Friedrich Singer and looking for any other abuses, by him and others."

I could almost see the FBI director dry washing his hands in glee. She'd be an inspector in no time, and a supervisory deputy within five years, if she played her cards right. "Washington," I said, dully.

"I was going to tell you in person."

"I see," I said, even though I didn't really.

"No, you don't."

"Look, Dana, you don't have to give a reason. I treasure the time we had. I'll never be able to tell you what you've done for me. I admire your mind, your wit and your heart. I lust after your body. I wish that it had gone differently."

"I do too," she said softly.

"Okay, that's what needed to be said, I think."

"I'll miss Marisol. She's going to be formidable," she said, quietly.

"Good luck with your new job, Dana."

She took an audible breath, "Right. You sound all in. Would you like me to come? Just to talk, I mean. I don't care about the case. If you need a friend. I still want to be your friend."

"Ow,"

"Oh. I really just said that, didn't I?" she asked.

"I'll pretend I didn't hear it."

"I'm just going to ask if you're going to be okay."

"One way and another. Sure," I tried for lightness in my tone, and failed.

She almost laughed, "Okay, hard ass."

"Rob/Friedrich Singer was a dangerous man with dangerous friends. Watch your back. Any idea of how he got Petersen done on short notice? Or do your people think it was set up long ago? Or do you think I did it?"

"Mention was made of the last possibility, not by me. You destroyed him, why kill him? As for Singer, we'll be working on that. We have all the time in the world." There was a silence that went on too long to be comfortable. "I should go. I won't forget to stay in touch with Marisol."

"Thank you. For everything, you know." Words just stopped coming.

Then she was gone, and I was listening to the electronic hum of a dead phone line.

It took me some time to get to my feet and clean up the cups from Larry's visit. That seemed right to me. It was like I was an empty but unwashed coffee cup. Sarah's phone call broke me out of my self-pity.

"What do you know about sleepovers?" I asked after we said hello.

"Is this an invitation?"

"Sure, then Mike can drop by and blend me into one of his sauces."

She laughed.

"Seriously, Sarah. 'Sol has asked about having one and I'm clueless. I mean do they just come over and go to bed?"

"Oh, you poor man. You are in for a long night. Look, Paul, how about if Mike and I drop by this afternoon, after 'Sol gets home from school? She and I can plan it, and come up with a list of things to get and do."

"If you do that, I will give you my secret recipe for three drinks, your choice."

"And when I do "The Talk," with her next week, what will I get?"

"Dinner for you and Mike, restaurant of your choice?"

"I was kidding," she answered. "Paul, is everything okay?"

"The important stuff is, I think. The devil's in the details. Maybe when you and Mike come over, I'll be able to talk about it."

"If you need to. Should we bring anything?"

"A healthy digestive system. I'll get something together for us," I answered. "Thank you, Sarah. I guess I could have called her friend's mom, but I'd feel pretty dumb."

"My pleasure."

"Thanks, Sarah. What time can you make it?"

"See you at six thirty."

"That'll work." I knew Mike would be arriving with one of his elaborate desserts. I smiled at the memory of the chocolate soufflé. Marisol's initial doubtful look at it ended when she tried her first bite and was replaced by some sort of prepubescent lust and a feeding frenzy.

One more call. I called Tim Foley at home, and got his answering machine. I thanked him, and invited him and Lois, the ex-stripper to come by for whatever.

I realized that keeping the human contact going was important. It had taken a murder and a threat to my family to force me out. The light was blinding, but once out, I had no desire to go back in.

It took a few attempts, before I reached my old friend at NCIS, "Al?"

"Paul? Jesus, you've been a busy boy."

"Al, I just called to thank you. Your guy kept me alive."

"Yeah, I saw the news. You've slowed down. He'd never have hit you when we were working together."

"I'm a bigger target, too."

He laughed. "Ain't it the truth."

I paused. "You know about all of it?"

"Yeah, buddy, it's all over the place. Singer, the Congressman's wife and daughter, you and the son. I have the gist of it."

"I think it's my fault."

"Someday, you and I will have to list all of the bad things that happened that aren't your fault, okay? "

"Is this going to be a long lesson, Professor?" I said.

"Shut up and listen. I wanted to say this to you for a long time. You were good, you know? You were probably the best interrogator I ever saw. You knew where the weak spots were, and you wedged them open, fast. You did it so bad guys couldn't do bad things."

"Afterwards, you'd pour out through your own ass, for being cruel. When we took too long to get the guy, you'd take the blame and bleed for days. Used to drive us crazy. You wouldn't talk it out. You'd just ex-sanguinate." He took a deep breath. "So here it is. Ready? Shit happens."

"You gave me a five minute lecture and it's a bumper-sticker?" I said.

"It's a great bumper-sticker? The way you think darkens you. Hard to just relax and enjoy what comes along."

"I hate it when you're smarter than me."

"You must hate it a lot."

"Fuck you very much. Al?"

"Yeah?"

"I still feel guilty as hell."

"Are all portagees this stubborn?"

"Yup, and we only let other portagees call us portagees."

"You can work on that," He paused, "Portagee."

After we hung up, I was sorting through some laundry, trying to think of mindless things to do, when the phone rang. I wanted the voicemail to take it, but I couldn't get a sleeve to turn right side out, unless the rest of the shirt went inside out. I heaved the damned thing across the room, and grabbed the phone.

"You miserable son of a bitch!"

"And hello to you, too, Sandra. How have you been?"

"I'm in water so hot, and so deep, thanks to you, that I may be reporting the Washington, DC annual flower show, and there isn't one."

"Does that mean that you don't want the exclusive interview anymore? And I'd bet that you don't want the cop, either, right? Am I right? How about the FBI?" There was silence.

"It's over?"

"As over as it will be."

"Wait one, then." She was serious and professional, again. I caught myself humming with the music the phone played while I was on "hold."

"I'll be up on the next available flight, which is in an hour, arriving an hour later at 'T.F. Green?' What the hell kind of name is that for an airport, anyway? I have to gather up Bill Latronica and a camera crew, so it'll be tomorrow at the earliest for the production work and pre-interview. How's that work?"

"I'll call DaSilva, the FBI and confirm. Chances are their superiors will want to be involved."

"Care to fill me in, some kind of advance information? Strictly deep background, I want to make sure that our legal eagles are ready."

I ran it down for her.

"You're a piece of work. I'll see you and the others, tomorrow."

"See you then."

I called DaSilva, explained what was going to happen the next day. "Great," he said in a lifeless voice, "I couldn't be more thrilled. Imagine, me on television and all."

"Trust me, Larry, your bosses will be thrilled. Call Dana and let her know?"

"You're a chicken. That makes me feel better. Hang up. I'll see you tomorrow."

I was on the phone, speaking with Doctor Debbie when Marisol came home from school. Mrs. Pina wasn't far behind. My house was in homecoming chaos, and we were deep in its throes when Mike and Sarah appeared at my door, carrying a container.

We laughed a lot that night, and Marisol ate herself into a stupor on little raspberry tarts and fresh whipped cream. Mrs. Pina grumbled her way through it and we smiled.

Chapter 32

My brush with fame and notoriety lasted longer than I expected. The interview went fine, and there were offers for books and other things. I turned them all down. In a month, it died out. Marisol's sleepover was a hit. There was a cacophonous four hours, dying down to two hours of giggling, with occasional laughter. I think they all crashed and burned by three or so. I was exhausted, Mrs. Pina was asleep on the couch, and I could hear my daughter's happy voice.

Maybe sleep was over-rated after all. It was a small price to pay. The morning after the sleep over party, I made a huge breakfast, and they went at it like a pack of happy young she-wolves. Their moms came to pick them all up, and aside from a couple of pizza boxes, a few empty soda bottles and random crumbs and popcorn kernels, they might never have been there. Marisol was tired, happy and let down all at once.

I took her to the Middletown beaches. I had to work that night, but the bar could wait. Tourist season was over, and we had the beach to ourselves. Barefooted, we walked at the edge of the water. The tide was rising, but there was no surf. We walked stiff-legged, driving our heels down to make clear footprints in the soft wet sand. She giggled when an errant wave washed over our ankles. She took my hand, stamping down hard trying to make deep, lasting impressions.

Neither of us looked back to watch the rising tide washing them away behind us. We looked at what we were doing, guided by the changing water's edge, only vaguely aware that the beach went on ahead of us.

Afterword

As it says in the front of the book, all characters are fictional. For the record, I've never heard a whisper of corruption from the Newport, Rhode Island police, nor from that city's Congressional Representative. I have thrown a drunk, boorish local politician, out of a bar, though. As far as I know, he's alive and well, and yes, he asked if I knew who he was. Yes, I did use the DJ's mike to ask for help with his identity. I've always been grateful for the opportunity to do so.

I've been to the locations mentioned in the book and took as few liberties with the geography as I could. The hotel bar is fictional, regardless of what you may think after a walk around Newport.

CPSIA information can be obtained
at www.ICGtesting.com
Printed in the USA
BVHW030504281120
594340BV00009B/801

9 781945 181795